# RIALTO

The Unbreakable Bonds Series

## JOCELYNN DRAKE
## RINDA ELLIOTT

This book is a work of fiction. Names, characters, places, and incidents are products of the authors' imaginations or are used factiously and are not to be construed as real. Any resemblance to actual events, locales, or organizations, or persons, living or dead, is entirely coincidental.

RIALTO. Copyright ©2019 Jocelynn Drake and Rinda Elliott. All rights reserved under International and Pan-American Copyright Conventions. By payment of the required fees, you have been granted the nonexclusive, nontransferable right to access and read the text of this e-book on-screen. No part of this text may be reproduced, transmitted, introduced into any information storage and retrieval system, in any form or by any means, whether electronic or mechanical, now known or hereinafter invented, without the express written permission of Jocelynn Drake and Rinda Elliott.

Cover art by Cate Ashwood.

Copyedited and proofed by Flat Earth Editing.

## Dedication

### Jocelynn

*To Rinda. Thanks for five years of crazy, explosive, sexy, duct-taped adventures.*

### Rinda

*To Jocelynn. This has been a blast and I look forward to many more adventures with you!*

## Acknowledgments

1 city
    4 men
    8 novels and 4 short story collections
    835,000 words
    Countless emails, phone calls, Skype messages, and cups of coffee.
    Miles of duct tape.
    And so many code names.
    When we started the Unbreakable Bonds series five years ago, we never thought we'd go on the amazing adventure that we have. We've fallen in love, laughed, cried, worried, revised, scrapped entire plots, argued, and laughed some more. We've gotten the chance to meet and talk with so many wonderful, enthusiastic readers.
    Thank you to everyone who has helped us, cheered us, and answered questions over the years. Thank you to everyone who took a chance on this series and followed us to the end.
    It's always hard saying good-bye to your favorite characters, but I'm glad that we got to share their lives over the past several years.
    Thank you.

# Chapter One

Ian stood back, chewing on his bottom lip. Every instinct was driving him to jump in, to offer a bit of advice, to tweak how he was holding the knife a tiny bit. But this was about letting go. He was the *chef de cuisine*, the Head Chef, and the *chef de cuisine* did not worry about training the new *commis*.

That was the job of the *chef de partie*, and Isabella was a fantastic line chef. Technically, she was one of his *chefs de tournant*, which meant that she was skilled and experienced enough to work all the various kitchen stations. She dove into each of Ian's new recipes and creations with amazing enthusiasm, eager to wow Rialto's guests.

But she also had amazing patience and a great way of clearly explaining things. She'd trained two other *commis* who had come into Ian's kitchen, but this one was different.

A gentle hand landed on Ian's shoulder, and he twisted to find his *sous chef*, Sean, smiling at him with a knowing amusement in his gaze. "He's going to do great."

Ian gave a little sigh and rolled his eyes at himself. Sean was right. Sean was pretty much always right.

But it was Wade Addams's first day as a junior member of Ian's kitchen at Rialto. The young man had been among the first he'd hired as a server nearly four years ago when he opened. Wade had suffered through a rough childhood, something Ian understood all too well, but he'd flourished at Rialto. Ian had watched the young man's confidence soar as he excelled at his job and became friends with everyone in the restaurant.

And in the evenings when the restaurant was quiet, Ian and Wade had bonded over a love of cooking. They swapped recipes and talked about new ideas and techniques.

Ian knew it was only a matter of time before Wade finally agreed that he was ready to move out of serving and into the kitchen.

Today, he was beginning his formal training. He was going to start as the *garde manger*, the pantry chef. It wasn't exactly an exciting position, since the *garde manger* was responsible for only cold dishes such as salads, but Ian had added a special duck pâté to the menu for that evening to give Wade a little variety.

"Of course he is. He's already a great cook without the formal training," Ian said stiffly, as if anyone could doubt Wade's skills.

"I was thinking that he's determined to impress you, Chef."

Ian could feel embarrassment heat his cheeks lightly. Okay, he had to admit that he had something of a fatherly relationship with his staff at Rialto. He'd met other chefs who ran their kitchens like militant dictators and expected the same brutal manner from their *sous chef*, but not Ian. The staff at Rialto were a second family to him.

And yes, he was younger than nearly everyone in his kitchen, but no one seemed to blink an eye at it. Cooking was his life. He'd proved himself time and again with his unique meals and by having the top-rated restaurant in the city of Cincinnati every year since they had opened.

"Have you decided whether you're going to keep him here at Rialto or move him to your new restaurant?"

Ian shook his head. "Wade is staying at Rialto. This kitchen is more formal and will give him the excellent experience he needs to expand his skills. The new place will be smaller, and most of the chefs will be accustomed to working multiple stations. I don't want to throw that at him yet."

Sean nodded, his eyes on Wade and Isabella. "I'm loath to suggest this because she's amazing, but have you considered Isabella for the *sous chef* position there? She's got the experience to handle whatever's thrown at her and knows when to crack the whip."

Grinning, Ian gave his own *sous chef* a little side-eye. "You'd be willing to give up your right arm so my new restaurant can flourish?"

"Oh, I plan to bitch and moan endlessly about it," Sean reassured him and Ian chuckled. "But she *is* amazing. She'd have your new place running efficiently. Plus, it would mean Rialto would finally have some real competition in this old town."

"I agree."

He loved having Isabella in his kitchen at Rialto. Sean and Isabella made a formidable team, keeping the entire kitchen working like a well-oiled machine. On the nights Sean was off, either Isabella or Ian slid into his place. Ian had to admit, things tended to be calmer on the nights that Isabella was in charge. Ian's presence seemed to put everyone a bit on edge; they all wanted to impress the Chef.

"I've been making up my final list of who I might consider moving to the new place and who I'd definitely prefer to keep at Rialto," Ian continued. "After the dinner rush this evening, can you stop by my office? We can go over it. I'd like to get your thoughts."

"Of course, Chef."

Regardless of what shifts were made, he'd need to hire new help for both kitchens, and highly trained chefs were not easy to find in Cincinnati. He was actually considering contacting a headhunter to search the top restaurants in New York City, Los Angeles, and Chicago. The only problem was that those people sometimes brought big-city bad habits and attitudes he didn't want in his kitchens.

Ian started to turn toward his office and stopped on a thought. "And bring a bottle of that Argentina Malbec the distributor gave us. I'm not putting it on the menu until we've both vetted it."

"Sounds like an excellent meeting, Chef," Sean said before he called out instructions to the *boucher*.

Orders were starting to pour in for the next rush. The slow and steady morning prep was giving way to the briskness of lunch. The kitchen buzz wouldn't die off until about two or three o'clock. More employees would stroll in; a second round of prep would begin as the dinner menu was brought out. It would all pick up again around five, and a controlled chaos would reign until almost ten.

But Ian didn't need to worry about the day-to-day activities within the kitchen any longer. Sean was an amazing *sous chef* and had everything under control. He had a similar view of the kitchen: the employees were family, not a small country to be dominated.

For nearly a year now, his attention had been split between planning his wedding and planning the opening of his newest restaurant in Over-the-Rhine. It was completely different from Rialto, but it would still have the Ian Pierce flare. Correction, the Ian *Banner* flare. He was still getting used to his new last name.

One key difference was that he was doing this restaurant on his own. Well, mostly.

Billionaire and best friend, Lucas Vallois had been a major investor for Rialto, supplying nearly all the money to get the restaurant off the ground.

This time, Ian had gotten the loans on his own, though Lucas had still managed to weasel his way in as a minor shareholder of Ian's new restaurant. Not that Ian could blame him. Lucas had made his investment back many times over on Rialto, and he was expecting to do the same with Ian's new place.

With the wedding a blissful success and the honeymoon even more enjoyable, Ian and Hollis had settled comfortably into a busy married life. Ian's main focus now was getting his new restaurant successfully launched in a few months.

Ian stopped on the way to his office, catching sight of his husband as he walked through the front door of Rialto. Even after four months, there was still a part of him that gave a less-than-dignified squeal at the thought that Hollis Banner was now his husband. They belonged together. Ian had felt it the first moment he spotted the former police detective standing in Lucas's penthouse, grilling his friend over a supposed mugging. The poor man had been sick as a dog and should have been in bed, but Hollis wasn't the type of person to let a little thing like a cold slow him down when he had his mind set on something.

As he strolled into the restaurant, Hollis winked at Carla and Anthony at the hostess stand, his grin wide and pointed directly at Ian. Hollis had a way of making Ian feel like he was the center of his entire world. Entire universe.

His man—his husband—was dressed in a pair of dark-blue jeans that were molded to his muscular thighs and were likely hugging his gorgeous ass just right. His black T-shirt was stretched over his wide chest and clung to his arms as he carried in a large box, balanced on his left shoulder. For early September, the weather was still more like summer than fall, with the temperature cresting each day at the mid-eighties, but the nights were becoming surprisingly brisk already.

"What are you doing here, Mr. Banner? Don't you have a job you should be at?" Ian teased as Hollis reached him.

"Is it so wrong that I wanted to see my husband at work?" Hollis replied. He leaned down and grabbed Ian's lips in a quick kiss.

Ian reluctantly let the kiss end and was already making plans to drag Hollis to his office, but he couldn't completely pull his eyes from the box Hollis was carrying.

"What's in the box?"

"I stopped by the house to pick up that paperwork we need notarized. Totally forgot it this morning," Hollis muttered as he lowered the box from his shoulder to hold it in front of his waist. "And I found this waiting on our doorstep. I think it's the extra copies of the magazine we ordered."

"Yes!" Ian shouted, pumping one fist in the air. He winced, pressing his lips together when he realized he'd broken the hushed tone of his restaurant.

Looking around, Ian spotted an open table off to the side of the dining area and waved Hollis over to it. As Hollis moved toward the table with the box, Ian hurried to Carla as she was already walking toward him with a questioning smile. "Could you get me some scissors, please?" She nodded and scurried off as fast as she could in her black pumps.

Ian joined Hollis at the table, practically bouncing on the balls of his feet. *The Cincinnati Edge* was a highly read magazine for the city that had regular features on important events within the city as well as its movers and shakers. Lucas had already had two write-ups in the magazine, including a big, glossy spread on his wedding almost two years ago.

When the editor reached out to Ian last spring asking if he'd be willing to sit down for an extended interview, Ian had been over the moon. The reporter had been so pleasant and funny that Ian had no problem talking about Rialto, the men he considered his family, and his sexy husband-to-be. The interview was just supposed to be about him, Rialto, and a little hint of the new restaurant he was opening at the end of the year, but it had all coincided with his wedding, so the reporter and photographer had also attended.

As a result, the three-page article turned into a massive eight-page spread with beautiful glossy pictures of his restaurant, home, and wedding. It was gorgeous and positively glowing. The reporter made his life sound like a fairy tale from a veiled rough start straight to the happily ever after.

And Ian couldn't argue with it. Sometimes he looked at his life, and it all seemed too good to be true. He'd been so lucky to have found Lucas as well as Ashton Frost and Rowan Ward. Those men were his cornerstone from which all the happy parts of his life had been built.

He worked hard for his success. He studied hard to become a great chef, and he'd studied even harder under Lucas's tutelage to be a great business manager. He'd managed to get over his past so that he could have an amazing life with Hollis. The magazine article was a stunning reminder that he'd achieved his dreams and so much more.

As they stood waiting for Carla to bring over the scissors, Hollis stepped behind Ian and wrapped his arms around his waist, pulling him in tight while pressing a kiss to his jaw. "So proud of you, baby," Hollis murmured.

Ian huffed a soft laugh. "We've already seen the article. It's been on newsstands for nearly two weeks. These are just our copies for the restaurant."

"And I'm still proud of my sexy, rising-star husband."

"Oh, God. The cute! It burns!" Carla teased as she approached them with a shiny pair of silver scissors in her hand.

Hollis straightened, only partially releasing Ian as they turned at the sound of her voice. "You're just jealous that Valerie hasn't made an honest woman out of you yet."

"And I'm fine to work at Valerie's speed," Carla said, her expression smug. "She's moved into my house and she's never getting out again, even if we never get married."

Ian accepted the scissors and smiled. "That's my girl."

"Yes, trap her in your kinky lesbian web."

"Ian, your husband is insane." Carla stepped closer as Ian cut through the tape securing the flaps of the box.

"That's why I love him." He put aside the scissors and pulled back the flaps to reveal two neat stacks of the magazine. On the cover was a picture of Ian lounging at a candlelit table at Rialto. He'd chosen a Prada suit for the Rialto photo shoot and gone for something more casual at home. His entire wedding party had been dressed in Armani tuxes for the event, even if he'd had to threaten Rowe with physical harm to get him into the suit in the first place.

"Oh wow," Carla whispered in awe. "They look beautiful."

"You don't think it's too pretentious to have them in the lobby for the guests?"

"No," Hollis said immediately.

"Definitely not," Carla added. "Your loyal customers will be excited for you, and everyone will feel a little more special because they managed to get a table at *your* restaurant."

"It all feels like a crazy dream." Ian reached into the box and started to grab a stack of magazines for Carla. She would be able to artfully decorate the restaurant's small lobby with them and keep more at the hostess stand to replenish as they disappeared.

Before he could get his fingers around them, there was a burst of noise from the front of the restaurant. They turned as one to see a bunch of men in what looked to be body armor, with weapons drawn, surge into the restaurant and immediately fan out. Customers enjoying their lunch gasped and cried out in shock.

Ian stood transfixed for a heartbeat, his entire body locked up in horror. It was a police raid. The police were storming his restaurant, but he couldn't imagine why. Horror gave way to rage as Ian spotted a man wearing a bulletproof vest rather than body armor with ICE emblazoned in yellow across the front.

It wasn't a police raid. It was fucking immigration.

Someone had called immigration on Rialto.

Ian charged across the restaurant, heading straight for the man with salt-and-pepper hair who was giving orders. He was vaguely aware of Hollis right on his heels, and he only hoped both of them didn't end up in jail. Neither were good about keeping their tempers when there was an injustice. And ICE storming Rialto was an absolute crime.

"What the hell do you think you're doing?" Ian demanded as soon as he reached him. Before he could even answer, there was a surge of outraged shouts from the kitchen. Ian almost darted toward the noise, but Hollis's hand landed on Ian's shoulder, holding him in place. Probably for the best if Ian wanted to avoid being accidentally shot.

"Are you the owner of this place, Ian Pierce?"

"Banner," Ian automatically corrected.

"Banner what?"

Ian growled. "It's Ian Banner now. I got married. And yes, I'm the owner. This *place* is Rialto, a five-star restaurant. I repeat, what the hell are you doing here?"

"We've had reports that your kitchen staff contains several illegal aliens. We've also got reports that drug smuggling has been operated—"

"I beg your pardon!" Ian shouted.

He took a step toward the ICE agent and despite being nearly a foot shorter than the man, the agent took a nervous step back. His hand dropped to his sidearm and Hollis pulled Ian away. Thank God, because he was leaping past rational thought. The idea that he was harboring illegal aliens was ridiculous, and to say his restaurant was involved in drug smuggling as well was ludicrous.

"You have no right to conduct a search of the premises without a search warrant," Hollis tossed out.

But the agent had been waiting for it, and he shoved the document in Ian's face. Ian snatched up the paper and tried to read it, but it was all legalese gibberish, and he was too pissed to try to decipher it. He handed it over to Hollis and waited. His former cop husband skimmed it, his frown deepening before he nodded at Ian.

"We advise that you stay out of our way while we question your staff and search the premises. We will be bringing drug-sniffing dogs to check over every inch of this place. If you try to hinder our investigation at any point, you will be arrested. Do you understand, Mr. Banner?"

"And do you understand if you bring *dogs* into my *restaurant* that I'll have to close everything down and throw out food in order to re-sterilize everything?" Ian snarled.

"No interference, Mr. Banner," the agent repeated, apparently not giving a shit that he was wasting both Ian's time and money.

"He understands," Hollis said sharply before Ian could continue, and it was for the best. He'd been about to call the man a goose-stepping idiot.

"Can we at least allow the guests to leave so you don't traumatize them with your antics any further?"

The agent gave a stiff nod before turning back to his men. Rage burned through Ian as he shrugged off Hollis's restraining hand, and he turned to a too-pale Carla. She was a second-generation Mexican American. She'd been born in the United States to parents who had naturalized years ago. But that didn't matter in today's political climate. Her skin was too brown for her to be a real American for some people.

"Hey, look at me," Ian said gently as he approached Carla. He took one of her shaking hands in both of his. "Nothing is going to happen to you. No one is taking you out of here today, I promise."

She turned tear-filled eyes on Ian. "But what if—"

"There's no what if. You're not leaving here. You're an American. You belong here. Everyone who works here belongs here. There is nothing illegal happening in my restaurant."

Carla nodded, looking reassured but still frightened. Ian couldn't blame her. There were too many horror stories of American citizens being detained because they *looked* foreign, regardless of their actual citizenship. It was fucking bullshit.

"Why don't you help Hollis escort customers quietly out of the restaurant? I'm going to call my lawyer."

Hollis's brow furrowed. "Sarah Carlton?" Ian nodded. "I don't think immigration is her thing. I thought she was mostly corporate law."

"Maybe not, but she's scary enough to take a chunk out of these fucking assholes."

Hollis smirked at him. "That is very, very true."

Sarah Carlton had been Lucas Vallois's lawyer for almost as long as Ian had known Lucas. She stood five-foot-nothing in her stiletto heels and looked as if a stiff breeze would knock her over, but the woman was an absolute shark. Men ran in terror from her, and Hollis had confided that half the Cincinnati police force was scared of her.

Luckily, she absolutely adored Lucas as if he were her own little brother. And lucky for Ian, that love extended to Lucas's family. Even if she couldn't do anything for him, she'd at least try to make sure that everything happening was by the book.

Turning away from the sounds of ICE agents rummaging through his kitchen and harassing his staff, Ian looked down at his magazine and frowned at his image on the cover. The presence of ICE in his domain felt like a dirty smear across his perfect dream.

∼

*Five fucking hours.*

It took Ian five hours to get rid of the ICE agents. They lingered in his restaurant as if they had nowhere else to be. And through it all, they found absolutely nothing. Not that Ian thought they'd find a damn thing.

Every one of his employees had a proper ID and credentials, proving they were in the country legally. Only Enzo was a foreign citizen, but he had all his papers proving that he had a visa to work legally in the United States.

And then the damn dogs. He loved animals but *not* in his freaking kitchen!

Sarah had come to Rialto immediately, but it was clear that there wasn't a damn thing she could do, thanks to the warrant. She'd stayed every minute though, making sure that not one of his employees were harassed or dragged off. The agents quickly learned to give the tiny woman a wide berth.

By the time the ICE agents were gone and Ian had his restaurant back, they were well into the dinner rush. But they couldn't cook. Too many people and dogs had trekked through the kitchen, touching the food, the counters, and the equipment. Everything had to be thrown out or scrubbed down.

To his chagrin, the restaurant was forced to close for the night so they could properly clean. Customers had to be called so their reservations could be canceled and rescheduled as best as they possibly could.

It was after midnight when the lights were turned off and the doors were locked. Ian sat alone in his office, exhausted and angry. He couldn't understand why anyone would make such a report against his restaurant. It was absolutely ridiculous. There was a part of him that wondered if ICE had even gotten the right restaurant, if it had all been a stupid mix-up. He tried to reassure himself that it was all over and that life would now return to normal.

Besides…he had a sexy husband to get home to.

## Chapter Two

City lights decorated the night, passing in a blur as Hollis focused on the road. A cool front had moved into Cincinnati, allowing Hollis and Ian to enjoy the drive with the windows down. Hollis had one elbow on the edge of his door and one hand lightly resting on the steering wheel. He glanced over and smiled at the way the wind ruffled Ian's once perfectly styled hair, a thoughtful expression on his handsome face.

"It was a good meeting," Hollis said as he guided them home from the foster parent training class.

After several long talks over the past months, they had decided to try and become foster parents. Ian had brought up how many kids were out there without loving homes, and they felt their home could be the perfect refuge from a difficult world.

It also didn't hurt that they were both plagued with worry about the kids they'd helped rescue from pedophile crime boss Boris Jagger. What had happened to the ones who hadn't had families? There were no forthcoming answers on that front, so they could at least take steps to help those struggling to find a warm, welcoming place to belong.

They did eventually plan to adopt and had discussed surrogacy, but this was the route they'd decided on to ease into creating their family. Hollis also looked at this as a chance to brush up on his meager parenting skills before they had their own kids. He'd helped raise his younger sibling, but that had been years ago. And the occasional babysitting of little Daciana Vallois wasn't exactly putting him on track to be father of the year.

Regardless of whether the kids that were placed in their home were there for a week or years, it didn't matter. They were both excited about this new step they were taking toward building a family.

The path to becoming foster parents wasn't easy. The process could take anywhere from six months to a year with classes, paperwork, and home visits. Up front they had twelve classes to go through. Each one was three hours long and happened twice a week. They were on week four, and rearranging their schedules for them was getting hard.

It was worth it, though. With each class, Ian had grown more and more excited, and Hollis loved seeing his enthusiasm. Normally, he left the long classes bubbling with excitement and talking a mile a minute about all the things they needed to do.

But tonight, Ian was unnaturally quiet. Hollis kept throwing him concerned glances as he drove back to the condo. Undoubtedly, his husband was worrying about the raid on the restaurant two days before, and Hollis didn't know how to ease his mind. Nothing had come from it, but the whole thing had thrown Ian off his game. And pissed Hollis off royally. He'd been in a mood since—one he couldn't seem to shake.

Their training class that night had been about agency policies and honestly, pretty damn boring. But still, it got them one step closer to their goal. Soon, they would be completing the home studies. They were on track to be foster parents in less than a year at the rate they were going.

"It was a good meeting." Ian sighed and ran his hand through his hair, then turned in his seat to face Hollis. "But I had no idea how dull a PowerPoint presentation could be. I kept picturing that incoherent teacher in Charlie Brown cartoons. Loved the way you nodded off."

"Thanks for that awesome jab to the ribs, by the way."

Ian's lips stretched into a wide grin. "Would you rather I let you snore?"

"Sleeping through most of that class would have been a blessing." Hollis chuckled. "I'm looking forward to being done with these. Three hours, twice a week is taking a toll."

"We only have two and a half weeks. We can do it." He suddenly frowned. "But it is a lot. I'm sorry about my mood lately. I can't help but wonder if maybe I *am* taking on too much. We have these classes, and we're supposed to be getting the condo prepped for foster kids. I've got the new restaurant happening, and now we have all this craziness at Rialto. Rialto alone is a huge job."

Hollis threw him a glance. "Which one would you stop?"

"That's just it. I don't want to stop anything. Well, I could have done without the ICE raid." He snarled, still so obviously annoyed about that. "But the rest is all important. And we have everything nearly ready at home anyway." He groaned and scrubbed both hands over his face. "Ignore me. I'm tired and worrying too much."

"I'm not going to ignore you. I'm worried about you."

"Don't be." Ian let out another long breath and leaned against the door. "I really am fine. Just frazzled tonight." His phone buzzed in his lap and Ian looked down at it, then snorted. "It's Snow again. This time he's asking about the officiant."

"Didn't he just text you half an hour ago about that?"

"No, that time it was about scheduling cake tastings. He honestly just wants to hire me to do the cake, and I told him that he and Jude need to go through an official cake decorator to make sure they get what they want."

"You love doing wedding cakes."

"I know. I'll probably end up doing it, but they could still go through the tasting at an actual cake shop to pick their flavors." Ian laughed. "I could tell Snow was grumbling on the other end without even seeing him."

"I thought he said he was doing all the wedding planning. Seems like he's hitting you up a lot."

"Oh, his exact words were 'How hard could it be?' " Ian laughed and texted something back to Snow. "He has no idea what he's doing. Stubborn ass."

Hollis frowned, kind of annoyed with Snow for bugging Ian with so many questions. Snow and Jude had gotten engaged just a few months earlier, but Hollis had heard through the grapevine that Snow's soon-to-be mother-in-law Anna was demanding that they start making official wedding plans. Things like setting a date, location, caterer, and whatnot.

Egotistical bastard that he was, Snow was convinced that he and Jude could handle it all, but it meant so many questions were flowing down to Ian. It would have been easier all around if they'd just let Ian do the planning, but everyone was worried about his time with the new restaurant, not to mention their training to become foster parents.

Rialto alone kept him busy, so the added stress of a wedding would have been too much. Well, according to the guys that made up Ian's unique family. He knew his husband—Ian would rather be planning that wedding himself. And it wasn't as if he didn't have fingers in it anyway. Not with how often Snow texted.

Stopping at a red light, Hollis reached across to touch Ian's hand in his lap. Ian turned his palm over and threaded their fingers together, giving him a sweet smile. Hollis's heart picked up as it always did when he was on the receiving end of that particular smile. It never failed to get a rise out of him and had from the very first time he'd seen it.

God, he loved this man.

When the light turned green, he didn't let go of Ian, using his other hand to steer until they reached their neighborhood. Ian's phone buzzed again. This time, he let out a laugh, then read the text out loud.

"*What the hell are 'Save the Dates'?*"

Ian shook his head and called Snow just as Hollis pulled into their driveway. He listened with half an ear as Ian patiently explained about the mailers and told Snow not to read any more online wedding planners.

"I'll get you a list of what you need to do," Ian finally said as he got out of the car. "No arguments. We'll use the list for mine—it's already done, and you won't have to do half of what I did. Yours isn't going to be…what did you call it? Oh yeah, isn't going to be as *extravagant* as mine." Sarcasm dripped from his tone.

He listened for a moment, then laughed. "If you don't watch it, I'm going to call Anna and tell her to help you. Next thing you know, it'll be a pink, rainbow, and unicorn themed wedding."

That warning seemed to shut Snow up, because Ian got off the phone as they walked inside the condo. They'd recently bought furniture, making sure everything was nice, new, and clean for when they got to foster a kid or two. The couch and love seat were hunter green, the chair and ottoman striped green and white. They'd even fixed up the one guest bedroom to be ready for a kid—hell, they were as ready as they could be. They just had to finish going through the training and home studies.

"Get everything situated with Snow?" Hollis asked as he tossed his keys into the bowl on the small table by the door.

"For tonight, anyway. He was going through online checklists and getting overwhelmed, poor guy. Some of those lists start out a year ahead. The Save the Dates mailings had him all jacked up because he supposedly missed that timeline. And he doesn't even have a date!" Ian shook his head and plopped down onto the couch, crossing one ankle over his knee. "He should let me do it."

Hollis scratched his jaw and flashed Ian his best crooked grin. "Weren't you the guy just minutes ago saying you were taking on too much? And now you want to add another wedding to that mix?"

"I like planning weddings, smartass." Ian smiled to himself. "Snow's would be my third one. I'm getting much better at them. Faster. Learning all the good shortcuts." A soft sigh slipped from Ian, but there was an underlying current of happiness in his tone. "Sometimes, I think I should have been a wedding planner because I find the whole process fun and interesting. Exciting, even."

"Then you wouldn't be the chef of the highest-rated restaurant in the city. And I wouldn't reap the benefits of all that fantastic food." Hollis patted his belly, then sat next to him and pulled him under his arm.

Ian sighed and stretched his legs out, putting his sock-covered feet onto the coffee table. He'd kicked off his shoes when they'd come in. "I'm still reeling over that damn raid. Someone had to have called it in, and I can't figure out who would do such a thing. It's driving me crazy worrying about it."

"Everything's fine. Even Sarah told you there's nothing to worry about now."

"Still, it shouldn't have happened, and having those dogs in the kitchen?" He growled softly. "I just hope we don't get any disgruntled reviews from the people we had to reschedule."

"Bad reviews happen, you know that."

"But over something like this? Something completely out of my control?" He sat up and faced Hollis. "I can't get it out of my head that someone actually turned us in. And all that stuff about drugs? *Drugs, Hollis!* The last thing Rialto needs is a rumor like that. We had people in the restaurant who heard all that when the agents first came in."

He stood and started pacing the room. Hollis watched his slim, agitated form as he moved, noting that his hands were clenched into fists at his sides.

"Rumors of drugs could hurt our chances of becoming foster parents, too!" he nearly yelled. He reached up and ran his fingers through his hair, leaving the brown strands sticking out all over the place.

He'd worked himself into a frenzy again. Hollis stood and walked to him. He placed his hands on Ian's shoulders, feeling the fine bones beneath his palms before sliding them down Ian's back to pull the man into his body.

Ian slumped against him, wrapping his arms tight around him. "Thanks."

"For what?" Hollis asked.

"For the hug. For knowing I needed one." He tilted his head and stared into Hollis's face. "You always know how to calm me down."

"I don't want you worrying about drug rumors. The fact that your restaurant only lost one night to the raid before opening up again will squelch any of those. Rialto will be fine. And this isn't going to hurt our chances at being foster parents. We've already gone through the background checks and everything else. It's all good."

Ian had worried incessantly about the background inspection, but his past with Jagger had never been public knowledge. It also didn't hurt that Ian had Rowe's tech specialist, Gidget, run a check, making sure that there was nothing from Ian's past that might throw up red flags. Gidget had confirmed that other than Jagger's attack on Ian at Union Terminal three years ago, there was nothing linking Ian to Jagger.

"I just want it so much," Ian mumbled against his chest as he leaned close again.

"I know, baby. I do, too."

Ian lifted his head. "Yeah?"

"You know I do," Hollis said as he bent down to kiss Ian. Ian's arms slid up around his neck and he stood on his toes to press harder into Hollis's mouth. That warm body felt too good against Hollis. He pulled away from Ian and stared at him, taking in the already blown pupils with a smile. "Enough of this worrying. I have a better idea. Stay right here."

He walked to the front door to set the security alarm, then flipped off the lights. The automatic night-light on the stairs came on, but he knew where Ian was. He walked to his husband and lifted him. Ian's legs automatically wrapped around his waist as Ian chuckled. Hollis knew he was laughing at being carried, but Hollis fucking loved carting Ian around.

"I bet I know what your idea is," Ian murmured, kissing Hollis's jaw.

"If it's stripping you naked and having my way with you, you get a cookie." He carried him up the stairs and into their bedroom, not setting him down until they were beside their bed.

Streetlights illuminated the room through the parted curtains. Ever since Hollis had found Dwight Gratton watching Ian through his window, he'd been unable to leave those curtains open. Ian didn't worry that it would happen again and kept opening them, but Hollis couldn't help it. He walked over to close them, hearing Ian's soft chuckle in the darkness.

Wanting to see his husband, he flipped on the low lamp next to the bed and walked to Ian, his hands going to the buttons on Ian's shirt.

Ian watched him as he unbuttoned and spread open the shirt, his brown eyes already glittering with desire. Hollis bent and kissed his collarbone, then his neck, opening his lips over Ian's pulse to feel it against his tongue. The scent of spices wafted up to his nose from Ian's afternoon in the Rialto kitchen as well as a little of his personal cologne. Ian always conjured up feelings of home and warmth whenever Hollis touched him.

Tilting his head, Ian gave a little purr as Hollis ran his lips over Ian's Adam's apple, up to an ear. Hollis nipped the fleshy lobe before moving to Ian's mouth. He could never get enough of Ian's mouth. Ian's nimble tongue came out to meet his, making Hollis moan in the back of his throat.

There was a taste of coffee from the cup Ian had enjoyed at the meeting, and Hollis chased the flavor down until he got only Ian. That was the best flavor of all. The kiss deepened, his hands moving restlessly over Ian's bare chest. He still felt like he'd won a prize, getting to put this man under his hands. He could never touch him enough. Kiss him enough. His love for Ian swelled in his chest as he pushed the shirt off Ian's shoulders and stroked his hands down the warm, silky skin of his back.

"Want the rest of our clothes off," Ian whispered against his lips.

Hollis pulled away and tugged his Henley over his head, then moved to the buttons of his jeans. His actions were hampered as Ian's hands came out to stroke his chest and stomach. "You aren't taking off your pants."

"Your body distracted me," Ian replied, kissing all over Hollis's chest. He licked a nipple, latched on to it, and sucked. "Such a gorgeous body."

Hollis's pants and boxers were still around his ankles, but he turned Ian and pushed him down onto the bed. He made quick work of ridding Ian of his jeans and underwear, then kicked off his own. Stretching out on the bed next to his husband, Hollis pulled Ian against him. All that warm skin made him close his eyes briefly before he opened them, not wanting to miss Ian's expressions as they made love. Everything he felt was stamped onto his face, and it made sex so much fun.

Ian watched him as he ran his hand down Hollis's side, then brought that hand across to wrap it around Hollis's cock. He stroked as he returned for more kisses and Hollis thrust his tongue into Ian's mouth. He cupped the side of Ian's neck, his thumb rubbing over his jaw. Ian had showered and shaved right before the meeting, so it was nice and smooth. His hand was hot on his dick and it felt so good, Hollis rocked into it.

"God, I can never get enough of you," Ian whispered. "Think it will always be like this?"

"Yeah, I do." He rolled Ian onto his back and came over him, nudging his thighs apart with his knee. He lay between Ian's slim legs and ground his dick against him. Ian's arms and legs wrapped around him, holding on tight before he let go and ducked his head to suck on Hollis's neck. Heavy emotion filled Hollis. He loved having Ian's mouth on him, loved the way he gave himself over to Hollis. Loved the pleasure Ian took in his body. Sex with Ian was always a revelation, a glorious buffet of feelings and sensations. He felt drunk on the man.

Hollis moved down, nipping and licking, relishing the tight muscles and soft skin. He sucked Ian's nipples, then the lines of his abdomen and the sexy hip muscles he couldn't get enough of. His husband was so damn sexy, his lithe form writhing in sensual pleasure as Hollis worshiped him with lips and tongue.

Ian's cock jerked against his chin and Hollis turned to run his nose along it, taking in the heady scent of Ian, the wonderful musk. He traced one of the veins with his tongue before going lower to lave Ian's lightly furred balls. He buried his nose in his pubic hair and took a long, deep breath before taking one of his balls into his mouth.

Ian cried out and spread his legs wider. "Come up here."

Hollis kissed the tip of his cock. He ran his tongue around the soft head, the sharp flavor of pre-cum making him suck Ian in deeper. When Ian tugged on him, he pulled off and smiled against his belly, then inched his way up Ian's chest, detouring to both nipples before he reached Ian's mouth. Hollis pressed him into the bed.

"Want you to fuck me." Ian nipped his bottom lip, sucking it into his mouth. "Wanna feel you inside me."

Hollis rolled them to their sides and kept going to get the lube on the side table. He stretched out on his back. "Sit astride me," he said as he coated his fingers in lube. Anticipation made his hand shake, and he spilled a lot of it on them.

Ian rose over him, staying up on his knees, and Hollis reached between his legs to rub his slick fingers around Ian's hole. He pushed lube into him with one finger, then two. He slowly slid those fingers in and out of Ian's body, watching his face as lust slackened Ian's mouth and caused his eyes to go half-lidded.

"So fucking sexy," he breathed as he breached his husband with his fingers. "So hot inside. Can't wait to get my dick in there."

Ian grabbed the lube and slathered it over Hollis's length slowly, stroking his hand up and down, squeezing it just right. The slickness felt so good, Hollis's mouth fell open and he gasped air into his lungs. He could come just like this, with Ian's hands on him and his fingers inside the man's ass. When Ian did that rolling hip move, Hollis changed his mind. He wanted in his husband more than he wanted his next breath.

He pulled his fingers out and grasped Ian's hips to position him over his cock. Ian guided him inside, slowly, slowly lowering himself onto Hollis. Tight, slick heat surrounded him, and he went still as heady pleasure swamped him. "Fuck, so tight."

Ian rose, using the strong muscles of his thighs, then lowered himself again, this time faster. He lifted and fell a few more times before Hollis was seated all the way inside him. He grasped Ian's hips and that was when he really did the hip rolling, driving Hollis out of his ever-loving mind. It rocked him deep inside his husband.

Ian clenched his muscles tight, gripping Hollis in a velvety hot vise at the same time.

"Fuck!" He threw his head back and gritted his teeth, pleasure making his vision go gray. He wanted to stay buried inside Ian forever.

"Yeah," Ian breathed. "So good."

Hollis brought his head down so he could watch Ian, watch the desire wash over his beautiful features. Ian rode him slowly, his hand on his own cock as he gasped and writhed on Hollis.

He could only stare up at the man, could only feel how hot and tight he was, see how gorgeous he was like this. It was Hollis's favorite position because he didn't miss anything. He liked all the ways he took Ian. From behind, bent over everything from the bed to the couch to the kitchen counter. He liked Ian on his back with his legs in the air.

But this would always be his favorite because he could watch his man take his pleasure. Could feel the ripple of his muscles as he worked himself on Hollis. Could watch the undulations of his graceful body. It was like watching Ian revel in his sexual glory and being, like he was claiming Hollis, and Hollis so wanted to be claimed by this man.

Ian sped up, his mouth open as he panted. His eyes shut and his head tilted back, his hand rubbing fast on his dick. Hollis felt scorched, inside and out. He dug his fingers into Ian's hips, watching him stroke himself, and felt the telltale tightening of his muscles as he grew closer and closer to the edge.

"That's it, baby. Come all over me."

Ian's brown eyes opened, his gaze locking with Hollis's. He raised up and down, the friction hot on Hollis's cock. The whole time he stared at Hollis, his breaths coming in short pants that increased as his movements did. When he suddenly went taut, Hollis felt that swell of lust and love he always experienced with Ian. Sex with other people had never been like it was with Ian, and he knew it was because of their deep connection. The love they had for each other.

A sharp cry of pleasure ripped from Ian's lips as he came all over Hollis's stomach and chest. Some of it hit his chin, and he let go of Ian's hip to swipe it up with a finger he sucked into his mouth.

Muscles clamped onto Hollis's dick as Ian rocked on him, and his hands slid to Ian's ass, his fingers roaming down to feel where they were joined. He felt himself thrusting inside Ian and groaned. He plunged up into the man over and over, felt his orgasm tightening his own body. When it crashed over him, he came hard inside his husband, pleasure curling his toes into the comforter underneath him.

Slumping over him, Ian slid in the mess he'd left on Hollis right before he kissed him. Hollis knew he tasted like Ian's cum and it was so erotic, he thrust his hips one more time. But he'd grown sensitive, so he slowly pulled out of Ian. He held on to the man, breathing hard and reveling in the bliss of a good orgasm.

"You fucked all the worry out of me," Ian murmured into his mouth. He pulled back and grinned at him. "Was that the plan all along?"

"I always plan to fuck you. Worry or not. I can't imagine a time when I won't be thinking about the next time I get to do this. It's always so damn good."

"It is, isn't it? Never felt anything like this with anyone else."

"That's why you married me." Hollis winked and raised up to kiss Ian again. His own lips were sensitive from all the kissing, but he didn't care.

"I married you for so many reasons, but yeah, that's definitely one of them." He buried his face in Hollis's neck. "Love you," he whispered.

"Love you too." Hollis wrapped his arms tight around Ian, relieved to feel his husband's pliant, relaxed body, knowing he'd let go of some of the stress.

Nuzzling Ian's soft hair, he breathed in his familiar scent, so damn thankful to have this life with him. He'd never expected to have anything like this and every single day, gratitude expanded in his chest. He didn't know what he'd ever done to deserve someone like Ian, but he wouldn't change a thing that had brought him to this place. He was a lucky, lucky man.

## Chapter Three

"I think you should go with easy to clean over expensive—at least until Daci is older," Ian said as he pushed the stroller between the different furniture settings in the store, hyperaware that a salesperson followed them at all times. It was as if he'd latched on the minute they'd walked through the front door and deemed himself their annoying shadow. Ian knew the poor guy worked on commission, so he definitely understood his drive to be attentive. It was just that he lurked too close, and Ian and Andrei could barely talk about a piece before he was jumping in.

The store was surprisingly busy on this beautiful, sunny Saturday morning and with so many people milling about the furniture, Ian guessed the salesman might be following Andrei out of recognition. He'd become something of a local celebrity, being married to Lucas Vallois. Or he could be trailing him out of appreciation for the gorgeous Romanian man.

Andrei, dressed in casual, loose jeans and a red button-down, reached to feel the arm on a copper-colored sofa. He had his wavy black hair pulled back in a short tail at the nape of his neck, and he looked well-rested and happy. Daci was apparently sleeping through the night now. "If Lucas were here, he'd go with expensive and just plan to replace anything ruined."

"We're more practical than Lucas." Ian smiled down at the baby as she cooed and rattled a toy in her stroller. She was nine months old and got prettier every day with her black curls and dark, dark eyes. A little replica of Andrei and it was no wonder Lucas was completely smitten with her. "You're so precious," he told her softly.

He didn't get to see her as much as he'd like with his hectic schedule, so he'd taken today off to spend it with her and her daddy while he shopped for new furniture for the house Andrei had built with Lucas. They were slated to move in soon, and while Ian's heart felt wrecked over them leaving the penthouse where they had so many memories, he knew it was time for his friends to get the bigger home. Especially since they planned to expand their family more.

Ian wanted that, wanted children. For good someday, but right then, he wanted to be a home for children who needed new families, at least temporarily. That was why he was going through all the steps to become a foster parent. He could offer so much love to them. Give back when he'd been so incredibly lucky to have found his own family.

But sometimes when he looked at little Daciana, he couldn't help but think of a tiny Hollis, and his heart swelled with want. She'd have wavy blonde hair and beautiful blue eyes. Maybe someday.

It had been wild watching Lucas and Andrei change so much as fathers. They doted on this little girl, and the change in Lucas especially had been something to see. He was no longer as hard-edged, was quicker to smile. The man had melded completely to married life and fatherhood and had never been happier.

And now, he was basically starting over in a whole new place. When he'd first told Ian they were selling the penthouse, Ian's reaction had been complete dismay. So many years he'd spent coming and going there. He'd *lived* there. That place still carried the remnants of home for Ian. But it was time…and he was happy to be searching for new furniture for the house with Andrei.

"I like these over here," Andrei said as he strolled to a brown set in the corner. Well, brown was too plain a word for the color that held a faint hint of red. It wasn't exactly maroon or burgundy, but it was close.

It reminded Ian of fall leaves. "This would go great in the new place, and I think Lucas would like it. It's certainly a lot warmer than the furniture in the penthouse."

"I like that furniture. I have great memories on that furniture." Andrei's smile was faintly wicked, and Ian could only grin back.

Yeah, he'd walked in on them a time or two with that furniture before he'd realized using his penthouse key without at least knocking first was a bad idea now. He still had it though, and more than likely he'd have a key to their new place. Lucas liked knowing his family had access to him whenever he was needed or wanted.

Andrei sat on the couch and spread out his arms. "It's comfy, too." He bounced a little, his grin turning into something infinitely private, and Ian had no doubts where his mind had gone.

Ian pushed the stroller between the sofa and coffee table and sat next to Andrei. The salesman took a few steps closer. "You're right. This set is nice. And it looks fancy enough for Lucas's tastes. Are you going to get it or bring him here for his opinion?"

"I may just get it. We're so close to the move-in date, and I don't think he really cares how I decorate the new house. It'll take me a while, big as that place is. And he's been extra busy lately."

"New business he's starting?"

Andrei gave him a look as if to say, "When isn't Lucas starting a new business?" and Ian could only chuckle. "When he is home, he just wants to spend time with us. No other worries," Andrei continued.

"The house is big because it's Lucas we're talking about here. Plus, he wants more children," Ian pointed out as he reached into the stroller to pick up little Daci. She gurgled and smiled at him as he sat her on his lap. Chubby little legs kicked out. She'd recently developed a belly laugh that had all his friends making fools of themselves to get her to crack up. "She's such a sweetheart."

Andrei looked at his daughter, and love shone from his eyes. "She is. And yes, Lucas wants more. At least one. He's even agreed to father our next child, though I had to talk him into it after seeing Daci."

"You do make pretty babies, Andrei."

Andrei reached for his daughter and she held her arms out. Ian shifted her onto Andrei's lap.

"What do you think, Daci? Like this furniture?" He kissed her cheek.

She made a bubble with her spit, causing Andrei to laugh and reach for a soft cloth he kept in the diaper bag on the back of the stroller. He wiped her mouth, then kissed her forehead. Watching the ex-MMA fighter go soft over his little girl warmed Ian's heart.

"So, you've made up your mind? Want to go find a dining table now?" Ian leaned over and ran his hand over the coffee table. "Are you going for just the couch, love seat, and chair—or are you going for the tables, too?"

"Let's look for other tables. These have sharp corners, and I don't want Daciana to get hurt when she starts pulling up on things."

Ian nodded and stood, his phone buzzing in his pocket. He pulled it out, read the text, and shook his head.

"Let me guess," Andrei said. "Snow."

"You know he decided to plan his own wedding, right?"

Andrei nodded.

"He should have just let me do it at this rate." He held out the phone so Andrei could read the text.

*Colors don't really matter, do they?*

Andrei chuckled as he slipped Daci into the stroller. "He was texting Lucas, too, until Lucas fired back that he didn't give a shit about any of that stuff either—just marrying me. That's why he'd left it all to you."

"Wonder if he's even tried hitting up Rowe." Ian should have insisted he do the planning. It wasn't like he hadn't already started the moment they announced their plans.

"That would be like asking a bomb specialist to plan the wedding."

Laughing, Ian started to put his phone into his pocket, but he noticed he had a new notification. He had alerts set for anything to do with Rialto because he'd worried so much about rumors after the ICE raid. When he saw it was just reviews, he nearly quit reading, but a one-star caught his eye. Then he saw there were several new ones and they were all one-stars. His gut clenched hard. Even knowing he shouldn't read them, he couldn't stop himself and his mouth dropped open with the second one.

"What's wrong?" Andrei asked, looking over his shoulder.

"There's a stream of bad reviews coming in for Rialto." He thumbed down the screen.

"Everyone gets a bad review here and there."

"Not seven in one day—not my place." He pointed to the second review. "And this isn't even real. We don't serve shepherd's pie. According to this review, the food took forever, the mashed potatoes were undercooked, and the service was terrible."

Andrei frowned. "Maybe you shouldn't read those."

"This one says the wine was off. We serve only the best wines, and I make sure they're all good." Ian growled, his eyes widening on the next review. He didn't say anything out loud because he hadn't told the others about the raid, but this review brought up animals in the kitchen and rumors of drugs. His heart beat so hard, he could hear it pulsing in his ears, drowning out anything Andrei might have said. His hands started to sweat.

This could hurt him. Hurt him badly.

Even as he read, more one-star reviews poured in. And there was absolutely nothing he could do about it. The walls narrowed around him as panic built in a tight, painful knot in his chest. He worked so hard to make that restaurant what it was, and yeah, low reviews had come in here and there, but never anything like this. His hands were shaking as he forced himself to shut down the phone and place it in his pocket.

Andrei rubbed his back. "I'm really sorry about this, Ian."

"There must be something I can do. I'll call James and see about reporting these reviews as fake," Ian said, mentioning his business manager, James Dunkle. The man had been with him since the opening of Rialto and was brilliant at handling much of the day-today ordering and human resources stuff Ian didn't even want to think about. "Or maybe hire a reputation management firm. It's so much easier to handle disgruntled people when they actually happen to be at the restaurant. If I have someone displeased, I can comp meals or offer gift certificates, anything. This is all happening online, and some of these reviews are for food we don't even serve. It's not really fair."

"It's suspicious."

It was. But Andrei didn't know about the raid, and some of those reviews had to do with that. He could imagine dissatisfied patrons being upset at getting caught up in the mess. He swiped a hand through his hair and closed his eyes, counting to bring himself back under control. When he opened them, he had a better handle on his emotions, though they boiled inside him. He'd meet with James and come up with a plan since he wouldn't just take this sitting down. "Let's enjoy the shopping trip. I can hardly get anyone to shop with me these days, and I don't want to ruin this. We're going to find you the best tables to go with that furniture."

Andrei's dark eyes held concern. "Are you sure you still feel like it? There's no hurry. We don't move in for several weeks yet."

He squared his shoulders. "I'm sure. I love shopping—you know that."

Andrei squeezed his arm. "I wouldn't want anyone else with me doing this. And Rialto will be fine. It's too good not to weather this little hitch. Think about that magazine spread you just got. That's great publicity."

It wasn't such a little hitch, not coming right after the raid, but Ian decided not to talk about it anymore. They found a set of tables with rounded corners that went perfectly with the furniture. They didn't find the right dining room set, but Andrei said they'd try another day. He put in his order with the happy salesman, and Ian played with Daci as he waited. It didn't take long since Andrei was buying everything outright and having it delivered.

As they pushed the stroller into the bright sunlight outside, he thought about how he could counteract the bad reviews. He knew there were companies that specialized in restoring reputations, but he knew little about them. Still, his heart felt heavy as they reached Andrei's SUV. Andrei had started driving this new car when he'd realized he needed the room for all Daci's things.

"How's the restaurant in OTR coming along?" Andrei asked as he got Daci out of the stroller and put her into her car seat.

"Good. Only a few months out now and I'm excited to be trying something with all new dishes. This place won't be as fancy as Rialto but more trendy, and the spot in OTR is perfect for that kind of restaurant. I'm calling it In Good Time."

Luckily, Rialto had been an easy five-star, and that had helped him get everything he needed to start the new place. Which reminded him of the bad reviews piling up.

"I should do something big," he said as he got into the passenger seat of Andrei's vehicle. "Some kind of splashy thing for the holidays. Thanksgiving and Christmas aren't that far off, and maybe I can counteract some of the bad reviews if I can't get them taken down."

"Sounds like a good idea," Andrei agreed as he got behind the wheel after storing the stroller in the back of the SUV.

Daci babbled in her car seat in the back as they got onto the road.

"You want to stop for lunch somewhere?" Andrei asked. "I'm starving."

"I feel the need to go by Rialto and see how things are going. Talk to James. Would you mind eating there?"

Andrei laughed. "I love it there. You know you don't even have to ask."

"Good. It'll give my staff a chance to coo over your sweet little girl, too. They love when you bring her in."

The whole time they drove to Rialto, the reviews played over and over in Ian's mind like a sickening film reel. The knot they left in his gut made him feel faintly nauseous, too. He was excited about opening the new place, but Rialto was his baby and he felt like all this was entirely too out of his control. He hated that feeling.

## Chapter Four

Hollis tucked his hands in his armpits and slouched a little lower in the passenger seat of the Merleau Detective Agency surveillance van. It figured that early fall weather had sneaked in when he was stuck in a van down by the river. He would have preferred to spend a cozy Sunday night wrapped around Ian in bed, buried under a mound of blankets and listening to his steady breathing.

Not that Shane Stephens was bad company. His boss at Merleau was a funny guy with a sharp mind. He would have made a good cop. As it was, he was already a much better follower of the rules than Hollis had ever been while on the force in Cincinnati or Atlanta.

Shane and his business partner, Patrick, had taken a big chance on Hollis when they offered him a job. Hollis had been a good cop. An honest cop. He'd worked hard to keep people safe and put criminals away, but it had become harder and harder to not cross certain lines when it came to stopping crime boss Boris Jagger. And it was damn near impossible the second Ian's past came to light.

But even with Shane's interesting stories about him and his live-in boyfriend or the even crazier stories of his father dating a man for the first time—a Ward Security bodyguard who also happened to be much younger—Hollis couldn't stop worrying about Ian. His husband was already stretched thin with the upcoming launch of his new restaurant and their plans to become foster parents, but the weird attacks on Rialto were ramping up Ian's stress.

Rialto was always a demanding business. Ian wasn't the type to just leave his restaurant in the capable hands of his employees; he needed to be there for nearly every decision.

For the most part, everything ran smoothly. The worst things that Hollis had been around for were some unexpected ingredient shortages and a really bad bout of the flu that had wiped out half the kitchen staff. That one had resulted in Hollis getting a crash course in working in a professional gourmet kitchen.

He prayed every damn day that he never had to do it again.

The bad reviews were annoying, particularly the ones Ian pointed out that were clearly fake. But every business had to deal with bad reviews. They had to be taken with a grain of salt. Sometimes you could do things to improve. And sometimes the person was having a bad day or was just a cranky bitch. Ian had to move forward, hire a reputation management company, and just keep being awesome. The packed reservation list and glowing professional reviews were proof that Rialto and its staff were amazing.

But when combined with the ridiculous ICE raid, Hollis couldn't deny that his cop senses were tingling. Not that he was ready to admit it to Ian. The phony reports to ICE could have come from the same vindictive bastard that posted the reviews. But instigating a raid was dangerous. Those agents stormed the restaurant with guns drawn. If someone had sneezed in that tense moment, they could have been shot. And what if someone didn't have their ID that day? In this political atmosphere, they risked being taken, and God only knew when they'd be released.

Maybe the asshole hadn't expected the tips to be escalated to a violent raid?

Or maybe they had and that was the point….

Hollis groaned and scrubbed a hand over his face. He was going around in circles and coming up with no new ideas. If this was all a horrible coincidence and amounted to nothing, then Hollis didn't want to bring his worries up to Ian. He had enough on his mind. Someone threatening his Rialto would send him screaming over the deep end.

"Go ahead, text him," Shane said.

"What?" Hollis blinked and looked around, trying to get his brain to remember why he was stuck in a van in the cold night air with Shane. *That's right. The stalking case.*

"That groan. I'm assuming you're worried about your sweet chef and fighting the urge to text him."

Hollis smirked at his companion. He'd told Shane about the ICE raid and the recent negative reviews. So far, Shane was shrugging them off as coincidence and bad luck. And maybe they were due for a little bad luck. Things had certainly been running in their favor recently. It had been months since any of the family had been shot or set on fire. God, Hollis wanted to roll his eyes at that thought alone, but when it came to Lucas, Snow, and Rowe, shootings and fires were kind of par for the course.

Their wedding had even been perfect. Hollis hated to admit that he'd been expecting something horrible to happen, but the worst thing was Daciana Vallois getting fussy during their wedding vows.

"Maybe," Hollis muttered.

"Text Ian. Then I can text Quinn guilt-free and tell him to get home to feed our cat."

Hollis snorted but pulled out his phone. With any luck, Ian would be fast asleep and wouldn't answer.

*It's colder than hell in this stupid van.*

He wanted Ian to be sleeping, but there was no denying that his heart picked up a little when he saw those three dots appear just seconds after the text was sent, indicating that Ian was replying.

*I'm lying across the entire bed, heating it up for you.*

Hollis huffed a soft laugh. He didn't believe that for a second. When Ian started out at night, he was curled up in a little ball on his side. But he was a restless sleeper even when he wasn't having nightmares. His husband usually spent a good chunk of the night plastered across Hollis while he was asleep.

*Naked?*

*Guess you'll have to come home to find out.*

Hollis tucked his phone into his pocket and looked over at Shane to find his friend smirking at him.

Shane set his phone on the dashboard. "Feel better?"

"I've moved from worried to physically frustrated."

Shane grunted. "They're all teases. Quinn sent an almost dick pic to prove he wasn't at the office."

"What's an 'almost dick pic'?"

"A fresh from the shower pic that gets a hint of pubic hair and tease of the root, but nothing else."

Hollis had to clap his hand over his mouth to keep his laughter from ringing out in the van. They'd been on surveillance for the past three hours. No reason to blow their cover by being careless.

And yes, he was grateful that Ian wasn't in a mean mood. His man knew all the ways to push his buttons and did it on more than one occasion to get what he wanted. Hollis fucking loved it, too. Loved Ian's sexual confidence. But he definitely hated when he was stuck in a van and couldn't put his hands on his lovely husband.

"We've got movement," Shane announced, his voice turning serious. He handed over his binoculars to Hollis and pointed with his free hand. As soon as Hollis accepted them, Shane grabbed the camera to start snapping pictures.

The case wasn't proving to be too complicated. The client had come to Merleau complaining that he was being followed and threatened. He didn't want to go to the cops until he had some kind of proof. The guy wasn't sure if his wife was trying to have him killed or if his business partner was trying to force him to sell his half of the business.

Tonight, they were outside the guy's business after he'd let slip to both his wife and business partner that he'd stashed some important financial documents in the office until he could meet with his lawyer.

"Doesn't look like the business partner," Shane muttered. There was an ultra-soft clicking noise of the shutter rapidly firing with each shot. "Maybe one of them hired out the dirty work."

Hollis lifted the binoculars and swung them over to the building. The back of the warehouse was well-lit, giving Hollis a clear view of the tall, skinny figure wearing a dark knit hat along with black pants and a leather jacket. But even from the distance, Hollis could clearly make out the devil tattoo on the man's neck.

"No fucking way," Hollis swore. He lowered the binoculars for a moment and blinked, his heart racing in his chest. He couldn't have possibly seen who he thought he saw. But there was no mistaking that tattoo.

"What? You recognize him?"

Hollis ignored Shane's questions as he stared through the binoculars again. He carefully focused the lenses, training them on the man's face as he paused at the door and looked around the open area to make sure he was alone. It was him. Hollis would have recognized Joey "No Nose" Pinscher anywhere. The man got the nickname because he apparently had no sense of smell. The guy usually stank to high heaven and was completely oblivious to it.

Hollis became acquainted with Joey when he'd worked undercover in Boris Jagger's mob.

"It's Joey Pinscher. He worked for Boris Jagger."

"What? Jagger? He's dead, right? I mean…"

"Yeah, Jagger's dead." Hollis would know. He was there when Ian finished him off before he could kill both him and Ian. That moment would haunt him forever. Terror and relief had run through him.

"Joey was a low-level creep for Jagger. Mostly ran errands, drugs, and worked as muscle here and there when it was needed."

Shane's voice was cautious as he continued to snap pictures. "Is this from when you were a Cincy cop? I know you were on the Jagger case."

That was an understatement.

"I spent close to a year undercover in Jagger's operation. That's when I met Joey, along with an entire cast of monsters I'd prefer to think were locked up in prison somewhere."

Hollis didn't want to think about Jagger. It didn't matter that the man had been dead for nearly three years. He always seemed to pop up in the back of Hollis's mind, reminding him of the horrible things he'd put Ian through. That Jagger and his entire operation were the reasons for Ian's nightmares.

Jagger conjured up endless tangles of helplessness and rage that Hollis couldn't shed. The old memories were always there, even if Ian refused to admit it. They gave his lover nightmares still and caused more than enough bad days. But Ian shrugged them off and pasted a smile on his face. He plunged himself into work, forcing them both to pretend that Jagger wasn't still haunting them.

And Hollis let it happen.

For the most part, they were happy. The nightmares were rare and so were the bad days. Hollis didn't want to rock the boat. He didn't want to be the one to force Ian to relive those horrible memories yet again. Not when their life together was going so perfectly.

He didn't want to admit that there were days he was afraid to let Ian out of his sight. That there were nights when Hollis had his own memories or something triggered an old thought from their early days together, leaving Hollis wanting to simply hold Ian and reassure himself that the man he loved most in the world was safe.

How was he supposed to explain to Ian that he was struggling with those old recollections when he knew that Ian had survived far worse?

So, they both pretended everything was okay.

But the appearance of Joey Pinscher was a sharp reminder that not everyone from Jagger's crew was locked up and far away from Ian.

*God, he wanted to scoop Ian up and carry him far from this fucking city!*

Far from all remnants of Jagger's world so they could start fresh where Ian would be safe.

But Ian would never leave his family. Never leave his beloved restaurant.

Hollis didn't want to leave their unique family either. As much as he hated to admit it, he loved Lucas, Snow, Rowe, and their husbands. Yet, Hollis would do anything to keep Ian safe.

"Fuck. Fuck. Fuck," Hollis muttered under his breath as he picked up his cell phone again. He looked down and quickly dialed a number he hadn't called in years. When the phone started ringing, he turned his attention back to the binoculars, watching the punk unlock the rear door and slip into the warehouse.

"Looks like he had a key," Shane grumbled. "Can't get him on B and E."

"No, but this is the guy that one of our targets hired to rough up the client."

"Banner, if you're calling me because you're going to jail, you deserve to stay there," a low, rough voice that brought a ghost of a smile to Hollis's lips grumbled.

"Kirby, you old dog. Did I catch you sleepin'?" Hollis teased. Taylor Kirby worked homicide with the Cincinnati PD. And thanks to the high body count linked to Jagger's men, their paths crossed on several occasions while Hollis was on the force. Kirby was a salty older cop who'd worked the CPD for nearly two decades. Damn good cop. And it was just lucky that he also liked Hollis.

"Yeah, I was sleeping. I'm on the day shift now."

"Slacker. Everyone knows the good shit happens at night."

"What the hell do you want, Banner? Some of us gotta work in the morning."

"I'm sitting here in this van working—"

"Are you in a van down by the river?" Kirby demanded suddenly.

Hollis glanced over to his right and sighed as he clearly saw the dark waves of the Ohio River. "Yeah."

"Ha! I won the pool! Oh, shit! Sorry, honey. Go back to sleep. Everything is fine." There was a sound of rustling fabric and a loud creak like Kirby was climbing out of bed while apologizing to his poor wife. A couple of seconds later, Kirby continued, his voice a whisper. "I knew you'd end up in a van down by the river."

"Ha. Ha. Focus, old man. This is serious."

"What's up?" His voice was sharp and the joking was gone.

"I'm working surveillance on a case. Looks like possible extortion and maybe attempted murder. I was surprised to see Joey Pinscher could have been hired for this job."

"No Nose?"

"The one and only. How did he escape the roundup after Jagger went down? Shouldn't he be locked up doing at least ten somewhere?" Hollis struggled to keep his voice light and even when he really wanted to grind his teeth in frustration. Joey had hurt plenty of people while working for Jagger. He should be rotting behind bars for far more than ten years, but here he was, running around free in Cincy.

"Joey slipped the noose. When Jagger bit it, all his little minions scattered like fucking cockroaches with the lights on. The DA was stretched thin, trying to tackle Jagger's entire organization, so they focused on his upper lieutenants in hopes of breaking any chances of someone trying to re-form his businesses. Low-level nobodies like Joey got a free pass."

"Fuck."

"Exactly."

"How many got through? How many other Joeys are running around the city?"

Kirby heaved a heavy sigh. "More than you want to know."

"Any way I can convince you to do a favor for an old friend?"

"I'm not getting fired for you, bastard. I retire in a couple of years with a full fucking pension."

Hollis winced. He was not going to cost Kirby his pension. The guy had definitely earned his retirement. But that didn't stop him from asking. "Just want a list of names. The ones that got away."

"I'll see what I can do."

"Thanks, Kirby. I mean it."

"Yeah. Yeah. Thank me with reservations at your boyfriend's fancy restaurant. It'll convince my wife that I can be romantic."

"It's husband now. You get me that list, and the dinner will be on the house."

Kirby chuckled. "Keep your fucking head down, Banner."

"You too, Kirby."

Hollis ended the call and looked over at Shane to find him paging through the pictures he just took. "We got what we need?"

"It's a start. We can show some of these to the client and see if he recognizes the guy. You've got us a name and some background.

We got nothing illegal yet for the cops, but I'm sure that's only a matter of time." Shane looked up at Hollis, worry clear on his face. "You and Ian okay?"

"We're good. Safe."

"You sure? You know that I'd do anything for you both. No questions asked."

Putting the binoculars in his lap, Hollis reached over and clapped his hand on Shane's shoulder. He'd never expected to find such a good friend in his boss, but Shane Stephens was a hell of a guy.

Fuck, Hollis was lucky to have so many amazing friends in his life. He needed to remember that he had these people to lean on. He might not be able to tell Shane the full story about Jagger and his involvement in Ian's life, but there were other men who knew everything. Maybe it was time for another "No Boyfriends" meeting with Andrei, Jude, and Noah. That trio could give him some much-needed perspective.

"We're safe. This is just to help me sleep at night. I think the whole weirdness at the restaurant has me a little rattled and jumping at shadows."

Just saying the words out loud helped. It was like rational thought was seeping in again. Jagger was dead. His goons were either dead, in jail, or scattered to the wind. They had no reason to go after Ian. The ICE raid had to have been a stupid mistake. The bad reviews were just a matter of poor timing. Or a bored internet troll. Everything was fine.

"Let's wrap this up," Hollis said as he tucked his phone back into his pocket. "I've got a sexy husband to get home to."

Shane hummed. "Yes. And I have a boyfriend who needs to learn how to take a proper post-shower picture."

## Chapter Five

Ian woke and turned over in the bed to look at Hollis, who was still dead to the world. His mouth hung open and little snores left his lips. They were adorable. As was Hollis's messy blond hair. He still remembered when Hollis had colored it while undercover and he was glad he hadn't done that again. Those chaotic, light waves were his favorite.

He snuggled closer and Hollis automatically pulled him into his bigger form. He also loved the way he held him while asleep and over the years, he'd gotten good at stopping Ian from leaving the bed and crawling around the condo. Not that he'd done that in a long, long time. Thankfully, those days seemed to be over. No more embarrassing wake-ups in the corners of the laundry room or bathrooms. He still occasionally had nightmares, but they were few and far between.

No, he was perfectly settled and loved every moment of it. Loved being married to this man and felt thankful every day for it.

He buried his nose in Hollis's neck, taking in the faint odor of sweat that overlaid Hollis's unique scent. Hollis hadn't taken the time to shower when he'd come home from his late-night surveillance. All he'd done was crawl into the bed and hold Ian. His skin had been cold, so Ian had been happy to warm him. He smelled so good like this, and Ian thought of waking him for some loving.

But he seemed so peaceful, he decided to wait. Ian wasn't due at the restaurant until nine that morning, though his *sous chef* and others were supposed to go in earlier today. He could just enjoy the snuggle time before he woke Hollis up a little later for sex.

His phone rang from the nightstand, and he cursed and rolled over to shut it down before it woke Hollis. But when he saw it was the restaurant, he quickly scrambled from underneath the covers and took the phone into the hall. It was way too early for problems there.

"It's Ian," he said as a huge yawn overtook his mouth. He walked down the hall, tugging up his loose boxers as he went.

"We're having a surprise health inspection," James said quickly, worry and annoyance coloring his tone.

"What?" Ian paused halfway down the stairs. "We just had one less than a month ago. It's too soon!"

"I know, but he's saying stuff about multiple complaints. You should maybe come down here."

"I'm getting dressed now." Ian hurried into the room to find Hollis sitting up and looking sleep-rumpled with the covers tangled about his legs.

"Come back to bed, GQ," Hollis said, his sleepy, rough voice laced with the promise of sex.

"Can't," Ian answered as he rushed to the closet.

"What's going on?" Hollis asked. He sounded instantly awake and ready to jump to Ian's defense.

"Health inspection and this time, he's come because of complaints. I have to hurry." He grabbed slacks and a white button-down shirt off the hanger in the closet and pulled them on. He buttoned the shirt as he raced into the bathroom to brush his teeth. Glancing in the mirror, he grimaced at his hair and worked to smooth it down with one hand while he brushed.

Hollis appeared in the doorway, naked as the day he was born, and if Ian hadn't been so worried, he would have thrown himself at that big, beautiful body. But instead, he eyed the man as he brushed his teeth, then gave up and ran a wet comb through his hair. He splashed water on his face, dried it off, and frowned at Hollis.

"Something's going on. It has to be. This is too many things too close together."

Hollis scratched the side of his head. "You think someone is doing this on purpose?"

"I don't know. I mean, all those reviews looked like they came from different places, but what if they didn't? And actual complaints bringing the health inspector to my door? I can't help but feel this is all related."

"My gut is churning, too, so you're probably right."

"I don't have time to figure this out now, though. I have to run." He kissed Hollis and scurried past him to hit the stairs. He didn't stop to have his usual coffee and rushed outside to his car.

The whole time he drove to the restaurant, his hands were white-knuckled on the wheel and his underarms were sweating. Dammit, he'd forgotten to put on deodorant. He had some stashed in his office, so he wasn't too worried about it. Luckily, he'd also showered the night before.

He parked his little Volt in his parking space and jogged inside the restaurant to find everyone standing around in the kitchen as the health inspector moved about. Sean looked positively livid as he stood with his arms crossed over his chest.

"Tell me why you're here again when you just did this a few weeks ago," Ian demanded, hands on his hips as he faced the inspector.

"Multiple complaints of food poisoning have come in since then."

"Since then, or have they been over the last week?"

The inspector, a small, thin man in khakis and a blue blazer, consulted his notes. "Looks like you're right. All in the last week."

"I haven't heard a thing about this." Ian waved his hand around the kitchen. "But go ahead, you know me. I follow all the codes to a T and keep everything in tip-top shape."

"I know, Mr. Banner, but I still have to do my job."

Ian watched as the man got busy. First, he washed his hands. He checked all their food storage, including using a thermometer to test the temperature of the freezer and refrigerator. He even tested the internal temperature of the food in the freezer. He looked over the shelves and saw they were clean and well-organized. He saw that all their prep tools were color coordinated to prevent cross-contamination. He checked the tableware and that there weren't any entry points for pests to sneak in. He did all the things he'd just done a short time ago.

He was damn thorough, and Ian was glad because he had nothing to worry about. He kept things exactly the way they should be. Rialto meant so much to him, and keeping it up to code was important to him.

The inspector stayed to watch them work as they began prepping for lunch. Ian's employees used the sink that was designated for handwashing often, and they kept everything separated the way they should. Several of them threw nervous glances at the health inspector, and Ian didn't blame them. He was like a dark presence, looming over them to ensure no one made a mistake.

Inside, Ian was a mass of fury. Hot acid kept flowing up his throat. He could no longer think these were all random attacks coming along at the same time. This was someone out to get his restaurant, and the thought was like a fist to his gut. He had another enemy and just when he had so many good things going on in his life.

Ian closed his hands into fists before he forced himself to jump into the fray. He put on his apron and thoroughly washed his hands before heading to the vegetable section to chop veggies for the lunch salads. Might as well help and keep busy while he was there early.

By the time the health inspector was done, Ian was quivering from all the repressed anger. Rialto had passed with flying colors, which he wasn't surprised about in the least. But still, the thought of multiple complaints made him sick. Something was definitely going on. He just wished he had some idea of why. His phone rang and he pulled it out to see Hollis calling.

He took the call in his office, happy to be in the privacy of the small room to decompress.

"How did it go?" his husband asked, and he felt warmth swell in his chest at the very welcome sound of that voice.

"Apparently, there were enough complaints about food poisoning to send the inspector here fast."

"Wouldn't you have heard something about that beforehand?"

"You'd think, but I didn't."

"It sounds like someone has it out for the restaurant."

"It does," Ian agreed as he sat in his office chair and rubbed his eyes. "What am I going to do, Hollis?"

"I don't know, baby. Don't think there's much you can do with the kinds of attacks you're getting. They're all being done through professional channels. You looked into one of those reputation firms, didn't you?"

"Yes." Ian sighed, his eyes gritty and irritated as he worked to blink back tears. James was looking into the top three companies who did everything from monitoring blogs to populating search engines with positive information. But the attacks were happening so fast, Ian felt overwhelmed. He just wanted to go home and crawl into his man's arms and forget about the world for a while. "I love you."

"I love you, too. Was sad when you had to take off so fast this morning. I was enjoying the cuddle."

"I thought you were asleep."

"It's hard to sleep when your perfect little body is against me."

"Aw, I'm not that little." But he did like their size difference and the way his husband could carry him around the condo. There was nothing like the feeling of safety in Hollis's strong arms. He sighed, hating that he had to get off the phone. "I should help with the lunch prep, but thanks for calling."

"We'll figure this out, Ian," Hollis said softly before he hung up.

Ian helped get lunch going and when everything was working smoothly, he walked out into his restaurant to see that all the tables were full, and people still waited to be seated. Word of all the problems hadn't gotten out enough to damage traffic at least. He'd ask

James to review the numbers over the past month, see if there had been any drop in sales or reservations.

As his eyes skimmed over the restaurant one last time, he spotted a friend at a table and walked to greet Lucas.

"I didn't know you were coming in today," he said as he stood beside the table.

"Got time to join me?" Lucas waved at the booth seat across from him. He was dressed in a gray classic Brioni suit, looking fabulous as usual.

"Of course." Ian sat and worked to bring himself under control. He didn't want to worry Lucas with his problems. "Andrei with Daci?"

"She's actually with the nanny today. Andrei is at Ward Security, and I'm headed home after this lunch. I've been pulling too many long hours lately. I miss her. But I wanted a good lunch and time with my friend if he had it first." He picked up his menu, then set it down. "What's the special for lunch today?"

"Parmesan bread pudding with broccoli rabe and pancetta. Lots of pancetta, so right up your alley."

"I'll be ordering that then." He waved the server over and smiled up at Johnny, who gave Ian a nervous glance. He was fairly new. He set down a water glass in front of Ian. Lucas already had his.

"We'll both have the special," Ian said, "and bring out the new Italian roasted coffee for us both as well."

"Will do, Chef." He hurried away.

"I've told him to call me Ian, but he forgets." Ian took a sip of his water, glad when it helped chase away the dryness in his throat from all his anger that morning. He forced himself to relax into the booth, enjoying the sounds of utensils and the voices of people around them. He glanced over to see that a lot of people were eating the special, and his heart gave a little pitter-pat of happiness. His restaurant was still going strong, despite someone's attempts to cause problems.

He looked up to find Lucas's gaze pinned on him, a frown of concentration on his handsome face. "What's wrong?" he asked.

"Do I look like something's wrong?" Because damn, he was working hard *not* to look that way.

"I know you better than anyone in this restaurant. So yes, I can tell there's a problem. Foster classes going well?"

This he could talk about. "Very. We're almost through with them, and then we have the paperwork and home studies and that's it. They are taking up a lot of time, though, and as you know, I'm busy getting ready to open In Good Time."

"Snow burning up your phone with questions?"

Ian laughed. "Not today, but he has been. Man should have just given in already. He needs to either hire a professional wedding planner or just let me handle it. He's probably driving Jude up the walls."

One corner of Lucas's mouth turned up. "Jude likes walls, so I'm sure he's dealing just fine. Never met anyone more perfect for our Ash."

"Isn't that the truth."

"If it's not the classes or the new restaurant, what is it?" Lucas folded his hands on the table and regarded Ian closely.

He thought of spilling everything that was happening, but he didn't want to talk about it yet. It would make it seem too real. So, he shrugged. "Just stressed from so many things going on."

Lucas narrowed his eyes; then he nodded. Ian had a feeling Lucas didn't buy it for a second, but he was letting the subject drop. Lucas learning to be less controlling and interfering was either Andrei's positive influence, or Lucas was realizing that he had his hands full already with a husband and a baby.

Thankfully, their food arrived, distracting them both. Ian took a bite of the crisp pancetta and smiled as Lucas dug into his food. He probably should have told Lucas about other items on the menu rather than let him have something so full of fat, but he knew the man mostly ate healthy at home. He'd had high cholesterol at one point, but all of them had ridden his ass until he did something about it and was now fine. He had that precious baby girl and gorgeous husband to be there for, so he hadn't argued too much. His friend was happy and he showed it every day. He hardly ever frowned, and he normally cut his working hours back. Little Daci couldn't have asked for better daddies.

"I'm thinking of having some kind of splashy Christmas party here in December. Maybe even serve some turkey specials through Thanksgiving. Something to give the restaurant a bump. Play up the holidays."

Lucas looked around, his gaze settling on the line of people still waiting to get in. "Looks like it doesn't need the bump."

"Gotta keep things fresh, you know. Keep people coming."

Lucas watched him closely, and Ian decided to change the subject before he lost his cool and started rattling off all the real worries he had about the restaurant. Those green-gray eyes probed like Lucas could tell he was holding back.

"How close are you to moving into the new place?" Ian asked.

"We're about two to three weeks out."

Ian looked up as Johnny dropped off their coffees. "Thanks," he said before picking up his mug to take a sip. The strong roast burst over his tongue and he sighed in pleasure, realizing it was his first cup of the day. He'd been so busy, he'd forgotten. And that would explain the slight headache he'd been dealing with. Well, other than the stress of the health inspection.

He looked back at Lucas. "Did Andrei show you the furniture we picked out?"

Lucas nodded. "It's nice. I like it. But I'm more interested in what's going on with you. You can say different all you like, but I can tell something's wrong. You're...agitated."

Ian sighed. He should have known he couldn't get anything past Lucas. Even with a husband and a baby, Lucas was all about taking care of his family. "We had another surprise health inspection this morning and apparently, there were complaints of food poisoning. I'm upset because one, I haven't heard any of those complaints myself, and two, we just had an inspection a few weeks ago. So, that was just one more thing on top of all the other things I have going on."

"So we were right to keep you from planning Snow's wedding. I knew you had a lot on your plate right now. In Good Time is what?

Months from opening and you still pull full hours here." He wiped his mouth with his napkin and set it next to his plate. "You do know that when there are children involved, hectic becomes a way of life, right?"

"Of course! I'll scale back by then. Just like you have."

"It's worth it. None of my businesses matter nearly as much as Andrei and Daciana. I know you, Ian. You'll fall in love with the first kids you foster."

"Don't tell me, there's a pool going on that."

Lucas cracked a grin. "Of course. Rowe started it."

"So, who thinks I won't fall in love with the first kids?"

"None of us—the pool is about how long it'll take. My money is on twenty-four hours."

Ian's laughter felt good. And Lucas was probably right about how long it would take him to get attached. He loved kids. He reached out and laid his hand on Lucas's arm. "Thanks for coming by today. I know you're supposed to come over Thursday with Snow for dinner, so it's a treat getting to see you twice this week."

Lucas patted his hand. "The treat is mine."

Ian relaxed back in the booth with his coffee and worked to shove his worries aside. It would all be okay. It had to be.

## Chapter Six

Hollis was reading the most recent reviews of Rialto when Ian returned home that night. The clock on the far wall said it was nine p.m. He should have made dinner, but he'd gotten distracted by the reviews, which were truly awful. Some held a sort of vicious glee he couldn't get past. Anger simmered inside him as he read another that was outright false. It was as if someone was just throwing out every complaint he could think of. Even though all the reviews came from different posters, they felt too much like a calculated move. The attack felt *personal*.

Worry for Ian gnawed at his stomach. This had to be hitting him so damn hard. He'd sounded defeated on the phone earlier, so Hollis planned to give him a nice evening at home with lots of cuddles.

The front door shut, and the keys hit the bowl before his husband walked into the kitchen where Hollis sat at the breakfast bar. Ian's shoulders, in his white button-down, were slumped and his hair was disheveled. Hollis set his phone aside, turned, and held open his arms. Ian set some sacks down on the counter and walked into them with a heavy sigh.

"Now that's what I've needed all day," he said into Hollis's neck as he wrapped his arms around his husband.

Hollis smelled his hair, taking in the familiar scent of food and coffee. He loved the way Ian smelled after a day at Rialto. And as usual, there were good scents coming from the bags on the counter. Something with a rich sauce. He nuzzled into the soft strands of his hair, then kissed his ear. "You doing okay, GQ?" he whispered.

"It was a long day." Ian tightened his arms. "I had a nice lunch with Lucas, though, and that made it better. But my employees are all spooked. Word of the bad reviews got out on top of the health inspection. And all this after the raid. I don't blame them for being nervous. If I wasn't so furious, I'd be a lot more nervous myself."

"I was reading the reviews, and I can tell some of them are completely fake. And there are so many coming in, they can't all be legit. Your idea that someone is out to get the restaurant is right. I'd like to look into this myself."

Ian pulled away to stare at him. His sweet face looked drawn, and there were shadows under his brown eyes. "As long as you keep me in the loop. I want to be one hundred percent involved."

"Of course. Why wouldn't I?"

"Because everyone seems to think I'm better off being left out of things. Do you know how many times my friends have left me out of their fun adventures? Not that this is fun, but you know what I mean." Ian stepped back and plopped his hands on his slender hips. "I'm tired of being overprotected."

"You mean you wanted to hang out in a nightclub while a bunch of hired hoods tried to kill Lucas and shot the place up? Or you wanted to ride along to DC with the Masters of Mayhem and take down a group of mercenaries?"

Ian rolled his eyes at Hollis's incredulous tone. "If Gidget hadn't shown the news footage, I would never have believed Rowe and Noah brought down an entire building."

Hollis dropped his head back and groaned. "Rowe even sounded disappointed that it was only a little building."

"Oh yes, only a few stories tall." Ian giggled and Hollis found himself feeling lighter. Talking about his "brothers" usually brought

Ian some happiness and relief. He turned serious, but the smile still lingered on his lips. "I don't need the danger and excitement that others seem to crave, but I want to be in the middle of things if it's about my restaurant."

Hollis brushed a lock of Ian's hair off his forehead. "Since this involves your business, you'll be party to anything I find. I promise."

"So, what can you do?"

He pointed to a notebook on the breakfast bar. "I've made a list of questions for you. Feel up to answering them now?" He eyed the sacks of food. "Want to wait on dinner and help me fold some clothes first? I know how you hate when I leave them too long and they wrinkle."

Ian nodded and chuckled. "Sure. Dinner will hold."

They walked into the living room where Hollis had left several baskets of laundry on the hunter-green couch. He flipped on a lamp and heard Ian sigh. He had to bite back a laugh. Yeah, he technically could have already folded the clothes, but most of these were Hollis's and he didn't give a shit if they weren't perfect. The other baskets were full of towels and sheets, and surely it didn't matter if those were wrinkled.

"We should probably start with the obvious," Hollis announced as he picked up one of his T-shirts. "Any past harassments or arguments with customers?"

Ian tilted his head and frowned before he shook it. "I can't think of anything. I mean even the few customers who had complaints were happy when their dinners were comped or they got free desserts. I've been wracking my brain, trying to come up with anyone who left that angry, and I am hitting a blank."

"What about employees? Any that you had to let go or who quit? Anyone you interviewed and didn't hire that could be angry?"

Ian folded a towel just so before he set it on the coffee table. He picked up another and tried to smooth the wrinkles out of it. "I did have to fire one employee. Ginger. She was disrespectful to my other employees. She was pretty pissed when she left, too."

"Ginger who?"

"Ginger Roberts."

Hollis stopped folding to write down her name. "So, that's one person who could be doing this. I'll see what I can find on her." He tapped the notebook with his pen. "What about rival restaurants? Ever hear any rumors that would give us a lead?"

Ian shook his head.

"Ever get into a scuffle with another chef over an ancient secret recipe? Old enemies from your cooking school days?"

Ian glared at him and Hollis couldn't keep his shoulders from shaking with mirth. While Ian was very serious about his cooking, Hollis couldn't imagine him ever getting into a fight with another chef.

"Have you been secretly watching those cooking reality shows again?" Ian teased. "You do know that crap is all staged. It's not real."

Hollis gasped loudly. "What? Are you serious? Not real?"

"Ass," Ian muttered, but it at least sounded like he was trying hard not to laugh at Hollis's ridiculousness.

"But I thought Anthony Bourdain had all these rivalries. And I thought there were a bunch of chefs who would get into fistfights on the proper way to prepare duck."

Ian relaxed even more. "Yes, chefs can get territorial, and there are a lot of us who can be…strongly opinionated on how to prepare certain dishes. But there aren't any chefs that I've started kitchen wars with. I actually don't know that many, and we're just on very light, passing-acquaintance terms."

"So…you've not pissed off any customers, you've got one potentially disgruntled ex-employee after being in business for four years, and you haven't started any wars with other chefs or restaurant owners," Hollis recapped with a wink.

"You're correct."

"Didn't Rowe set up security cameras?"

"I have outside ones in both front and back, but it would take forever to watch all that footage." He paused his folding. "I wonder if Gidget could work some of her tech magic. Figure out a way to go through those tapes without having to watch every second, though I don't know what we'd be looking for."

"Anything that stands out. Anyone leaving pissed—that sort of thing. Or anyone who returns to the area frequently but doesn't go in. And if we're going to use Gidget, then we could get Quinn to look into the IP addresses of these bad reviews. Maybe he could find something. I'll see if I can get Shane to sweet-talk his boyfriend into helping us."

Hollis noted that Ian had gone still, his hands tightening on the towel he was in the middle of folding. It was clear that some new thought had occurred to him, and Hollis was waiting for him to finally voice it.

"If we ask for help from Gidget and Quinn, Rowe is going to find out about what's happening," Ian started, his voice low and thoughtful. "And if Rowe knows, then you know it's going to be only a matter of minutes before Snow and Lucas find out."

Hollis stopped in the middle of reaching for another shirt and straightened. Ian wasn't one to hide things from Rowe and the others, except for maybe his poor sleeping habits. All four men leaned heavily on each other and were always eager to help each other out. They'd want to know that Ian was having trouble. "You don't want your family to find out? You know they'd be happy to help."

"And you know their form of *'help*,'" Ian said irritably. "I would get pushed to the side where it was safe while they handled everything."

There was absolutely no argument Hollis could give to that. It was the truth. Everyone in the family was incredibly protective of Ian. They did whatever they could to keep Ian as far from danger as possible.

And Ian had just wrangled a promise out of him to keep Ian at the center of their investigation. There was little chance of them getting the same promise from Rowe and the boys.

A slow, wicked smile spread across Hollis's lips, and Ian arched one brow at him in question.

"What are you thinking?" Ian asked.

"Shane could ask Quinn not to tell Rowe about his little research project," Hollis suggested.

"You mean co-opt Quinn to work secretly for us? That's devious. I love it!" Ian gave a wicked little laugh and rubbed his hands together.

"What about Gidget? Do you think you could talk to Gidget without Rowe knowing it?"

Ian straightened and crossed his arms over his chest for a moment before starting to tap one finger against his pursed lips as he thought. It took only a few seconds for a smile to spread across his lips. The wicked thing was sending blood straight to Hollis's cock. Ian didn't have a damn evil bone in his body, but when he was in the mood to be a little sneaky…fuck, Hollis lost his freaking mind every time.

"I was just thinking that I haven't brought food to the Ward Security team in a few months. Maybe it's time to try out a few new recipes."

Hollis shook his head as he chuckled. There was no better way to distract all the employees of Ward Security than to have Ian bring in trays of free food.

They both returned to the piles of laundry in front of them, smiling to themselves.

"There's no way to track down who reported you to ICE or who got the health inspector on your ass today. I already looked into that."

Ian nodded. "Okay, but at least Quinn and Gidget could give us some good leads. We've got a starting point. And that's way better than just sitting here, waiting for the person to strike again."

Ian stacked more towels on the coffee table, then reached for the basket of jeans. Hollis learned to wash those all on their own now after he'd ruined a couple of Ian's shirts. He used to just throw everything in together, but Ian had been absolutely horrified. A smile crossed his lips as the memory drifted through his brain. He picked up another T-shirt and quickly folded it, noticing it was mostly rolled up. He saw Ian eyeing the shirt and chuckled. He refolded the T-shirt the way Ian liked that time.

Ian grinned at him.

He couldn't keep his hands off his man then. He yanked him

close to his body and kissed him. Ian's lips were soft and warm and he lingered over them. "You're so fucking cute. You want to redo everything, don't you?"

"No," Ian mumbled into his mouth. "Maybe just a few of those shirts…" He looked up at Hollis. "Thanks for doing so much laundry. Were you off today for some reason?"

"Because we've been pulling some night shifts—both of us—I took off this afternoon to catch up on things around here."

"I still don't know why you can't fold things as soon as they come out of the dryer when they're nice and smooth."

"I was preoccupied with what's going on with you. I hate seeing you so upset."

Ian hugged him, then stepped away to grab a sheet. This time, no matter how much he smoothed it, the wrinkles weren't coming out, and he was obviously holding back a scowl.

*So. Damn. Cute.*

"You really think this could be Ginger? She was definitely pissed when I had to fire her, but she was such a…horrible person. She fooled me completely during her interview, and I still feel bad about that."

"What kinds of things did she do?"

"She was rude to the other servers and especially to the kitchen staff. At first, she didn't do it in front of me. But I caught on pretty fast when she started slipping up. Plus, people started putting in complaints about her—even some of the customers. She would take too many breaks and not get to the tables fast enough. Mostly, she just pissed off people who work for me. She was constantly picking at them. But she was only there a month. This seems like a lot of anger for such a short time."

"You never know with people. Maybe she pissed off a customer enough for this."

"I don't know. I made sure each and every one of them left happy when I was there."

Hollis pulled out a shirt that had turned into a wrinkled mess and realized it was Ian's again. He turned over the basket and dug out the things that could be wrinkled, like underwear. Since he was finding a lot of Ian's shirts in the basket, he'd just throw them into the dryer and fluff them.

Ian didn't say a word as he watched him carry the load to their laundry room. Hollis grinned the whole time he fed the clothes into the dryer. It honestly didn't bother him that his GQ was so particular about his clothes; it was one of the things he loved about him.

When he walked back into the living room, he found Ian had moved on to the kitchen and was getting down plates from the overhead cabinets. They clinked onto the counter. He doled out food onto each one, then set them out. Steam still rose from the pasta. Hollis recognized the spaghetti Bolognese and his stomach growled.

Ian never complained, but he went out of his way to keep Hollis from cooking. Not that he minded. Ian might have his quirks, but he was warm and caring and so damn hot—Hollis still had trouble believing he had such a wonderful husband. They'd built a family he was proud to be a part of.

He walked to Ian and tilted his head back. Brown eyes met his and Hollis smiled as he leaned down to softly kiss Ian's lips.

"What was that for?" Ian whispered.

"Because I love you and all your little quirks."

"Hating wrinkles isn't a quirk."

"Yeah, it kinda is." He kissed him again. "But you've got a bunch."

"What other quirks do I have?"

"You like your fashion. You like being in charge in the kitchen." He dropped his voice. "Sometimes, you like being in charge in the bedroom. Have to say, I love those times." He winked. "The toothpaste has to be squeezed from the bottom up. Your car has to be perfectly neat at all times. Want me to go on?"

"Those are all normal things."

Hollis laughed. "To you they are."

"Your car could use a good cleaning."

"That it could. Come on, let's eat."

They ate their dinner at the breakfast bar while Ian continued to try and come up with anyone who would be angry enough to go after Rialto. Outside of the conversation topic, sharing an intimate late-night dinner with his husband was one of Hollis's favorite things, and he kept his gaze on Ian. He would never tire of looking at the man, never get over how lucky he was. The thought that someone was deliberately hurting Ian's business turned his stomach and despite being hungry, he didn't eat a lot of his meal.

They cleaned up together, put away the folded and fluffed laundry, and Hollis pulled Ian down for some snuggle time on the couch. He flipped on the television to find *Star Wars* playing and settled back with Ian against his chest.

It didn't take long for Ian to fall asleep. Hollis kissed the top of his head before flipping off the television. They both had early days tomorrow, so he woke Ian enough to get him into bed and then finally let himself relax. He held his husband close as he drifted off to sleep.

## Chapter Seven

Ian sat in the driver's seat of his Volt and rubbed his palms on the legs of his pants. His hands were sweating. His freaking hands were sweating! This was ridiculous. He was never nervous to stop by Ward Security, particularly when he had a huge load of food in tow.

But then, he wasn't usually planning to do something sneaky. He wasn't a sneaky person. Rowe, sure. Half the man's DNA had to be made of underhanded genes. Noah was the same way. Snow could be devious when he wanted to be, but it wasn't often. Lucas didn't have a prayer. Well, he could be when he needed to be, but Lucas was generally all bluster and bombast when he wanted to catch someone off guard.

And then there was Ian. He didn't feel that he was particularly strong at sneaking, and right now, he was attempting to do it past the sneakiest man he'd ever met.

Taking a deep breath, Ian released his seat belt and climbed out of the car.

"Ian!"

Ian jerked around at the sound of an excited voice. Dominic Walsh was striding toward him with his hands thrown up in surprise.

The bodyguard with the flame-red hair and handsome face was the company's prime practical joker and all-around fun lover. And he was the perfect distraction.

"Dom!" Ian shouted with a wave.

"What are you doing here?" As he got within a few feet of Ian's car, he drew in a deep breath and released a happy groan. "Oh, God! Did you bring us food?"

"Yep."

Dom grabbed Ian in a brief hug, but Ian could also feel him leaning over his shoulder, peering into the rear window of the car to check out the large pans that were occupying his back seat. "What's the occasion? Is it Rowe's birthday?"

"No, I was tinkering with a new recipe, and I thought I'd use Ward Security as guinea pigs."

Dom laughed and released Ian. "We are the worst guinea pigs and you know it. Bunch of oversized bodyguards in desperate need of nourishment at all times. We inhale everything you bring to us."

"True, but sometimes I need a judge who already loves me before I seek out the harder ones."

"Ahhh…a confidence boost. I gotcha. Anything I can help carry?"

"Lots, actually." Moving the driver's seat forward, Ian grabbed a large pan and handed it to Dom. "Why don't you take this in and send out whoever you can find in there? I've got more stuff in the trunk I could use a hand with too."

"We've got you." Dom set off quickly across the parking lot, humming happily to himself.

Ian had made way too much for this simple little mission, but he'd been nervous thinking about trying to sneak past Rowe, Noah, and even Andrei. Those three men were the kings of devious and observant. They kept an eagle eye on Ian when he was around, and he could only think to distract them with food. Lots and lots of it.

Usually when he cooked for Ward Security, he brought enough to feed fifty, even though there were usually far less in the office. Most of the bodyguards would be in the field with clients, but the ones in the office tended to eat enough for two people.

Ian had just popped the trunk when he heard new voices in the parking lot. He turned back toward the building to find six tall, muscular men pouring out of the front door with looks of excitement on their faces. They acted like they hadn't been fed in a week, and it was a great ego boost. Rowe's men loved Ian's cooking.

"Ian, you spoil us," Sven stated as he reached the car. The Viking-like man towered over Ian, gracing him with a soft smile. Sven was an absolute gentle giant…unless you were threatening his boyfriend, Geoffrey, or any of his family at Ward Security. Then he turned into something quite scary.

"I thought you guys were due for some spoiling." Ian laughed. Some of the tension flowed from his shoulders as praise poured over him for the smell of the delicious dishes and how happy they were to see him again. He might be on a mission to secretly enlist the help of Gidget, but Ward Security was a safe place. These were Rowe's people. His friend trusted these people with his life and the lives of his own family.

It took only a minute to get the other four chafing dishes pulled out of the car and divided up while the last two men lucked into dessert and a box of plastic utensils and other serving items. Ian followed behind the crew with a small box with something special for his ultimate target.

When he reached the main open floor of the building, he found Rowe and Noah setting up a couple of long tables they pulled out whenever Ian brought in a meal.

"Ian! You should have called ahead," Rowe admonished as he straightened from securing the last table.

"Did you eat already?" Ian asked. It was not even noon yet, but he guessed that some people could have taken an early lunch.

"No, of course not. We just would have been set up and looking for you."

Ian snorted. "If I'd have called ahead, it wouldn't have been a surprise."

"I would have still acted surprised."

"Me too!" Noah chimed in.

"You're both insane," Ian said before hugging Rowe and then Noah.

He'd grown accustomed to seeing them close. It was rare for them to be far apart at any time, and Ian was glad for it. A day didn't go by when Ian didn't miss Rowe's wife, Mel, who'd been killed in a car collision, but he was glad that Rowe had found love again with Noah. He deserved to be happy, and Ian knew that Mel would have been ecstatic to see Rowe so happy and loved.

Stepping away from Rowe, Ian set the box in his hand on the floor under the table and out of sight so he could work on setting everything up. The men had learned the hard way to stay back during this process. Ian knew just what needed to be done to get his food set just right. The presentation wasn't ideal, but these guys didn't care about the look. It was all about the taste, and Ian was determined to always have his food taste amazing.

Once everything was laid out, he looked up at the men standing dutifully before him, waiting for the okay. "I made a duck *confit* stuffed ravioli with a spicy red sauce as well as a crab and creamy vino ravioli. There's a fall salad with a balsamic vinaigrette and roasted root vegetables in a new spice mix I'm trying. Garlic bread with a nice cheese mix is on the end. And, of course, cannoli for dessert. Enjoy!"

"Damn, Boss." Garrett groaned. "Can we reschedule the training sessions for tomorrow? I don't think I'm gonna move after this lunch."

"We'll push it back an hour," Rowe said and then added under his breath, "Maybe two."

Conversation filled the room as employees from the various departments gathered in the main room of the company. They all chatted while they loaded up their plates. Ian kept his eyes open for the triplets—what Rowe lovingly called his IT team. All reformed hackers…sort of…they knew their way around anything tech.

He was briefly distracted by the appearance of Andrei at his side. The former Romanian bodyguard turned COO of Ward Security had a knack for just sort of appearing out of nowhere. Ian couldn't decide if he was the more dangerous one to watch out for or Rowe. Probably both.

But that was hard to remember when Andrei didn't even look at the silver dishes as he walked to Ian's side and pulled him into a hug.

"This is a nice surprise!" Andrei said as he released Ian.

"I was in the mood to try out some new recipes," Ian said with a smile.

"We're always happy to be your test subjects."

"How's Daci? Ready for my cooking yet?"

Andrei chuckled, his expression changing from joy to pure poppa pride. "We're getting there. I think she's going to be ready for at least a little of Ian's infamous Thanksgiving."

Ian clapped a hand over his mouth. He hadn't even given a thought to Thanksgiving. Where the hell was he going to put all the people? It wasn't just the addition of Andrei's daughter to the table in her adorable high chair, but Lucas had mentioned having his sister and niece fly in for the holiday. Ian also wanted to bring in Hollis's family. He'd become quite close to Hollis's mother, mostly over the phone.

"Already planning it in your mind?" Andrei teased.

"I was just thinking that there might not be enough room at my place, and I hate to think of people being forced to sit in separate rooms."

"Lucas and I would like to offer our house. The formal dining room will be big enough, I think." Andrei hesitated, looking a little unsure. "We know how important Thanksgiving is to you, and we don't want to upset your plans."

Ian wanted to laugh. What Andrei was trying to say was that Ian was completely irrational and bit of a high-maintenance diva when it came to Thanksgiving. Ian always wanted the holiday meal to be perfect, and he refused to let anything stand in his way. Okay, yeah…so maybe Hollis was a little right about his quirks.

"Having it at your house would be perfect. There will be plenty of room for everyone without us feeling cramped."

"And the kitchen is twice the size of Lucas's old one. Plenty of room for you to work."

Ian sighed happily. Lots of counter space. Double oven. Large range with a water spigot for soups. He'd seen the plans and it really was a dream kitchen, which was ridiculous because Andrei and Lucas rarely cooked.

Ian loved his house and he did like his kitchen for most small home projects, but when it came to cooking for his family, there was never enough counter space. If and when he and Hollis found a new place, it was going to have a much larger kitchen. It was his one and only requirement.

"Did I hear someone mention Thanksgiving?" Rowe chimed. In one hand, he clutched a heavily mounded plate. Ian wanted to laugh. That man was not going to be moving later. He could easily imagine Rowe stretched out on the big leather couch in his office, sneaking a nap in. Probably wrapped around a snoring Noah.

"We're planning to have it at Lucas and Andrei's this year because there isn't enough room at my place," Ian replied.

"Does a bigger kitchen equate more grub?"

"We're not hiring a forklift to get you back out of the house," Andrei muttered before stepping in line to fill his plate.

"Noah and I would just move in until we could leave on our own," Rowe said.

"I haven't thought about the menu yet." Ian grabbed a plate and piled a little of the salad and duck ravioli on it. He wasn't hungry, but he knew that Rowe would badger him until he ate something. "My main concerns have been the new restaurant, our foster parent classes, and Snow's wedding."

"I thought you said you weren't planning Snow's wedding," Noah said before shoveling a forkful of ravioli into his mouth.

"I'm not…officially."

With his plate in hand, he followed Rowe and Noah up to Rowe's office. Once there, Rowe grabbed some bottles of water out of the mini fridge he had tucked in the corner.

"What does that even mean?" he asked as he handed Ian a bottle. "Not 'officially' planning the wedding."

"It means that while Snow is content to take charge of his wedding and supposedly make all the decisions with Jude, he's still texting me every day with these crazy questions. Last night, he was asking about location weddings and if I thought Mykonos was better than the Seychelles. Like anyone wants to blow an entire day changing from one plane to the next, trying to get to a wedding. This morning, he was asking if it was unrealistic to ask people to drive an hour from the site of the ceremony to the reception because he found this interesting place deep in Kentucky for the ceremony."

"He's out of control," Rowe grumbled. "He texted me pictures of china patterns two days ago. China. Fucking. Patterns. Like I know a damn thing about china and place settings for weddings!"

"Have he and Jude picked a date yet?" Noah inquired.

"No!" Rowe and Ian said in unison.

"They can't make up their minds," Ian continued. "One minute they want a fall wedding, and then it's a winter wedding in a tropical location. Then it's spring, but they don't want to do any of the usual spring wedding things."

Rowe grabbed his bottle and cracked the seal on the cap. "I thought Lucas and Andrei were bad with postponing their wedding."

"Yeah, but once they finally settled on a date, Lucas and Andrei were good about making quick decisions and sticking to them."

"Only because they were having sex every time they signed a contract or handed over money. Twisted fucks."

"It was romantic! They were excited about starting their new life together."

"There is one important thing we haven't even discussed yet," Noah said, stopping their complaining. "The bachelor party."

Rowe nodded solemnly. "True."

"You can't plan that until you know when the wedding is," Ian argued.

"We can at least start the brainstorming," Noah replied.

Rowe speared a vegetable and pointed it at Ian. "Your bachelor party was amazing, but I think we really need to make Snow and

Jude's epic. I don't think anyone ever expected Snow to settle down, so we need to make it massive."

"What? Vegas?"

Rowe shook his head at Ian's suggestion. "There's a big security conference there next year, and I can't risk getting banned from the city before that."

Ian closed his eyes and fought back a groan. Rowe was dead serious. He truly believed he would get banned from the entire city of Las Vegas if he had a bachelor party there. Ian was pretty sure he was right.

"We could do Tahoe. Or Atlantic City," Noah said.

"Miami," Rowe said slowly, lifting both of his hands into the air. "Beach. Nightclubs. Gambling. Those cool airboats on the Everglades."

This time, Ian did groan. One of their drunk asses was going to get eaten by an alligator. It would be amazing if they all made it to the wedding.

"You guys make bachelor party plans. I'm going to check on the food downstairs and call the restaurant," Ian said as he gathered his mostly empty plate and bottle of untouched water.

"Problems?"

"Nope," Ian said quickly and then winced inwardly at himself. That sounded guilty. "We're training some new cooks and trying a new wine distributor. Just want to check on everything."

*Not a lie. That was not a lie,* Ian mentally repeated to himself. What he told Rowe was entirely true. Those just weren't reasons Ian would ever call into the restaurant to check on things.

Rowe offered up a wave and turned to Noah, talking about a drunken club crawl through South Beach.

Ian walked out, breathing a sigh of relief until he got down the stairs. He threw his plate into the trash, checked the food to find that nearly all of it was gone, and grabbed the little box he'd tucked away. Glancing around, he casually strolled down the hall and hurried up a back staircase to the second floor. This was the only way he could get to the IT office without crossing in front of Rowe's open doorway.

As he reached the hallway, he leaned slightly out and peered carefully around the corner to make sure neither Rowe nor Noah had popped out of Rowe's office. When he was sure the hallway was clear, Ian silently hurried down the hall and darted into the IT office. He wasn't at all surprised to find that all three of them were at their desks, either empty plates or nearly empty plates sitting next to their keyboards.

"Ian!" Gidget squealed. "This ravioli is amazing!"

"Shhhhh!" Ian said, wincing. "Rowe can't know I'm here."

The sweet woman who looked and talked like a kindergarten teacher covered her mouth with her hand and stared at him with wide eyes. Gidget—or rather, Jennifer Eccleston—had been with Rowe since almost the beginning of Ward Security. She was absolutely brilliant when it came to computers, but then they were all geniuses.

"I'm pretty sure Rowe knows you're here," Quinn snickered. "You can't enter this building with a mountain of ravioli and him not know."

"I mean in here," Ian said, his voice barely over a whisper. "I need a favor. But Rowe, Noah, and Andrei can't know about it. Especially Rowe."

"What kind of favor?" Gidget asked quietly.

"Does this have to do with…" Quinn started but his voice drifted off.

"Yeah."

Quinn immediately spun around to face his computer monitors, his head down. He already knew about the attacks on Ian's restaurant. Shane would have enlisted his help to research the IP addresses of the bastard who posted the bad reviews.

"Is this the secret project you won't tell us about?" Cole accused, glaring at Quinn over his monitors.

"I'm not talking," Quinn said.

"I am." Ian held up the box in his hand. "And I brought a bribe just in case you needed persuading."

Quinn's head popped up. "For me too?"

Ian opened the box displaying three individual strawberry-and-chocolate tarts. He didn't make desserts often. They weren't his strength, but for Rialto and secrecy, he'd been willing to try something new and special. He offered the box to Quinn, who quietly celebrated as he pulled one delicate tart from the box.

Turning, he offered the box to Gidget, who looked at it while chewing on her bottom lip. She was torn between the treat and her loyalty to Rowe.

"What do you want me to do?" Her voice was cautious and hesitant. Ian felt guilty about asking her. She and Rowe had suffered a falling out a few years ago, with good reason, but Ian doubted that she wanted to cross him again. Rowe wasn't big on second chances.

"Just review the security footage outside of Rialto."

Her brow instantly furrowed, confusion clear on her gamine face. "That's it?"

"And if you find anything, you have to tell me. If I decide to involve Rowe, I want to be the one who tells him."

"I...don't know," she hedged.

"If it's really bad, you can tell him, but I'm not expecting really bad."

"Define really bad."

Ian grinned at the woman. "Jagger-level bad."

Gidget nodded. "That's fair." And she snatched up a dessert.

Ian turned toward Cole. He didn't know the quiet man as well. Cole looked as if he were a bodyguard with his broad chest and shoulders, but he loved working behind his computer, according to Rowe. "Can I bribe you on retainer for a potential job later?"

"Similar level of sneaky?" Cole asked while eyeing the tart.

"Yes. Nothing to jeopardize your job, I promise."

Cole nodded and accepted the last dessert.

Ian turned and found that Gidget had pulled a spare chair over to her desk. She patted the seat and smiled at Ian. Dropping down into it, he rolled closer so that he wasn't easily visible to the door and kept his voice low as he explained everything that had been happening at the restaurant recently: the ICE raid, the bad reviews, and then the report to the health department.

Gidget nodded, jotting down some quick notes as he spoke. The first thing she suggested was checking the IP addresses on the bad reviews. Ian smiled and discreetly pointed at Quinn. She chuckled and shook her head.

"So, you mentioned you want me reviewing the security footage?"

"Yes. Hollis and I think this could be someone who's at least been to the restaurant. Probably recently. There are cameras outside the front door and back delivery door. We were wondering if you could cook up some kind of…I don't know…search parameters so that a computer scans all the footage looking for suspicious people. Or maybe someone who left angry."

"I could do something like that," Gidget said with a nod. "It wouldn't be precise, but it would give us something to work with. Far easier than watching hundreds of hours of tape."

"Probably look for repeaters too," Cole chimed in. "The person could have returned several times to the restaurant, obsessed or maybe casing the place."

"How far back do you want me to look?"

Ian twisted his fingers together and frowned. "I'm not sure. The ICE raid was over a week ago, and we figure that even after someone submitted reports, it would take a couple of weeks at least for them to pull something together."

"So, three weeks?" Gidget suggested.

"I'd consider a full month. Just to be on the safe side," Quinn said.

Gidget nodded and made a few more notes.

"I really appreciate this. I don't want to get you in trouble with Rowe. We'll tell him eventually. It's just that he, Lucas, and Snow tend to blow everything out of proportion in favor of wrapping me in cotton and tucking me away in a closet."

"They worry about you," Gidget said diplomatically.

"I get it and I appreciate it, but this is my restaurant. I'm going to protect *my* restaurant."

"We're happy to help any way we can. No bribe necessary," Cole said.

"But your bribes are always appreciated," Quinn quickly added.

Ian relaxed a little as he chatted with the triplets for a few more minutes. Just talking to them made him feel like he was taking some steps in the right direction. If there was anything that could be done on computers to track this person down, they would be able to uncover it. He was just tired of wracking his brain over who it could possibly be.

Plan in place, Ian poked his head out of the door and peered down the hall. With it empty, he walked to Rowe's office where he found Rowe stretched out behind his desk, appearing half-asleep. Noah was on the couch and not looking much better.

"I'm guessing lunch was good," Ian teased.

"Amazing," Rowe groaned.

"I've never had duck like that. Sooo good," Noah added.

"I better get back to Rialto." Ian waved a hand at him when Rowe acted as if he was planning to get to his feet. Rowe instantly stopped and lounged in his chair again with a happy moan.

"Leave the trays. We'll clean up and someone will run all your stuff to the restaurant tonight."

"If you're planning to grab seconds, you're too late," Andrei said suddenly. Ian gave a little jump, surprised to find the dark, sexy man standing directly behind him. "I overheard Dom saying he was planning to lick the pans clean."

"Well, no rush. We've got plenty at Rialto." He leaned over and gave Andrei a quick hug before he hurried toward the stairs.

Had there been something in Andrei's smile? A twinkle of knowledge in his dark eyes? Did he see Ian coming from the triplets' office? Overhear something? The man just seemed to have a magical way of knowing things.

Ian shoved the thought aside, calling it paranoia. Andrei didn't know anything. His secret was safe for now. He and Hollis were investigating this case themselves. Ian was handling the problem with his restaurant with just Hollis. No Snow. No Lucas. No Rowe, Noah, streams of colorful duct tape, code names, or explosions.

And most importantly, no one leaving Ian alone on the sidelines while they had all the fun!

## Chapter Eight

Ian opened the trunk of his car and shoved one hand through his sweaty hair. It was almost October and the temperature had hung out in the low nineties all day. When the hell was fall finally going to arrive? Only the nights had been cool so far. Luckily, the sun had set and the air was finally growing more comfortable, even if his clothes were already sticking to him.

He surveyed the collection of reusable grocery bags overflowing with food in his car that needed to be hauled into the condo. It had been just over twenty-four hours since he'd successfully sneaked through Ward Security and enlisted the help of Gidget and Cole. No word yet on the results of the security video, but Ian knew it was going to take some time. It wasn't just a lot of hours to go through, but hundreds of people came and went through the restaurant.

But for now, things were quiet and Ian would take a slice of quiet while he could.

Tonight Hollis was working late with Shane, so he had Snow and Lucas stopping by. He needed guinea pigs for some new dishes he was considering for the Over-the-Rhine restaurant. Of course, it also gave him a chance to deal with some of Snow's wedding questions in person. With any luck, he and

Lucas would be able to force Snow into actually picking a goddamn date. Nothing could be accomplished until that was finally done.

Rolling his eyes heavenward, Ian knew that despite all their frustrating qualities, he wouldn't have his life any other way.

He glanced at his watch and did a quick calculation in his head. There was enough time to get everything inside and put away before grabbing a quick shower. Lucas and Snow would be arriving just as he got out. The recipes he was thinking of didn't take long at all to prepare.

Looping the bags on both shoulders, he grabbed a few more in his hands before turning toward the condo. It took some more wiggling and shifting to get the key into the lock, but he finally managed to open the back door that led into the kitchen.

Thank God no one was around to see that little grocery dance. People would think he had no common sense. Tossing the keys onto the counter, Ian freed up a finger to turn off the security system on the house.

As he stepped across the threshold, he paused at what sounded like the scrape of a shoe on the deck behind him. Ian smiled and started to turn, sure that it was Hollis surprising him, but he never saw the person behind him. Never got the chance to turn around.

Pain exploded across his head. Blinding white light flared before his eyes, and Ian could feel himself falling. Mentally he reached out to catch himself, to stop his tumble, but there was nothing to grasp on to. He was falling and he couldn't stop it. Darkness swallowed him up and the last thing he remembered thinking was that he wasn't alone.

Someone was in his home.

∼

IAN WOKE TO PAIN AND HUSHED VOICES ARGUING OVER HIM. THE voices were growing angrier by the second, which was adding to the pain in his head. *What the hell?*

Lifting his hand, Ian gingerly rubbed his head. Everything was so blurry in his mind. Couldn't remember where he was or why he hurt.

"Easy there. Go slow."

The arguing stopped the moment he moved, and some of the pain in his head eased as he instantly recognized Snow's soothing doctor tone. Always authoritative, but when it came to the small group of people he loved, there was a gentleness that was rarely heard.

"He needs to go to the hospital." That was Lucas. Stern and dictatorial, but it was all a poor mask for the anger and worry that was slithering among his words.

"Are you seriously trying to tell me that I don't know whether Ian needs to go to the hospital?" Snow snapped. He continued, his sarcasm growing heavier with each word. "I'm sorry, where the fuck are your diplomas? When the hell did you sneak in four years of residency in between your attempts to take over the world?"

"He's got a fucking concussion. He needs to go to the hospital." Lucas was not backing down.

"No hospital," Ian croaked.

"See?" Snow said.

"Since when do you give a shit what the patient wants?"

Ian blinked and rubbed his eyes. He lowered his hand and looked around the room to find that he was lying on his couch with Snow sitting on the edge at his hip. Lucas was pacing back and forth along the front of the couch, lines of concern digging deep into his face.

"What happened?" Ian asked. He started to get up, but Snow placed his hand to his shoulder, holding him in place. There was worry in Snow's blue eyes, but his expression was one of removed professionalism. He was in doctor mode. As soon as he was sure Ian was okay, he'd easily slide into angry, irrational Snow.

"Answer a few questions for me," Snow said. He pulled out a small penlight and flashed it in Ian's left eye and then right. "What's your name?"

Ian sighed. He'd been through the concussion thing before with Snow. "Ian Banner."

"What day is it?"

"Thursday. Ugh. September...twelfth, I think. I have no idea the date." Everything was starting to come in clearer the longer he was awake. If he had a concussion, it was pretty damn mild.

"Who's the president?"

Ian glared at Snow, but Snow didn't budge. "A douche-nozzle. Can't you ask me something else?"

Snow's lips twitched slightly as if he were fighting a smile. "When is your husband's birthday?"

Ian didn't hesitate. "August twenty-ninth."

Snow looked over at Lucas, who threw up his hands. "Why are you looking at me? I don't know his birthday! *My* husband's birthday is October seventh."

"I'm right. Now someone tell me what's going on. The last thing I remember was coming home and carrying in the groceries."

Snow released Ian's shoulder, and Ian scooted so that he was sitting up against the arm of the couch. Lifting his head, he carefully touched the back of it, finding a lump and some crusted hair.

"We're hoping you can answer that question for us too," Lucas said. He stopped beside Snow, his arms folded over his chest. "We arrived a few minutes ago to find you flat out on the kitchen floor just over the threshold with some blood on the back of your head. Someone hit you from behind and knocked you out."

"Who?" Ian asked and then winced when he realized what a stupid question that was. They arrived after he'd been knocked out. They wouldn't have a clue.

"We didn't see anyone. When we pulled up, we noticed the groceries in your car."

"How long was I out?" Ian looked down at his watch, trying to remember the time when he'd gotten home.

"We don't think long. Your ice cream hadn't even started to melt yet."

"Oh, shit! All the food!" Ian tried to get up from the couch, but both Lucas and Snow lurched forward, holding their hands up to block him.

"No!" they said in unison.

"You need to rest for a while longer and help us figure this shit out. We can deal with the food later."

Ian opened his mouth to argue that he wasn't going to let all his food go bad when Rowe's angry voice echoed through the house.

"What the hell happened?" Rowe demanded as he stomped through the kitchen toward the living room.

"That's what we want to know. What happened to your fabulous security system?" Snow snarled at Rowe as he appeared in the living room. Right on his heels was a worried Noah. The other man gave Ian a questioning look and Ian nodded with a weak smile, wordlessly informing him that he was fine.

"My security system is fucking fabulous!" Rowe shouted.

"I turned it off as I came in the door," Ian said wearily. He paused and rubbed his temples with both hands. "I think he struck right after I turned off the alarm."

Ian closed his eyes as the reality of what happened started to sink down on him. Someone had watched for him to return home and had been smart enough to wait until he'd turned off the security system before he was attacked.

But at least a few minutes had passed between the attack and Snow and Lucas's arrival. What had happened in those unconscious minutes? Had he been touched? Had his home been ransacked? Robbed?

Oh God, where was Hollis? He wanted Hollis there to wrap his arms around him and tell him that everything was going to be fine. That they could handle it all together.

Opening his eyes, he looked around the room at the gathered family. "Did anyone think to call my husband?"

He was met with awkward silence and guilty looks. Ian was about to blast them when Noah held up his phone. "I've got it!" he shouted and started to head toward the kitchen again.

"Be sure to tell him I'm okay!" Ian called after him.

"We're sorry, Ian. It wasn't intentional," Lucas murmured. "We've only been here a few minutes and wanted to make sure you were okay first. We didn't know whether to tell Hollis to come here or the hospital."

"But you called Rowe?"

Rowe at least had the good sense to wince a little. "I might have already been on the way over. Heard you were cooking for Snow and Lucas."

Ian let it go. He shouldn't have been surprised that Rowe and Noah were just going to "happen by" on a night that he was already cooking for Snow and Lucas. It certainly wasn't the first time and definitely wouldn't be the last.

"Rowe, can you do a sweep of my house? See if it looks like anything was touched?" Ian asked calmly.

"Got it," Rowe said and he was gone in a flash.

Ian turned his attention to Snow. His heart was pounding in his chest so hard that it was difficult to speak. He didn't want to get the words out, but he had to know the truth. He'd always wonder if he didn't ask.

"When you found me…" Ian started at a whisper.

"Not one piece of clothing looked disturbed on you," Snow answered immediately. "Your attacker didn't touch you. I swear."

Ian released a loud, shaky breath. Snow leaned forward and pulled him into a strong hug that threatened to break bones, but Ian didn't care. He snuggled close and sighed. It was nice to feel his comfort and strength. Lucas's hand landed on the nape of his neck and squeezed before a kiss was pressed to the top of his head. The only thing that would make this better, that would put his world back on the right course, was Hollis. And he was sure his husband was already racing to him.

Ian released Snow and with a little grumbling, finally got to his feet. His head throbbed, but he didn't want to keep sitting there on the couch. He had too much nervous energy, too many questions rattling around in his brain. The feeling of being trapped and helpless would go away only if he was moving.

His head throbbed and the world swayed a little when he stood, but he found his footing again and moved to the kitchen. When he arrived, he discovered that Noah was bringing in the last of the groceries from his car and setting them on the counter. He smiled at Ian reassuringly. That man was just too sweet for Rowe.

"Hollis said he's on his way and will be here in about twenty minutes."

"Thanks, Noah." He knew better than to try to call Hollis himself and talk him out of abandoning Shane while on a job. Hollis would only feel better when he finally laid eyes on Ian and saw for himself that his husband was safe.

When Rowe arrived back in the kitchen and announced that it looked like nothing in the house had been touched, Ian set them to work putting the food he didn't immediately need away in the pantry and fridge. He grabbed the cutting board and knife to start chopping up vegetables.

"Ian, you need to take a break. I don't think you should be cooking right now," Lucas gently advised.

Ian snorted at him and kept working on the prep. "You really think anything else is going to help me calm down right now?"

"True." Lucas sighed. Pulling out a chair at the breakfast bar, he sat down and rested his arms on the counter. "All right, tell us everything. Did you see or hear anything?"

"Did you notice being followed while you were out at the store?" Noah added.

"No." Ian paused and sighed. "My mind was on a hundred other things. No one has been after me for years. My mind was on the foster classes, the new restaurant, the problems with Rialto. I didn't—"

"Whoa! What problems with Rialto?" Rowe interrupted, holding his hands up in the air.

Ian clenched his teeth together in frustration. He'd really wanted to deal with this on his own. Well, just him and Hollis, actually. Lucas, Snow, and Rowe liked to exclude him from all the interesting and dangerous stuff as their overprotective way of keeping him safe. But this was his restaurant, dammit!

Reluctantly, he launched into a quick retelling of everything that had been happening at the restaurant—the ICE raid, the fake bad reviews, and the reports to the health department about supposed food poisoning. Though Ian felt a small amount of glee in informing Rowe that he had already secretly gotten the help of his

IT team. Noah snickered and Rowe crossed his arms over his chest as he thundered softly like a little black raincloud.

"Why didn't you tell us all of this when it started?" Snow demanded. Ian winced at the hurt and betrayal in his voice.

"We're family," Rowe groused. He still looked like a redheaded powder keg ready to explode. "We're supposed to be honest with family. We're always there for each other."

"Yes, and I'm sorry I hurt your feelings, but you have to admit that your way of taking care of things sucks for me."

"What are you talking about?" Rowe asked.

"You cut me out of everything. You leave me out and shove me aside. This is *my* restaurant," Ian said, tapping his chest with his index finger. "You leave me out in the name of protecting me, but you never do that when it comes to Snow, Lucas, or Rowe. Or even any of your spouses. You're all right in the middle of the shit and explosions."

"But you've never trained for that," Snow countered.

"Neither has Jude."

Snow sighed. "And I pray that he's never in the middle of the shit and explosions ever again."

"Whatever. And I don't want to hear any more of that Army training crap from you two," Ian said, pointing the knife in his right hand at Lucas and Snow. "It has been *decades* since either one of you was in the Army."

Ian stood with his hands pressed into the center island counter, watching as the four other men in the room exchanged looks. Oh, Ian knew he had them trapped between a rock and a hard place. He welcomed their attempts to wiggle out. They weren't going to work. Not this time.

"Ian, we're just trying to keep you safe. After everything that you've been through—" Lucas started, but Ian simply shook his head.

"This isn't just an attack on your restaurant any longer. Someone came here and physically attacked you," Snow picked up when Lucas fell silent.

"You need a fucking bodyguard with you again," Rowe growled. "I'll check the roster. I'm sure—"

"No! Absolutely not!"

"And an upgrade to the security system," Noah said. "I don't remember if we've got a camera that has a good view of this rear door and the driveway."

Rowe nodded. "At the very least, we need to make sure that everything is still recording even when the system is disengaged, just in case we get another smart asshole on Ian's tail."

"No more food for any of you!" Ian shouted above the talking.

The response was absolute silence for several seconds.

Lucas was the first to find his voice after that stunning announcement. "What are you talking about?"

"You're all banned. If the only thing you value me for is my cooking, then you're cut off if you aren't going to treat me like an equal in this family."

They all started to argue with him at once, but their words stopped when he held up his hands. "I'm serious. I get it. The Jagger shit and my past, it's bad. Really fucking bad. Years and years of therapy bad, but I'm not an invalid. I'm not so fragile that I'm going to break when things go sideways. If you guys try to exclude me from shit on this, I will cut you all off. No more Rialto food. No more surprise lunches." He paused and looked over at Rowe. "And I'm definitely not cooking Thanksgiving."

The deafening silence in the room was broken by clapping. Ian twisted around to find Hollis standing in the doorway, a lazy grin on his face.

"Proud of you, babe," Hollis said before squeezing between Rowe and Snow to reach Ian.

Ian let Hollis's arms engulf him, pulling him in tight. He could feel the tension trembling in his body despite the smile on his face. He'd been worried and it was only now that Hollis was holding him that his husband could find some relief.

"I'm okay. I promise. Just a conk on the head. Nothing more," Ian murmured over and over again. He tried to be strong, but Ian couldn't deny the tremor in his own voice as he spoke. There was a

# Rialto

bundle of fears he wasn't dealing with yet and probably wouldn't until he and Hollis were alone that night.

"Ian," Snow said softly, drawing Ian's head from Hollis's chest to look at the surgeon. "We are sorry we made you feel like you weren't an equal part of this family. We never meant to do that to you."

A lump of old pain and new joy grew in Ian's throat as he released Hollis and walked over to Snow, grabbing him in a tight hug. "I know."

Lucas added, "We want to keep you safe, and we tend to take it overboard when it comes to you…because of Jagger."

Ian turned and hugged Lucas. He hated that he'd hurt them, but this conversation had been a long time coming. They were spending far too much time trying to protect him and not enough actually including him in on the crazy things in their lives. He was tired of feeling like an outsider.

"And while we love your cooking, we love you more," Rowe said. "If I've got to choose between never having your cooking and keeping you safe, I'll always choose your safety."

Ian moved to Rowe and hugged the grumbly lunatic, then pulled Noah in for good measure.

This was his family. He knew they loved him and would do anything for him, but they also needed to let him take the same risks and chances they took.

Ian stepped away from Rowe and wiped his eyes, feeling relief and maybe a little silly.

"Now that we've got that out of the way," Ian said with a laugh.

"How do you want to handle this?" Lucas asked, and Ian couldn't deny that the question felt great. They were willing to leave things in his hands.

Ian walked back over to where Hollis was standing by the center island, a questioning look in his dark eyes. Ian leaned against Hollis, inwardly smiling when his husband pulled him in tight. They were a single unit. Just how he wanted it.

"Right now, Hollis and I are following a few leads. Gidget is looking at people who've visited the restaurant. Quinn is trying to track the person behind the bad reviews. And Hollis is digging into my last disgruntled employee."

"Sounds like a good start," Rowe said with a nod.

"What are you doing about your safety?" Snow pressed.

"Until now…not much," Ian admitted. "But until now, everything was directed at the restaurant. I'll admit that I was kind of wondering if I wasn't the target. If maybe someone on my staff was the real target."

"But now we have proof that this person is out to hurt you. And not just financially or your business reputation. This was an attack at *our* home on you." Hollis's arms tightened around Ian as he spoke, his voice growing more urgent.

"I know. But I still don't want a bodyguard."

Noah took a step forward, one hand outstretched toward Ian. "Would you at least consider letting us look at the security system? See if there's something more we can do or add to make sure you're better protected?"

"Yes, that would be fine." Ian could at least agree to that for both of them. While Ian might be the ultimate target, he wouldn't put it past this person to threaten Hollis with harm if it meant hurting Ian.

"And maybe stop back in for a refresher on self-defense."

Ian narrowed his eyes on Noah. "You're pushing your luck."

"If not for yourself, then do it for Hollis. The poor guy is just starting to enjoy married life."

Ian groaned. "Fine. Two self-defense sessions at Ward Security just to brush up."

Hollis tightened his arms around Ian and lowered his head, brushing his lips across the edge of his ear. "Thank you, baby."

Ian closed his eyes and pushed down a sigh. Anything for Hollis. If it made Hollis happy, he'd do it. And it probably was a smart idea to knock some of the rust off his skills.

"So the plan is to let you follow up your leads, and we're going to wait until you need us?" Lucas asked.

"Yes. We've got this for now. Oh! And Snow needs to plan his own damn wedding. I've got enough to do."

Snow's mouth dropped open while Rowe and Noah nearly fell into each other laughing.

"What? Jude and I are totally planning the wedding on our own," Snow argued.

Lucas placed a hand on Snow's shoulder. "You're texting all of us. Even me. I'm sure Ian's getting the most. You're outsourcing your wedding and afraid to commit to any decisions."

At least Snow had the good grace to blush a little.

"Go! Get out of my kitchen while I cook," Ian said with a laugh. "Go figure out Snow's wedding while I make food."

With some grumbling, the quartet relocated to Ian's living room while Hollis lingered behind.

"Do you have to return to Shane and the case?"

"I should. I hate to leave him shorthanded and without backup, but I had to hold you to make sure you're fine."

Ian lifted up on the tips of his toes and lightly kissed Hollis again and again until his lover grabbed him and deepened the kiss to something desperate and hungry. When they parted a minute later, Hollis hummed and gave him a slightly wicked grin.

"Oh, you're so fine," Hollis purred.

"And I'll be happy to prove how fine I am to you later. For now, go back to Shane. I've got plenty of company to keep me safe tonight."

Hollis cupped the side of Ian's face, rubbing his thumb across his cheek. "I know you find it annoying, but they really are trying to keep you safe."

"I know."

Hollis kissed the tip of his nose. "Sometimes it sucks to have so many people love you," he teased and then left through the door again.

Ian smiled to himself, instantly missing the feel of Hollis against him. The smell of his cologne lingered in the air, and Ian wanted to wrap himself in it. His husband was right. He might chafe under their overprotectiveness, but it all came from a place of love.

## Chapter Nine

Hot water pounded down on Hollis's head as he closed his eyes and leaned into the stream. He braced both hands on the tile and rolled his shoulders, hoping the water would take away some of the stress eating him alive. He'd spent the evening in a surveillance van with Shane when all he'd wanted to do was be home with Ian. He needed to find out who was out to get Rialto.

No, that wasn't quite right anymore.

Someone was out to get Ian. Tonight's attack had been intensely personal. His hands closed into fists as he thought of how much worse it could have been. What if that person had hit him more than once? He imagined Ian lying alone and dying on the kitchen floor. His heart clenched, panic clawing at his insides. Ian was his whole damn world, and the thought of losing him terrified Hollis.

And all this right on the heels of seeing one of Jagger's enforcers.

Ian wasn't completely safe.

While Hollis understood Ian's frustration with everyone treating him like a kid, he couldn't help but want to take care of him. He'd liked the idea of a bodyguard, dammit. But he also understood how

Ian felt, and he had the utmost respect for those feelings. Still, he was walking on a fine line here and he hated it.

He growled and turned under the spray, opening his eyes when a gust of cool air hit him as Ian stepped into the shower with him, naked.

"I'm okay. Wanna see?" His smile was warm but his brown eyes held concern. He brought his slim body close, his hands on Hollis's hips. "I figured you'd be in here, worrying. You tend to take extra-long showers when you do."

"How's your head?" He kissed Ian's temple.

"Just a slight ache, nothing really all that painful." He tightened his fingers on Hollis's hips. "My dinner with the boys turned out nice once they all calmed down."

Hollis ran his hands up Ian's shoulders and cupped his neck. "I'm so pissed this happened to you in our home."

"I know, but there's nothing you can do about it now."

"Oh, there's plenty I can do. Ian, I liked the idea of you having a bodyguard."

"Hell, no. The last thing I want is another one of those following me around. Rowe is upping the security system, and I'll just have to be more vigilant when I'm coming and going, that's all. Pay attention to my surroundings. Not get lost in my thoughts. You know…like normal people." He smoothed his palms up Hollis's chest, curling his fingers in the hair. "I don't want you to start getting overprotective again. We'll figure out who's doing this."

"You bet your ass we will."

Hollis picked up the body wash and started soaping Ian, his dick hardening as he ran his palms over the lissome body of his husband. He had no intention of doing anything about it though, not when Ian's head probably hurt more than he was letting on.

But Ian had other ideas as he wrapped his fingers around Hollis's cock. "I need you tonight," he said softly.

Hollis shook his head even as he gasped at Ian's grip. "I don't want to hurt you."

"You won't. We can take it slow and easy, but I want to feel you in me. Want to feel safe and loved."

"You are so loved, Ian Banner. More than you can possibly imagine."

"Show me."

They got out of the shower and dried off. Hollis watched Ian the whole time, loving the lean lines of his body. He was so damn sexy, he took Hollis's breath away. When he held out his hand, Hollis took it and followed him into their bedroom. Ian let go, turned on a lamp, and crawled onto the bed, his gorgeous, round ass on display. He looked at Hollis over his shoulder and the come-hither smile on his face reeled Hollis in. His feelings for the man were this tangled mass of lust and love and appreciation that swelled in his chest and threatened to steal his breath. But he also felt worry over Ian's injury and he hesitated.

Then Ian stretched out flat on the bed on his stomach and slowly spread his legs, revealing that dusky, pink hole.

Hollis grabbed the lube and dropped it onto the comforter. He crawled behind Ian and stared at the beauty before him and wanted his mouth all over him. He started with Ian's calves, kissing them, enjoying the soft hair, then nibbled on the sensitive skin behind his knees before moving up to knead the taut, round globes of his ass. He kissed the dimples right over his cheeks and nuzzled up his spine until he reached the back of his neck.

"So fucking hot," he whispered into Ian's ear before he nipped it. He was careful around his head, still worried about jostling him too much.

Ian turned so they could kiss. He pressed against Hollis, his body feeling wonderful underneath him. Muscles shifted under sleek skin.

"How's your head, baby?" He kissed his nape.

"We can take this slow and I'll be fine. Need you."

Hollis came up to his knees, gaze roaming the body spread out before him. He reached down and spread Ian's cheeks, further revealing the tight hole he couldn't wait to be inside. But first, he wanted his tongue there.

"Yeah," Ian breathed.

He licked around it slowly, then speared his tongue inside, tasting soap from their shower and the unique flavor that was all

Ian's. He kneaded the globes of Ian's ass as he moved his tongue in and out. Ian shoved up into Hollis's mouth, crying out. Listening to his husband made the sweetest sensation move through Hollis's heart. He'd never get enough of Ian as long as he lived.

Hollis grabbed the lube and coated his fingers before slipping two of them inside Ian. He pushed them deep. Ian was now writhing on the bed and panting. Hollis was so turned-on, pre-cum oozed from his dick as it ached to get inside. But he took his time, also loving the feel of Ian's smooth walls around his fingers. He watched his fingers disappear inside his husband, watched the way Ian lifted into each thrust, his movements fluid and graceful.

"Love watching you like this," he said under his breath. "Holy shit, you're gorgeous."

"Want you inside me," Ian groaned. "I'm okay, I promise."

Slicking himself with lube, Hollis came over Ian and nudged his opening with the tip of his dick. Heat surrounded him as he pushed inside. There was nothing like this, like the feel of Ian around his cock. Soft, slick walls enveloped him and he pushed deeper, bracing his hands on the bed on either side of Ian. Ian pushed back into him, making him go even deeper. Hollis groaned and flicked his hips, knowing he was rubbing over Ian's prostate. The man loved sex like this, loved when Hollis held him down.

"Yeah," Ian gasped. "Move inside me."

The tight, wet heat went to Hollis's head and he rocked into Ian, his rhythm disjointed as pleasure surged through him. It raced through him like wildfire, and his movements picked up as he sank into that delicious heat over and over. He leaned down, pressing his lips to Ian's back, tasting sweat.

Ian moaned and moved with him, his hands coming up to brace against the headboard. He undulated his hips, driving Hollis mad with how hot he was. Ever mindful of Ian's injury, Hollis slowed down his movements, the deliberate thrusts bringing him closer and closer to the edge. He didn't want this to end, so he gritted his teeth and pulled out. Ian went still, glancing over his shoulder in question.

Hollis wanted to turn him over but worried about the pressure on his head, so instead, he drew Ian up to his hands and knees. He could reach around and stroke Ian's cock like this. Ian quickly got with the program and positioned himself in front of Hollis. Hollis couldn't resist running his fingers over Ian's hole, still soft and open from their lovemaking.

He pushed back inside that tight heat and groaned.

"Fuck." Ian's voice broke on the word and he tightened around Hollis.

Hollis lubed up his hand and reached to wrap his fingers around Ian's cock. The satiny skin felt so good against his palm, and he tightened his grip and stroked. Ian grunted and spread his legs more, his hips moving in rhythm with Hollis. The tight clutch of his body, the sleek muscles moving underneath his skin, all of it dazzled Hollis. He rubbed his thumb over the tip of Ian's cock, feeling the slick wetness of pre-cum. It was all so hot, he felt close to blacking out. A ragged moan left his lips as he worked to get air into his lungs.

He leaned down and opened his mouth over Ian's skin. "There's nothing like this," he whispered. "Nothing."

"I know." Ian looked at him over his shoulder, those beautiful brown eyes hooded with lust. "Love this. Love you."

"Love you so goddamn much."

Hollis stroked Ian faster, loving the glazed look that filled his expression. He pressed as deep inside him as he could, his eyes rolling back into his head. He wanted to pound the man hard but kept up the slow, careful movements that were really just as good. He could pay attention to every sensation like this.

Ian clenched around him and he grunted as he felt his orgasm hovering on the edge. He wanted Ian to come first, so he stroked down to his base like Ian loved, then twisted his hand on the way back up to swipe his thumb over the tip again.

"Oh!" Ian cried out, squeezing his ass.

"I'm coming. You first, baby."

"It's there. I'm there!"

Ian's whole body tensed up and he yelled as he came, spilling over Hollis's hand, his hold around Hollis's dick like a vise. Hollis's movements stuttered and he shoved into Ian three more times before pleasure rushed through him. He grasped Ian's hips and held on, riding the waves, his vision going black as he squeezed his eyes shut. He shuddered and couldn't stop his hips from pushing into his husband a few more times before he started to feel too sensitive. He slowly pulled out and collapsed on the bed next to Ian, who plastered himself over Hollis. He wrapped his arms tight around him, kissing his temple. "Want me to go get a towel for cleanup?" His words came broken through his harsh breaths.

"No, I like it like this." Ian nuzzled his chest. "Is it just me, or does it feel like that's getting even better?"

"Always good," Hollis panted. "Always."

They lay there, catching their breaths, sweat cooling on their skin.

"I never knew sex could be like this before you," Ian said softly, stroking his hand down Hollis's side.

His weight felt good on top of Hollis and he tightened his arms. "Sex wasn't like this before you. It could be good, but nothing feels like the way we do together. And yeah, it seems to be getting even better. Don't know if I could live through it improving more."

Ian chuckled and kissed his chin. "Not to sound cheesy, but I'm pretty sure love has something to do with it."

"Oh, there's nothing cheesy about that." Hollis nuzzled into Ian's hair, taking in the scent of sweat and shampoo. He thought of him lying on that floor. Defenseless. "I would die if something happened to you."

"Nothing is going to happen to me. I'll be paying better attention from here on out."

"Yeah, but he came into our damn home. I can't get past that. This is our sanctuary from the world, you know?"

"It still is. We're beefing up security, and I doubt he'll return. He knows we're on to him now. Or her. We don't know who we're dealing with."

"True. I haven't found anything on Ginger yet, but I'm looking." He looked down at his husband and stroked his hands over the silky curve of Ian's back. He gently tugged Ian so their faces lined up, and he kissed him. Ian's lips were so soft and warm, and he slid his tongue into his mouth. Ian was his home. His everything. Every single day, he thanked the universe for putting this man in his path.

Ian kissed him back, his hands coming up to frame Hollis's face. "Mmm. We keep this up, and I'll be ready for round two."

"As intriguing as that sounds, I think you should rest."

Ian sighed and snuggled down onto his chest. "As long as you lie here with me, too."

"I'm not going anywhere."

He held his husband long into the night, relishing his weight on him, his scent, and the soft brushes of his breath over Hollis's skin. He didn't sleep for a long time, too wound up and worried.

## Chapter Ten

Over the next four days, Ian felt like he was going to crawl out of his skin. The constant worry made his muscles ache and nausea creep through his stomach. The physical toll this was taking surprised him, but the emotional toll was worse. He still couldn't believe someone had attacked him in his home and whether he liked it or not, Hollis was checking in with him a lot more often than usual. So were his friends.

It did warm his heart that he had so many people who loved him.

But he couldn't kick the worry over Rialto, couldn't stop wondering who it was and what exactly they were after other than destroying his livelihood. Why they'd physically attacked him. Ian wracked his brain constantly, trying to come up with who it could be and kept hitting a blank.

He spent those days at the restaurant, reassuring his employees, and keeping an eye on the foot traffic, which still hadn't lessened. Either people weren't paying attention to the reviews or they just didn't care. As of right then, it seemed his business might weather the storm. But he couldn't ditch the bad feeling that followed him around like an evil shadow.

When Rowe called a meeting Monday afternoon at Ward Security, Ian and Hollis drove there together. Ian frowned at the trash in the back seat of his husband's blue Chevelle as he got into the vehicle. He gave Hollis a look.

Hollis glanced at him as he pulled the car out of their driveway and smirked. "Hey now, this is my space and I keep it the way I like."

"You like having all this junk in your car?" Ian picked up a bag that had come from a fast-food restaurant. "And are we going to have to talk about your diet when I'm not around?"

Hollis's grin was wide. "No, it doesn't bother me to have this stuff in the car. It gets cleaned out eventually. As for my diet, you know it's mostly good, but every now and then a guy just wants a Big Mac."

Ian rolled his eyes and tossed the bag into the back seat as Hollis laughed.

"I hope they've found something," Ian said as he watched the city scenery go by.

Hollis reached across the seat to touch his hand. That little contact helped to settle the swarm of butterflies trying to escape his stomach.

They arrived at Ward Security and walked inside the building to find a self-defense class going on. Noise filled the big, open space, and Ian had to wonder if a lot of the men and women in the class joined it because it was being run by Sven. The man was a beautiful giant with his long blond hair and massive, muscular form. Ian loved his much smaller boyfriend, Geoffrey. Ian glanced around to see if Geoffrey was hanging around and spotted him off to the side, talking to a group of people.

Geoffrey saw him and jogged over, his blond hair flopping over his eyes. He threw his arms around Ian's neck. They'd become friends over the years, so he was no longer surprised by the blond man's effervescence. Or the stuff that sometimes came out of his mouth. Geoffrey lacked a filter and as usual, he didn't disappoint.

"If it isn't the famous Chef Banner. I saw that magazine spread of yours and was wicked jealous. Mine wasn't nearly that big. My spread, that is." He winked. "I haven't yet had the chance to explore how we rate in other areas."

Ian shook his head. He knew Geoffrey was one hundred percent faithful to his boyfriend, so the man was just fucking with him. "I saw the article about you and your big sale. How's the new app doing?"

"It's in the final stages now and just awaits a launch."

Ian waved toward Sven, who was demonstrating how to break out of a hold. It was with a very small woman, so he was being obviously gentle. "You come to all his classes?"

"When I'm not working. I just *love* watching him work. So damn sexy." He gave a demonstrable shiver.

Hollis chuckled, his hand on the small of Ian's back. "I think half his class is here for the same reason. Some are pretty blatant—just watching."

"What do you mean half?" Geoffrey laughed and pointed at his boyfriend. "There's a reason Rowe has Sven lead this course." His expression grew serious. "Why are you here? Are you getting a bodyguard? Is there a reason you need one?"

"No, I have a meeting with Rowe and the triplets, that's all."

Geoffrey lowered his voice. "Listen, I've seen the reviews lately and just wanted to say that anyone who has half a brain could tell they're not true, that someone has it out for your restaurant."

It didn't make him feel better knowing anyone had seen the damn reviews, fake or not. "Yeah, it's pretty obvious. Figuring out who is the hard part."

"Is that why you're here? I'm being very nosy, aren't I?" He grinned and it was so cheeky, it made Ian smile. Geoffrey had zero remorse when it came to being nosy and curious. "I'll let you get to your meeting. Sven and I have reservations at Rialto next weekend, so I'll see you there."

They said good-bye to Geoffrey and took the stairs up to Rowe's office. Rowe looked up at them when they walked in, his red hair a disheveled mess, a scowl on his rugged face.

"Hey," he said. "Just a sec and we'll head over to the triplets' room." He poked at the keyboard of his computer a few times, cursed, then stood up. "I will forever hate the paperwork part of this business."

"I'm with you there," Ian said. "It amazes me how much paperwork goes into a restaurant when all I want to be doing is cooking and talking with the customers."

"I prefer being out in the field and leaving Andrei to this crap, but I took more of it on since Daci's arrival." He went to the door. "I hope the triplets have some good news."

They walked down the hall to a big room filled with electronic equipment and a conference table. Gidget was on her computer with Quinn leaning over her chair and pointing to something on the screen. He looked up. "Hey, Ian. Hollis."

Gidget waved them over to her computer. She had several screens around her, and she pointed to one that was frozen on a scene from behind Ian's restaurant. "The only thing suspicious on the tapes was this guy painting graffiti on the brick at the back of Rialto." She frowned at Ian. "It would have helped me if I'd known I was looking for a graffiti artist."

"Wait, when did you deal with that?" Hollis asked, coming around to look at the screen.

"I didn't say anything about it because it happened right after the magazine came out, and it was your standard hate stuff. I dismissed it entirely—just painted over the words. It's not like I haven't dealt with that kind of thing before. Since opening Rialto, I think we've been hit with this kind of graffiti about a half dozen times." Ian squinted at the image.

"But if this happened recently, when all this other stuff is going on, it's important," Rowe pointed out. "Do you recognize this person at all?"

"How could I? They're wearing a hoodie. But it's too big to be Ginger. She was tiny."

"It's not a tall man, but a man nonetheless," Gidget pointed out. "Look at the ropey forearms." She zoomed in on the arms. "Also, whoever this is uses drugs. See the track marks?"

"I don't think we're dealing with Ginger in any of this anyway," Hollis said. "She took a job in Louisville and has been out of town this whole time. Took me some time to track her down." He looked at Quinn. "What about the IP addresses?"

Quinn shook his head. "That's a dead end. Tracked them back to a library."

"So we have no leads?" Rowe barked out. "We're hitting a wall on this. Any ideas on who would want to hurt you, Ian?"

"Hollis and I have already gone over this, and the only person we came up with has been out of town this whole time. She could still be putting out some of those reviews, but I can't help but feel this is all coming from the same person. The only logical explanation is another restaurant owner, but why come to my house and physically hurt me?"

Rowe nodded. "You're right, that was too personal." He paused and chewed on his lip a moment as he stared at Ian. "I hate to say this, but what about someone from your past? Not everyone who worked for Jagger was arrested."

Ian wrung his hands. "But that's been such a long time. Why would anyone carry a grudge that long and why start attacking me now?"

"Who knows?" Rowe answered. "It could be anything. They're still out there."

Hollis cleared his throat. "They are, Ian. I saw one of them not too long ago while on surveillance with Shane."

"You did?" Ian frowned as his gut began to churn. Anger pierced his belly. "Why didn't you say anything?"

Hollis reared back at his tone. "Because I didn't want to worry you."

Ian shut his eyes and counted to ten while his fury grew into something that blacked out the corners of his vision. "I'm never going to be safe, am I? Never going to be free. Here I am working on building this life with you and my restaurant and…kids." His eyes opened as he focused on Hollis, and he knew his expression was bleak. "How do we bring foster kids into our lives if we're still dealing with this shit?"

Hollis grabbed his shoulders and squeezed. "We don't know this is coming from one of Jagger's men. Like you said, that's a long time to carry a grudge, and why have a grudge against you to begin with? You were a victim."

"Maybe because I killed him?"

"It's been years." He tried to draw Ian into a hug, but Ian pulled away. He was still pissed Hollis hadn't told him about seeing someone from Jagger's crew. He was pissed over the entire situation, and he stalked away from everyone and ran his hands through his hair.

"I can't bring kids into my world. I should have never thought I could."

Rowe came to him and cupped his face. "If anyone in this world deserves to have kids, it's you, so don't you dare give up on your dreams over this. We'll figure it out."

But Ian was inconsolable. He stepped away from Rowe and returned to the computer screen. He looked at the hooded figure and tried to make out anything familiar about him, looking for tattoos, a glimpse of a face. Whoever it was, he wasn't really that much bigger than Ginger, but he agreed that it was a man and a drug user. He'd seen marks like that in the past. "Can you run this back a bit? Does his face show up at all?"

"No," Gidget answered. "I've slowed it to a crawl and watched the whole thing. He's extra careful, like he's aware he's being filmed. What did the graffiti say?"

"Homophobic slurs. But I can't imagine someone being so upset that I'm gay, they'd go through all this. I mean, that kind of hate can't still be real, right?"

"Hell yeah, it could be." Rowe scowled. "All this started right after the magazine article came out, you said?"

Nodding, Ian hugged his arms around himself because he still couldn't believe someone would hate who he was enough to try and destroy him. "Then this could be anyone. We have absolutely nothing to go on. No leads at all."

"We know it's a man, and we know he's a drug user." Hollis

walked to him and again tried to draw him into a hug, but Ian tensed up, causing his husband to frown.

"That's not enough," Ian said, drawing in a shaky breath. "It's just not."

## Chapter Eleven

Ian shrugged off his jacket and hung it in the hall closet. The trip to Ward Security had been more painful than he'd been expecting. He'd thought they'd be able to walk away with some lead or clue as to why he was being targeted. But the information that came out of the meeting had left him feeling sick to his stomach and so damn frustrated.

Jagger.

No matter what he did. No matter what he achieved. No matter what he tried. It all came crashing back down to Jagger.

The fucking bastard had been dead for almost three years, and he was still interfering with Ian's life in some way.

It wasn't fair.

He hated to think of it that way. He knew that life wasn't fair. That it wasn't supposed to be fair, but there had to be a line where things sort of evened out or there was some kind of balance that kept people from running through the street screaming.

Since Lucas, Snow, and Rowe had saved him, Ian had worked hard to live his best life. The guys had given him countless opportunities to pursue his dreams. He'd studied the culinary arts, opened an amazing restaurant in downtown Cincinnati, moved out on his own, taken down a crime boss's operations, dated, found the love of his life, and gotten married.

Now he was on the cusp of starting a second restaurant and becoming a foster parent with the hope of one day starting his own family with Hollis.

But it all felt like it was on the brink of falling apart because of something to do with his stupid past and Jagger's organization.

Hollis walked into the living room with his phone in his hand, scrolling through something as he flopped down on the sofa. "Don't forget that we've got another foster parent class tomorrow night," Hollis murmured. "It'll be good to have those done."

"Why bother?" Ian grumbled.

"What? What are you talking about?" Ian looked up to find that Hollis had lowered his phone and was now sitting on the edge of the cushion. His expression was both hurt and confused. "Do you not want to be a foster parent anymore?"

Hollis's question was like a knife to the heart. Yes, he wanted to be a foster parent. There was little in the world he wanted more. There were so many kids in desperate need of a safe place. After losing the love of his parents and being sold to a pedophile, Ian knew the value of being loved and cared for by someone. Knew what it was to go to sleep with a sense of safety and the feeling of being protected.

"Why should we bother? We can't keep any kid that we bring home safe," Ian replied, frustration and pain battling it out in his voice.

"Ian..."

"Don't! You have to be realistic about this. Kids in the foster care system are going through some rough stuff. They've already been through enough in a place they call home. It's supposed to be safe there, but obviously it isn't if they're in the foster system. How can we offer them safety?"

"Our home is safe."

"Really? Does it feel safe to you? Does our life feel safe to you? We've got security cameras outside our home and a state-of-the-art system inside our home. I've been attacked on more than one occasion in my life. God knows how many times you've been attacked."

"Most of the attacks on me happened while I was a cop. I'm not a cop anymore," Hollis quickly threw out.

"And Rowe keeps threatening to have a bodyguard follow me around. How exactly is that going to look to a social worker? You, me, the kid or even kids, and a freaking bodyguard!"

Hollis took a deep breath and stood. "Ian, you're upset. It's been a long few days. We didn't get the kind of good news we were hoping for when we met at Ward's. But it doesn't mean we need to toss all our plans in the trash. If you think logically about this, you'll realize you're overreacting. Our home is safe. We're safe. We're safe as any other family out there. No family can promise that nothing bad will ever happen. Everyone takes precautions against the worst. That's why we lock our doors at night and wear seat belts when we ride in the car."

"Yeah, and what kind of precautions does the average family take against Jagger's former crew? What kind of precautions are they taking against former drug dealers, murderers, extortionists, and pedophiles? Did I miss that on the home prep list between locking away the household cleaners and putting covers on the wall sockets?"

Ian could see the muscle ticking in Hollis's jaw—a clear sign that Hollis was on the edge of finally losing his temper—but Ian didn't care. He was hurting and angry. He needed Hollis to be angry and hurting with him. Needed Hollis to understand that everything they were working so hard for was falling apart.

"That's not our life anymore," Hollis snapped.

"It is! You just didn't see fit to tell me about it. How could you? How could you not tell me you saw one of Jagger's men?"

"Because we don't talk about Jagger!" Hollis exploded. The pain and rage had Ian stumbling back a step in shock. Hollis shoved both his hands through his hair and paced away from Ian, but he couldn't go far before he was forced to turn back. His face was flushed and his eyes glistened.

"Can you even tell me how many times we've talked about Jagger since his death?"

"No. Why should we?" Ian replied, but his voice had lost some of its confidence and bravado. Even he couldn't pretend complete ignorance.

"Because it's a festering fucking wound between us."

Ian wrapped his arms around his middle and took another step away. Old pains and anxieties came creeping in. Flashes of ancient, ugly memories he'd never fully be free of. "I don't want to talk about Jagger. It was a nightmare. You weren't there. I just want to move on."

"You keep forgetting that I *was* there. Yeah, I only spent a year in Jagger's organization, but it was enough to see what went on in his house. It was enough that I could very clearly see the kind of hell you were living day in and day out. I saw those fucking pictures that Dwight Gratton had of you. Those memories flash through my head at odd times, and I want to kill them all over again. I hurt for you, but I can't talk with you about it—the one person who would understand—because it's going to hurt you."

Ian pressed the heels of his palms into his eyes, rubbing them hard against the burning tears that were trying to break free. He hurt for Hollis and the memories he was forced to carry. He hurt for himself and the past he couldn't completely shed. "I-I just want to move on. Create a better life."

"So do I. I don't want to hurt you, so I pretend everything is okay. The same way you pretend that you're fine. Or pretend that the nightmares that get you out of bed to cook at four a.m. have nothing to do with Jagger."

Ian balled his hands into fists and turned to glare at Hollis. "Is rehashing the past really going to make things better?"

"Maybe. If it means that you stop pretending and running, then yeah, we need to talk."

"What the hell are you talking about? Who's running?"

"You are! You were planning the new restaurant at the same time as our wedding. We were barely back from our honeymoon before you started researching what it takes to be a foster parent.

You didn't pause to think what our schedules were already like. You just jumped right in. You are running from one thing to the next so that you never have to sit still, never have to think about the things that are bothering you from your past."

"I'm done putting my life on hold for Boris Jagger and Dwight Gratton and all those fucks from my past!" Ian shouted, pointing behind him where all the rest of his bad memories waited. "I'm going to be thirty this year. I want to finally live my life."

"What? All at once? You got eggs that are suddenly going to go bad if you slow down just a little?" Hollis taunted.

"Fuck you!" Ian shouted, hating the tears he could hear in his voice. "I'm done waiting. I waited for Jagger to lose interest in me. I waited for the guys to finally start letting me live my own life. I fucking waited for *you*!"

"And fuck you for making me feel like I can't talk to you about shit! For making me walk on eggshells so I won't interfere with your plans for the perfect life."

Ian stormed out of the living room with a dismissive wave of his hand at Hollis. Stomping to the bedroom, he slammed the door shut behind him. He couldn't talk to him anymore. Couldn't even look at him. Hollis wasn't listening to him. Talking about Jagger wasn't going to fix anything. It wasn't going to erase his past or suddenly make everything better.

He dropped down on the floor and leaned against the side of the bed. His head throbbed and his throat felt raw from fighting back the tears. It was their first serious argument. They'd had some small blowups over the past few years, usually about Ian taking risks and Hollis being overprotective.

But this one was different. It was the first time he'd ever said, "Fuck you!" to Hollis like that. How could Hollis keep something as big as seeing a former Jagger goon from him? Telling him wouldn't have been the same as demanding to know what his life had been like in Jagger's house. Or how often he'd been forced to fuck the man. Those things he didn't want to talk about, didn't want to relive in his head.

Ian scrubbed his hands through his hair. Even if he didn't talk about them, Hollis knew of them on some level because of his time undercover. His husband was forced to deal with that knowledge with no outlet. And the idea that Hollis felt like he couldn't talk to Ian gutted him so deeply. He was always there for Hollis. No matter what. How could he think that he couldn't talk to Ian?

Except that talking about it forced Ian to think about it, relive it, and that would cause Ian new pain. Something Hollis never wanted to do.

What the hell were they supposed to do?

Go to counseling?

Jesus, they both obviously needed it. Solo and together.

Ian had gone to a therapist for a few years after coming to live with Lucas and the others. She'd helped him deal with a lot of shit and move on so that he'd feel safe in life to pursue his dreams. But he'd stopped before the final confrontation with Jagger and never returned. Old wounds had been reopened and never truly closed again. God only knew the wounds that Hollis was nursing since they didn't talk about this stuff.

*Hell.* They'd been married for only a few months and they needed to go to counseling already. Ian was sure he couldn't feel like a bigger failure.

But then, most couples weren't dealing with a past like Ian's. Most couples weren't dealing with old memories from an evil crime boss. Most couples weren't dealing with a lunatic trying to destroy Ian's restaurant and possibly his life.

Didn't matter. Ian didn't give a shit about other couples or what his family might think. The only thing that mattered to him was Hollis. He wanted Hollis to be happy. He didn't want Hollis hiding his pain anymore. Didn't want to hide from his own.

He needed to fix this.

## Chapter Twelve

Ian gave up trying to sleep several hours later. Hollis never came to bed, and Ian assumed he'd gone to the guest bedroom to sleep. Either that or he'd sacked out on the couch. They hadn't slept apart since they'd first moved in together, and he felt the loss like he was missing a limb.

Heart aching, Ian got out of bed and walked down the stairs. Hollis wasn't on the couch, and Ian knew he wouldn't be able to sleep until he did something to fix the rift between them. Hollis meant more to him than anything else in the world.

He could start with chocolate.

Hollis loved anything and everything chocolate. His favorite dessert was something as simple as brownies.

Ian padded into the kitchen and started getting the ingredients for his double fudge. He set out the eggs so they'd be closer to room temperature while he got down the cocoa, baking soda, sugar, vanilla, and more. He melted butter and started the water to boil. He'd just whip up a batch of these and present them for breakfast. Chocolate for breakfast was bound to get him back into Hollis's good graces. Or at least talking again.

He couldn't believe what he'd said to him. That he'd actually said "fuck you" to his husband. Ian never blew up like that. The only time he ever yelled was when he was arguing with Lucas or Snow, and even that was rare.

Shame pinched his chest as he preheated the oven and began to assemble the ingredients. He didn't use his loud mixer, whipping the batter by hand. By the time he got the pan into the oven, his hands were shaking and he thought of waking Hollis to apologize. But the man needed his sleep, so he stayed in the kitchen.

Soon, the rich scent of fudge filled the condo. Ian leaned against the counter and shut his eyes. He rubbed them hard, feeling so out of sorts. He didn't know what to do with himself. Sleep called to him, but he needed Hollis more, and their argument sat like a rock in his stomach. Cooking was his only solace, so he decided maybe two chocolate things were better than one. He could make some cookies, too.

He opened his eyes and jumped when he saw Hollis standing in front of him. He wore nothing but a pair of boxers, his big body so damn welcome, Ian's shoulders slumped as he took a step toward him. Hollis held open his arms and Ian fell into them, wrapping his own tight around Hollis's back.

"I'm sorry," they said in unison.

Ian laughed and buried his nose in Hollis's neck. "Did I wake you?"

"No, I couldn't sleep. The wonderful scent coming from the oven brought me downstairs. I guessed you were doing what you always do when upset. Cooking. I'm sorry you're so sad, but whatever that is smells delicious."

"You don't recognize your favorite brownies? I thought chocolate might help me apologize better."

"You don't have to apologize in any special way. You're going through hell right now and we have nothing to go on, so it's frustrating and upsetting. You're so strong to be holding it together as much as you are." Hollis pressed his lips to Ian's forehead. "I'm sorry I lost my temper earlier."

"We both did. I think this has just been building inside me, and I felt ready to explode. Shouldn't have done it all over you."

"I'm here for the bad as well as the good. I'm here for everything. I love you so much, Ian."

"I know." He pulled away so he could see Hollis but kept their lower bodies together. "We both need to do a better job of talking."

Hollis frowned, sadness creeping into his beautiful blue eyes. "I don't want to hurt you."

Reaching up, Ian gently laid his hand against Hollis's cheek, rough with whiskers. "I know, but I don't want you hurting either. Don't want you to feel like you're alone and have no one to talk to. That kills me. You're the most important thing to me in the whole world."

Hollis closed his eyes and leaned his cheek into Ian's touch. Ian could feel some of the lingering tightness leaving his hard muscles as he relaxed further against Ian. "Thank you," Hollis whispered. Those two words were choked with emotion, and Ian could feel a knot forming in his throat. He never wanted Hollis to be in pain for any reason.

"And when we're done talking, I can always make brownies," Ian said. When Hollis opened his eyes again, Ian nodded his head toward the oven with a small smile.

"I don't give a damn about the brownies. You're all I need. I only followed the smell because it let me know you were awake down here."

"I was about to make cookies, too."

Hollis framed his face with his hands and kissed his nose. "The brownies are more than enough. Like I said, I don't need them. I just need you. I always need you."

"I don't like it when you sleep in the guest room. We need to make a pact that we never go to bed angry from here on out."

"Done. Couldn't sleep in there anyway. I need you with me."

Ian leaned against him again, wallowing in the knowledge that neither of them was able to sleep while angry. He looked out the kitchen window at the darkness outside and felt like they were cocooned in their own perfect bubble. He sighed and kissed Hollis's shoulder. "We really do need to talk about our feelings when it comes to my past with Jagger. I'm sorry you felt you couldn't tell me about seeing one of his enforcers."

"I was shocked to see him, to be honest. I thought of saying something, but like I said, it's just not something we ever talk about. I had no proof that he had anything to do with what's happened with Rialto, and I didn't want to upset you more."

"I'm thinking of trying therapy again," Ian said quietly. "If this has shown me anything, it's that I haven't gotten past it all myself."

"If you think that'll help, then I'm all for it."

Ian looked up at him and smirked. "But it's not for you, huh?"

Hollis grimaced. "I'm not sure therapy and me would be a good mix. I can try if you truly want me to, but just knowing we're pulling all this out into the open is good for me. I don't want to fight with you about any of that. Honesty from here on out is needed."

"Agreed." He grinned up at his husband. "Neither of us lasted long in our first real fight."

"It sucked. I was just lying in there and feeling like an idiot. Missing you." He kissed Ian and pulled him in tight to his body. Since Ian was only in pajama pants, their chests slid together and Ian loved feeling all that warm skin and hair. Hollis deepened the kiss, his tongue winding with Ian's.

The oven timer dinged, and Ian reluctantly pulled out of his husband's arms. "Hold that thought." He quickly checked the brownies to see if they were done, pulled them out, and turned off the oven. He held his hand up to Hollis. "Time for makeup sex?"

"Hell yeah," Hollis breathed as he pulled Ian back into his body. The kissing took on a new level of passion then, and Ian knew they were both feeling the guilty remnants of their earlier argument. He wanted all that negativity out of his head, so he wrapped his arms around his husband's neck and threw everything into their kiss. Tongues slid together and Hollis's hands stroked up and down his spine before he gripped Ian's hips and ground against him. Ian could feel how rigid Hollis already was and pressed hard against him.

Hollis groaned, kissing his jaw to his neck. He sucked the skin into his mouth briefly before moving to Ian's shoulder and opening his lips over skin. "Love you," he whispered reverently. "No more fighting."

"No more," Ian agreed as he nuzzled into Hollis's soft hair.

Hollis returned to his mouth, sliding his tongue between Ian's lips. Ian opened wide for him, and the kiss went on and on until they had to pull back to gasp air into their lungs. They stared at each other for long moments, the passion between them scorching Ian from the inside out.

Ian stared just a bit longer before he kneeled and pulled down Hollis's boxers until Hollis could kick them off. He took hold of his beautiful cock and licked the end, the flavor of pre-cum bursting on his tongue. The tile was cold under his knees, even through his pajama pants, but he didn't care. He buried his nose in the pubic hair at Hollis's root and took in the scent of his man. Musky and warm—it was his favorite smell in the world.

Hollis stroked his hair, then grasped his head and led him back to his cock. Ian took him into his mouth, using his tongue to love on the silky skin. Hollowing his cheeks, he took Hollis deep, relishing the sound of Hollis's moan above him. He pulled him deeper and worked to swallow around the head, choking as Hollis moaned again. His husband loved it when he choked on his dick, and Ian wanted to smile but his mouth was too busy.

He wrapped his hand around the base and went to work, bobbing his head as that slick cock slid in and out of him.

He loved giving Hollis head, loved the sounds that came out of the man, loved that he could bring such pleasure to him.

When Hollis tugged him to his feet, he blinked at him in surprise. "Not good?"

"Too good," Hollis growled as he set Ian up on the breakfast bar.

"This isn't hygienic at all," Ian muttered, though he really didn't care. He'd scrub the place down in the morning.

Hollis stepped between his legs and ravished his mouth, his big hands stroking Ian's chest, then his back. He cupped the sides of his head and tilted it, his mouth going to Ian's neck. Ian shivered, loving kisses there and when Hollis opened his lips over his pulse, he held his breath. Hollis returned to his mouth, spearing his tongue deep inside Ian.

"I hate it when we fight," he murmured against his lips.

"We don't do it often, thank goodness." Ian licked into Hollis's mouth, wrapping his legs around Hollis's waist and his arms around his neck. "And we've never had one like that."

Hollis abruptly picked him up and walked toward the stairs.

"I have to cover the brownies," Ian said as he held on.

"Fuck the brownies. I want you so much. We'll be lucky to get up the stairs."

Ian smiled and went back to kissing his husband. Hollis was so damn strong as he carried Ian to their bedroom. He put him on his feet next to the bed and leaned down to tug off his pajama pants. He kissed Ian's legs, then his hips, before stopping at his cock. He licked it and pulled it into his mouth, his hand coming up to cup his sac.

"Agh," Ian breathed as he dropped his head back and sucked air into his lungs. One of Hollis's hands went around to cup his ass, and he pushed Ian into his throat. Ian fucked into his mouth, loving the feel of his tongue sliding around him. He was so wet and so tight. It all felt so fucking good.

When Hollis moved up to his mouth, he sighed against his lips. They were going to be okay, and it wasn't just because of the sex. Neither had made it through one night mad at the other, and his heart warmed at the realization that their relationship was that strong.

Hollis devoured his mouth, his kisses deep, hot, and wet. Ian stood on his toes and opened wide for Hollis's tongue as he stroked his hands over Ian's shoulders and down. Hollis gripped his ass and ground against him.

"What do you want, GQ?"

"You. Just you." Ian turned and bent over the bed. "Like this."

Growling, Hollis grabbed the lube and brought his slick fingers to Ian's hole. He rubbed around it, leaning over to kiss the small of Ian's back. He nuzzled the skin as he dropped soft kisses there, his fingers slowly sliding into Ian's body.

Ian groaned and spread his legs more, bracing his hands on the bed. When Hollis entered him, he held his breath at the sting, knowing that pleasure would soon follow. The last time they'd made love he'd just been hurt, but he was fine now, so he hoped Hollis would pound him into the mattress. He loved when the man came over him and pinned him down.

Hollis didn't disappoint and before long, he was ramming Ian's prostate and making him see stars. He howled into the bed, gathering the covers in his fists. Hollis's fingers dug into his hips as he held him and thrust into him over and over.

Fuck, Ian loved this.

Sweat built on their bodies and Hollis grunted when he bottomed out inside Ian. "You feel so damn good," he said on a moan.

Ian looked over his shoulder to find Hollis watching where their bodies connected. It was dark in the room with only lights from outside filtering through the blinds, but Ian's sight had adjusted enough to see the glazed lust on his husband's face. He loved him like this—loved when he gave over to his pleasure and took Ian like this.

He leaned over Ian's back and sweat dripped from his chest. He lifted Ian onto the bed and crawled up behind him on his knees before spearing into his body. Ian lifted and reached behind him to touch Hollis's face and Hollis grasped his chin, his fingers going into Ian's mouth. He sucked on them, gasping at a particularly strong thrust.

Hollis pulled out his fingers and reached to wrap his hand around Ian's dick. Ian cried out, the dual sensations rocking his whole damn world. He pushed into Hollis's hand, then back onto his cock, so fired up, he hovered on the edge of his orgasm. When it hit, he yelled and shuddered and came all over Hollis's hand and the bed. Hollis stroked him through it, groaning softly behind him.

"So fucking hot," he panted, pulling out and using some of Ian's semen to stroke himself before pushing in. Ian gasped and cried out again, coming up to reach behind him for Hollis. Hollis's wet hand held his chest as he sucked on Ian's neck. His rhythm faltered, and his breaths picked up until he was panting hard in Ian's ear. Then he went mostly still with only his hips rocking into Ian as he groaned long and loud. Ian felt him pulsing inside him as he quivered with the force of his orgasm.

He loved feeling Hollis lose it on him, loved knowing he affected the man as much as he affected Ian. Ian collapsed onto the bed, grimacing at the huge wet spot he'd left. But he didn't have time to relax before Hollis was hauling him up and into the bathroom. Hollis turned on the water and when it was hot enough, he stepped into the spray with Ian.

They washed each other slowly, their gazes mostly locked, and it was so intimate and loving, Ian didn't want to ruin the moment with words. Though they needed more words. After they dried off, he stripped the ruined comforter off the bed and grabbed a blanket out of the closet to replace it.

Crawling into bed, he held his arms out for Hollis, and Hollis settled on his back and pulled Ian half on top of him.

"We still have baggage," Ian whispered against Hollis's chest. He swirled one finger in the hair there before looking up to meet Hollis's gaze. "I'm going to call tomorrow and make an appointment for me."

"If that's what you need, then it's important. I should have told you about seeing Jagger's enforcer. Should have realized you're strong enough to handle that kind of information." Hollis palmed his back, softly running his fingers over Ian's skin.

"I am. I'd gotten too relaxed about things since Jagger's death. It was nice to not be looking over my shoulder all the time, and I resent that I'm having to do so again." He sighed and snuggled closer. "I don't want to spend my life doing that, so we have to get to the bottom of this."

"And the foster classes?"

"We'll finish. We've come too far to stop now, and I still want it. I let my anger speak for me earlier. My anger and fear. But I am worried. I won't bring in any children until this situation is resolved."

"We *will* resolve it. I promise."

Ian sighed and kissed Hollis's chest. "No more yelling at each other, either. I didn't like it."

"Me neither, baby," Hollis whispered, nosing into Ian's hair. "We should try to sleep. Maybe tomorrow things won't feel as bleak."

"They don't now. As long as you and I are good, I can deal with the rest."

"I promise, we're good. Hell, we're great."

Exhaustion pulled Ian nearly under before he remembered something. "I never covered the brownies," he murmured.

He fell asleep to the deep, rumbling chuckle in Hollis's chest.

## Chapter Thirteen

Hollis stood to the side, smiling as he watched Ian talking animatedly with another couple they'd made friends with in their foster training class. It turned out that they were unable to have their own children and were now looking to adopt but wanted to start out as foster parents. They were currently chatting about the anxiety and stress of preparing their home for the first check to make sure they'd made all the necessary changes to accommodate young children. He and Ian had yet to go through that, but it was coming soon. They'd agreed to get through the mandatory training classes first.

Reaching into his pocket, Hollis pulled out his phone and turned it on. The classes were the only time they both turned off their phones as a way of making sure there were no distractions. The world could get along without them for three short hours. Right?

He looked up from his phone as Ian started to make sounds of wrapping up his conversation when Hollis's phone started buzzing and vibrating like a thing gone mad in his hand. He stared at it, his brow furrowing as missed calls and frantic texts started rolling in.

"Everything okay?" Ian asked. His hand came to rest on his bicep, his gentle touch meant to soothe.

"Turn on your phone. I've got calls and texts from James as well as Jude. Something bad happened."

Ian released him and immediately reached for his phone. Hollis shoved his own phone away and grabbed Ian by the shoulder so he could get them both walking toward his car while Ian dealt with whatever was happening on his phone.

He'd just gotten Ian into the car when his phone finally booted up and messages started scrolling through along with missed calls. "James, Jude, and Isabella for me."

Hollis shut Ian's passenger door and hurried around the car to jump behind the wheel. The Chevelle roared to life, and Hollis carefully backed out of the parking spot, planning to head directly to Rialto, though he couldn't understand how Jude Torres was involved in anything to do with the restaurant. Had he and Snow stopped there for dinner and something happened?

"Oh, God!" Ian gasped, his fingers partially covering his mouth as he pressed the cell to his ear. Hollis could only guess that he was listening to a voice mail. "Go to UC hospital."

"What? What happened? Is Snow okay? Jude?" Hollis demanded.

"Wade and Sean were attacked in the parking lot as they were leaving tonight. They were both taken to UC."

A heavy weight sank in Hollis's stomach and he stepped on the gas so that they sped down the quiet street. They were no more than fifteen minutes from the hospital, but Hollis was determined to get them there in ten. "Fuck. Are they okay?"

"James said he didn't think it was too serious, but he sent them both in an ambulance to get X-rays and checked by a doc."

"Which would explain Jude. He and Rebecca must have been the ones to get the call," Hollis said, mentioning Jude's perpetual partner in the ambulance. He hated to admit that he relaxed a little to know that it wasn't their small family that had been attacked. Jude was a great guy, and even grumpy Snow was growing on him. Particularly when he and Snow teamed up against Lucas.

"I'm calling James to get more details."

Hollis nodded and turned his attention to getting them to the

## Rialto

hospital as quickly and safely as possible. Though he was also keeping one eye on the rearview mirror to make sure no one was following them. The bad reviews and report to the health department were annoying and financially troubling, but whoever was out to hurt Ian was definitely stepping up their game. First the physical attack on Ian at their home and now a physical attack on two of Ian's employees. He wasn't sure if this was just a scare tactic or something more. They needed to figure out who the fuck was doing this and why. It had to end now.

Hollis was only half listening to Ian's conversation with his business manager as he mentally ran through their options for securing Rialto and protecting the other employees.

"Thanks, James. We're pulling into the garage now. We'll be there in a few minutes," Ian said as Hollis started looking for a place to park.

"What'd he say?"

"Both Sean and Wade are in for X-rays now. Sean definitely has a concussion, so they'll probably be keeping him overnight for observations. He's not happy about that."

"He knows your insurance will cover it." Hollis glanced over at Ian to find his husband giving him a look that said he was being obtuse.

"Sean doesn't want to be away from the restaurant any more than I do. He knows I'm going to make him take some time off to recover."

"Is everyone at Rialto a workaholic?"

"Pretty much."

Hollis pulled the car into an open spot and shoved it into park. He pointed his finger at Ian. "You're a bad influence."

"I know. I know," Ian muttered as he threw off his seat belt and climbed out of the car.

"Did James say anything about who attacked them?"

"No." They started to quickly walk toward the area marked as the emergency room. "Sounds like they didn't see who it was, but it was just one attacker. Apparently he knocked out the light over the parking lot and attacked them with a baseball bat, then got away. The police have been called and are checking the area. They're also going to keep a squad car in the area until everyone has left for the night. James has already called someone to replace the light."

"Shit."

"Why go after Sean and Wade? I thought this was a personal attack on me," Ian demanded, lowering his voice to a near whisper as they entered the hospital.

"Because attacking your people hurts you too."

Hollis looked over at Ian to see the pain, anger, and helplessness clearly etched onto Ian's face. It was working, too. Ian was more shaken up about the attacks on his employees than he was about the attack on him in his own home. Enough had happened to Ian over the years that he'd learned to shrug off personal physical attacks, but attacks on his family and restaurant were deep wounds that he didn't quickly get over.

"This is a clear attack on you and your business," Hollis murmured. "Do you want to take this to the police? You've got a definite case now."

Ian's fast steps slowed to an almost halt, and he stared up at Hollis in surprise. It was clear that he'd not considered it yet. Hollis could almost see the thoughts zipping around in his mind as he weighed the pros and cons. It took only a couple of seconds for Ian to shake his head.

"No. Not yet, at least. The police are keeping an eye on the restaurant, and we can ask Rowe to send over some bodyguards as well so that everyone at Rialto is safe."

"I worry about the people at Rialto, but my main concern is *your* safety," Hollis pressed.

"I know, but what if Rowe is right, and this is someone from Jagger's old crew? That's going to raise a lot of questions as to why I'm being targeted when very few people know I have a connection to Jagger. I don't want my past getting out and dragged through the news if I can help it. We can take precautions. I just want to get more information first before I willingly blow up my life."

Hollis wrapped his arm around Ian's tense shoulders and pulled him against his side as they continued to walk. "Then we'll keep it in the family," Hollis whispered as they started down the hall again.

He understood Ian's desire to keep his past hidden. The strong man at his side had worked far too long and hard to rise above that sordid ugliness and make a great life for himself. If the world found out the truth, they would never let him move on. He'd forever be labeled Jagger's victim. No one would care about his other accomplishments. It wouldn't matter if he was the world's greatest chef or owned a string of five-star restaurants that had lines of people waiting to get a table.

Ian deserved better than that.

As they reached the waiting room, they found Jude talking to a pretty brown-haired woman in the same uniform as Jude. This had to be the infamous Rebecca. Jude straightened from where he was leaning against the wall when he spotted them and ended his conversation with the young woman. They waved and Jude turned to meet them, a tentative smile on his lips.

To say that Jude was a fucking catch was an understatement. The dark-haired man with the swarthy skin and constant five o'clock shadow looked like he should be modeling clothes and not riding in an ambulance, covered in blood and other fluids. If Hollis had never met Ian, then yeah, he would have definitely hit on Jude, convincing them they'd have a wild night. But Jude had eyes only for his General, just like no one would ever catch Hollis's attention but his husband beside him.

"They're okay," Jude said before Ian could even speak.

Ian breathed a deep sigh of relief and Jude immediately pulled him in for a brotherly hug. "I'm so glad you were the one called to the scene," Ian replied.

"Honestly, I wasn't really needed. Don't get me wrong. They took a good beating. Sean definitely has a concussion, and it looks like Wade has a few fractures. Maybe some internal bruising. But I wouldn't expect either of them to be here for more than a night just for observation."

"Thanks, Jude," Hollis said. Jude wouldn't normally share patient information, but they all knew Ian was about to barrel into those rooms and get the information from his employees. It was better that they weren't allowed to sugarcoat it for Ian. They would both need some time off work to recover.

"Do you think this is related to the recent problems that Snow was telling me about?"

"Very likely."

Jude turned his attention to Ian, but there was something assessing in his gaze, as if he were slipping into paramedic mode the same way that Snow went into doctor mode. "How are you doing? Recovered from…"

Ian quickly waved a hand at Jude. "I'm fine. Just fine. Recovered. It was nothing."

"He had a concussion," Hollis corrected.

"A small, baby one. Not even worth mentioning."

"All concussions are worth mentioning," Jude said firmly, but his expression softened. "I'm glad you're okay and so are your people. If you need anything, you know that Snow and I are here for you."

"We know. Thank you."

Jude stepped backward and turned toward the double doors leading into the emergency department. He flashed his badge in front of a reader and the doors automatically opened. He led them through the busy room with people rushing from one place to the next. Curtains were pulled around half of the beds.

"Is Snow working tonight?" Ian asked, following after him.

Jude nodded. "In surgery now. It'll probably be a few hours."

"Busy night?" Hollis asked.

Jude shrugged a shoulder. "Not really." He paused in front of a pulled curtain and flashed a little grin. "At least it's not a full moon."

Ian started to open his mouth, but Hollis didn't know if he was going to tease him or ask if that old superstition was true. From his years as a cop, Hollis could confirm that shit really did get crazy when the moon was full. And he was sure that just by close association, so did the ER. But Ian never got the words out as Jude poked his head in the closed-off area and asked if whoever was in there was up for a visitor. They didn't hear the reply. It didn't matter because Jude had pulled back and was waving for them to enter.

Lying on the bed, they found Wade in his uniform from Rialto with small splatters of blood on it. He was a little pale, and one arm was now wrapped up from fingers to elbow. At his side was Jackson Kent, a bodyguard for Ward Security and Wade's boyfriend.

"No! I told them not to bother you," Wade cried as he saw Ian. "You had a foster parent class tonight."

Ian hurried around to the side of his bed and placed a gentle hand on his shoulder. "And this is exactly where I should be. Everyone at Rialto is my family too. Now, are you okay? What has the doctor said?"

"I'm fine. I swear."

"He has a hairline fracture in his arm and wrist. Also a couple of bruised ribs," Jackson said, his voice barely more than a growl.

"I'm going to have James rotate you off the schedule for a week, give you some time to heal and recover."

"No!"

"Wade, you need rest. Your body must heal. The kitchen will still be there and waiting for you when you're healthy."

"But Isabella was going to teach me some of her grilling techniques this week," Wade argued, just shy of hitting a whining tone.

Hollis turned to the side, his lips pressed tightly together to hide his smile from Jackson and Wade. He wondered if Jackson knew what he was in for yet. Wade was just a younger version of Ian, and there was no way of getting Ian out of the kitchen unless Hollis appealed to his sexual appetite. Then again…maybe Jackson had figured that out.

Jackson leaned down and pressed a kiss to Wade's temple. "I'll talk to Andrei and Noah, see if they can work me out of the schedule for a week so I can stay home with you."

"I don't need a freaking nurse. I'm fine." Wade had moved from whine to pout.

Jackson leaned down and whispered something in Wade's ear that made his eyes go wide and his cheeks flush. Hollis couldn't stop his snort, and even Ian was looking anywhere but at the couple. Yeah, Jackson had definitely figured out how to handle Wade and his cooking obsession.

"Fine. You can stay home with me," Wade mumbled.

Ian patted his shoulder, and Hollis swore it looked like he was trying so damn hard not to laugh. "It looks like you're in good hands. I'm going to see if I can find Sean. I'm glad you're okay, Wade."

"I am."

"I heard them taking Sean to get a scan of his head. He probably won't return for a while," Jackson added.

"Ian, what's going on?" Wade asked, stopping their departure. "The person who attacked us kept shouting at us to stay away from Rialto. If we came back, he was gonna kill us."

Both Ian and Hollis were at his bedside again in an instant, shocked expressions on both their faces.

"He spoke to you?" Hollis asked, his voice low.

"Yes. Kept threatening both Sean and me." He nodded at Hollis and then turned his attention back to Ian. "I'm not leaving. That asshole isn't scaring me off."

"Thank you, Wade." Ian started to reach for his hand, but he was on the side of Wade's injured hand, so he opted for his shoulder again. "I really appreciate it."

"What's going on? Is this linked to what's been happening recently? With the raid and the bad reviews?"

Ian sighed. His gaze darted over to Hollis, and his heart broke a little bit for his lover. Ian didn't fucking deserve this shit.

"I think it is." He paused and licked his lips. "Someone recently attacked me at my house." Wade gasped and Ian quickly held up a hand, stopping the barrage of questions that was undoubtedly coming. "I'm fine, I promise. I was knocked out, but Snow and Lucas found me a short time later."

"Do you have any idea who's doing this?" Jackson demanded. Hollis bristled at his tone, but he tamped down the urge to snap at the bodyguard. It wasn't just Ian's life that was in danger anymore. The attacks had now reached Ian's employees.

"No. We're following up some leads, and we're getting help from Rowe's triplets," Ian said. Jackson nodded and seemed to relax a little more now that he knew Ward Security was involved.

"We need to tell Rowe about this," Hollis said.

Ian shoved a hand through his hair, leaving it standing up in various directions, but he nodded. "Agreed. We need more security for the restaurant, both for the customers and the staff. I don't want anyone to not feel safe at work."

"I don't think he's going to have any problems getting volunteers," Jackson said with a little smirk.

Ian's brow furrowed. "Why do you say that?"

"Sven might have bragged about how well you kept him fed during the two times he worked as your bodyguard."

Hollis chuckled and Ian's shoulders shook a little with laughter. "Yes, whoever gets 'stuck' with Rialto guard duty will be fed," Ian replied.

They stayed and chatted with Wade for a little while longer until a nurse finally came with Wade's paperwork for his release. They'd given him a prescription for a mild painkiller and instructions to schedule a follow-up appointment with his regular doctor as well as an orthopedic doctor.

Ian and Hollis then found Sean, who'd been moved to a regular room for the night. He wasn't at all happy about the situation, but he seemed clearheaded with some internal bruising like Wade.

Neither Wade nor Sean could give a good description of the attacker. Only that he was male, thin, and about the same height as Ian. They were just lucky that it didn't appear to be one of Jagger's old muscle who specialized in breaking bones. They also hadn't talked to the cops yet, but Hollis was sure someone would be around to question both Sean and Wade. And to see Ian.

With a great deal of reluctance, Ian told Wade and Sean to be honest with the cops and tell them everything they remembered. Even the threats. Ian didn't want the cops involved, and Hollis had to agree with him, but it was an extra set of eyes watching over Ian's people at Rialto.

They stayed with Sean for a while, making sure that he was comfortable and didn't have any new information that Wade hadn't already told them. Sean would definitely be taking some time off. He was about as grumpy as Wade had been about it…

well, before Jackson gave him some incentive to lounge at home for a few days.

It was late when they silently walked out of the hospital and to Hollis's car, both of them deep in thought. They didn't see Snow or Jude as they left, but Hollis was sure they were both busy doing their jobs. Tomorrow there would be more phone calls and questions. And for once, Hollis welcomed them. They needed all the help they could get. The problem was growing more dangerous by the day, and they had too few leads.

They didn't speak again until they were home. Hollis turned off the security system and locked the door behind them. While Ian hung up their jackets, Hollis quickly swept through the house, double-checking to make sure that nothing had been disturbed while they were gone. It shouldn't have been possible, but since the attack on Ian, Hollis couldn't relax until he made an entire pass through the house.

Luckily, Ian said nothing about it, understanding that it was something to make them both feel more secure.

Hollis returned to the first floor to find Ian in the kitchen, which wasn't surprising, but he was staring off into space.

"Babe?"

Ian shook his head as if pulling himself out of a spiraling thought. "This has to be someone from Jagger's old crew."

Hollis nodded. He'd been thinking the same thing on the drive home but hadn't figured out how exactly to broach the topic with Ian yet.

"It's the only thing that makes sense. Another restauranteur? Competition? I can't imagine that person would turn to violence. Bad reviews and even the health department stunt, sure. But attacking me? And attacking my staff? That's too extreme for most normal people."

"But Jagger's crew are made for violence," Hollis agreed.

"Dammit," Ian swore softly. "I can't believe my past is coming back to hurt *my* people. This shouldn't be happening. Shouldn't be possible."

Hollis walked around the island that separated them and pulled

Ian tightly into his arms. "This isn't your fault. You haven't done anything to cause this. This fucker is insane. You can't be blamed for that."

"But—"

"There are no buts for this."

Ian wrapped his arms around Hollis, dropping his hands down to cup his ass, which brought a smile to Hollis's lips. "Except that you've got a really sexy one."

Hollis pressed a kiss to the top of Ian's head. "And only you get to touch it."

"What are we going to do? Besides add more security, of course."

Hollis swallowed back a sigh. He would have liked one quiet, happy evening at home with Ian, but it was clear that wasn't going to happen until they caught this fucker. They needed to take care of this problem.

"How about you grab that Bordeaux you've been wanting to try and two glasses? Bring them into the living room. I've got something a friend sent me today."

Ian pulled away and gave him a questioning look before he nodded. Hollis released him and walked into the home office he'd set up in a corner of Ian's office. He woke up his laptop and quickly opened the email that his friend from the CPD sent him. There were several pages, but he only needed the top sheet. He printed it off and went to the living room, where Ian was pouring them a glass of the dark red wine.

"What secrets have you been keeping?" Ian asked when Hollis appeared.

"No secrets. A cop friend emailed me this today, and I was going to show you tomorrow morning. I wanted us to have one quiet night together."

Ian opened his mouth, looking as if he planned to apologize, but Hollis glared at him as he stood over Ian. Ian snapped his mouth shut and smiled at him. There would be no more apologies from Ian. This wasn't his fault.

Sitting down on the couch beside Ian, Hollis handed over the paper.

"What's this?" Ian asked, his eyes already skimming over the list.

"Those are all the people who were known to work for Jagger who are still living and free in the Cincinnati area."

Ian's eyes went wide, and his mouth dropped open. "So many? There have to be at least thirty people here."

"I found out that after all the chaos, the DA was forced to focus on the most dangerous of Jagger's people. His lieutenants. Those who were most likely to restart his business interests."

Ian gave a little nod, his eyes skimming down the list. "I understand."

He was taking it far better than Hollis had expected. Hell, he was taking that news better than Hollis had. The former cop had been ready to march down to the DA's office and knock them around for what they missed.

"I thought you could look over the names. See if there's anyone on there who might be angry with you. Anyone you might have had some contact with in the past."

"Well, I guess the good news is that I don't recognize at least half of these," Ian murmured. "I'm guessing they joined Jagger after I left. Do you have a pen?"

Hollis jumped up and quickly searched out a pen. He dropped back into his seat and handed it over, watching closely as Ian placed little stars next to three names—all of the former enforcers for Jagger. He drew a big circle around one name that made Hollis's stomach drop.

"The ones with the stars are the ones that I had the most contact with. They'd at least know me, but I don't know that they'd necessarily be angry with me. Ernie Bowling…he was close with Jagger. Ran a lot of jobs personally for Jagger. If he's upset about Jagger's death, then yeah, he'd be pissed at me."

Hollis sighed and scrubbed a hand over his face. "Ernie Bowling is a monster, Ian. We couldn't get any dirt on him that would tie him to specific deaths, but we were pretty damn sure he whacked several people for Jagger."

Ian looked up at Hollis and smiled. "I think we should talk to him."

Hollis didn't even try to hide his skepticism. "Ernie is taller than me. There's no way he was the attacker tonight."

"I know, but I have a feeling Ernie still has a lot of contacts. He could have heard something. I think he's the best starting place."

Hollis had to agree, but they weren't doing it without a hell of a lot of backup.

## Chapter Fourteen

Ian shoved his hands into the pockets of his brown leather jacket and tried like hell not to look as out of place as he felt. He'd been to dive bars with Rowe on more than one occasion over the years, but Goodtimers was even more dive-y than Rowe would have liked.

The smell of old, stale beer and cigarette smoke was thick in the air, and Ian was sure that it was already clinging to his skin. Thick darkness blanketed the interior so that it was nearly impossible to make out the faces of patrons. Not that anyone probably wanted to be recognized.

Hollis walked just a step in front of him, looking far more at ease in the place. But then he'd admitted before they arrived that he'd been to the bar a few times when he'd worked undercover in Jagger's organization. The place had been a favorite of some of Jagger's lower-level goons.

Apparently it still was.

Ernie Bowling was sitting at the bar, nursing a beer. It looked like he had one eye on the small TV mounted up in the corner, running the evening news. The man was massive. Even bigger than Ian remembered. Ian was sure he stood an easy six five, maybe even six seven, and was wider than a double-door refrigerator. He could palm Ian's face with his monster hands.

"I think he got bigger," Ian whispered.

"We've got your back," Rowe replied calmly in his ear.

Hollis had been insistent that they not go in alone, and Ian was so damn glad he'd listened. There couldn't have been more than half a dozen people in the place, including the bartender that stood behind the bar, looking half-asleep on his feet. No, all of Ian's attention was on Ernie. Even if he wasn't armed, the man could plow through Hollis and him like they were made of tissue paper.

Rowe and Noah were stationed out front, across the street. Sven was out back to cover the rear door, while Royce was hidden somewhere in the darkness of the interior of the bar. It had been decided that with his scruffy looks, he could pass for someone who could belong in such a place.

Unfortunately, Royce's boyfriend, Marc Foster, had been visiting Ward Security when that comment was made, and he'd not been amused. He asserted that his adorable boyfriend did not look like a low-life thief or drug dealer, which led to them briefly disappearing off somewhere for a quiet moment.

Just the memory of the stiff and proper Marc defending his lover while the usually growly Royce melted as he watched nearly made Ian chuckle. He couldn't think of two people who were bigger opposites, but they appeared to simply fit together. Of course, there were whispers that Marc's past wasn't entirely prim and proper. Something about an art heist and trolling sex clubs with Snow in the old days. Not that Ian wanted to know any of the details.

As they walked through the bar, the plan was for Ian to grab a table while Hollis went and ordered a couple of beers. They wanted to see if he remembered Hollis from when he worked at Jagger's. They weren't sure if Hollis's cover had been blown with everyone, and if Ernie thought Hollis was an old compatriot, he might start talking. That was assuming he didn't notice Ian in the first place.

But as they crossed the bar, Ian changed his mind. He wanted Ernie to notice him, to remember him. The monster of a man hadn't directly terrorized him. Never laid a hand on him, but the dark threatening looks had been there. The threat obvious. If Ian had stepped out of line, Ernie was right there to knock him back into place.

Ian had never been tempted to test him. A big part of surviving Jagger's place was making sure he didn't attract more attention than necessary. He didn't want anyone looking at him, thinking about him. If they forgot, then they didn't try to touch.

But those days were over. He wasn't going to be scared anymore. He had Hollis right beside him. Royce was somewhere behind him. Rowe, Noah, and Sven were just a short distance away. He was safe.

Hollis motioned toward a small, rickety table that looked like it hadn't been cleaned since Clinton was in office. There was no way in hell Ian was touching that nasty thing. Stepping around Hollis, Ian took two big strides toward the bar, almost instantly closing the distance between him and Ernie. Hollis hissed and grabbed Ian's shoulder, trying to stop him, but Ian shrugged off his hold.

"What the fuck are you doing, Ian? That's not the plan!" Royce said in a low, harsh whisper.

"What the hell is going on?" Rowe demanded, panic filling his voice. He was blind to the events inside of the bar and was waiting for the signal to storm the place. Ian suspected that Noah was just barely keeping Rowe on the street outside.

He poked Ernie three times with his index finger in his meaty shoulder, and it was like poking a sleeping giant. Ian's heart was pounding as if it had gone mad in his chest. Breathing became difficult, but Ian held it together, using his anger and frustration as fuel for bravery.

"Hey!" Ian said sharply. "You remember me?"

The mountain of flesh slowly turned on the stool and looked down at Ian. His meaty face was a mask of boredom for a moment, and he looked like he was about to tell Ian to fuck off when recognition lit his features, transforming them into expressions of surprise…and joy.

"Ian! Holy shit! Ian!" he shouted. Ernie dropped off the stool faster than Ian had thought possible and grabbed him up in massive arms, pulling him into a tight hug. He was hugging Ian.

Behind him, Ian was vaguely aware of both Hollis and Royce shouting for the man to drop him and step back.

Ernie released him and put his hands up. "What the fuck is this?" he demanded.

"Whoa! It's okay!" Ian jumped in front of Ernie the moment he got his brain wrapped around the situation. Ernie didn't want to hurt him. The big guy seemed genuinely happy to see him. "It's okay. He's not a threat. Everything is fine," he repeated as much for Hollis and Royce as he did for the others outside who were likely running to stop what they likely thought was an attack.

"Ian?" Ernie asked.

Ian looked over his shoulder at the huge man and gave him an apologetic look. The whole scene looked ridiculous. Ian was defending someone easily twice his height and weight against two other big guys with guns drawn.

"Sorry, Ernie. We thought you might be the person out to destroy my restaurant and maybe kill me."

"What? No! Of course not!"

Both Hollis and Royce lowered their guns, their expressions becoming a bit sheepish. Hollis said something quick to Royce, and the bodyguard gave a little wave to Ian before leaving the bar. The other patrons continued to stare at them for another couple of seconds before turning back to their beers now that all the action was over.

"What's going on?" Ernie asked.

Ian looked around and finally decided on a table toward the rear of the bar that looked a little less disgusting than the others. He motioned for Ernie to accompany him. As the three of them settled at the table, Ian made quick introductions, but it hadn't been necessary.

"Yeah, I remember you. I thought I heard you were a cop," Ernie said with a grin.

"Ex-cop now. Private detective," Hollis corrected.

"Nice gig. And you ended up with Ian here?" Ernie continued, pointing at Ian. His smile grew even bigger, and Ian was sure that Ernie was a secret softie. "That's great."

"Look, someone is out to ruin and hurt Ian, and we're pretty sure that it's someone from Jagger's old crew. There's more of them running free in the city than we expected," Hollis said. His voice was hard and serious. The man was in no mood for a reunion. There was nothing positive about Ian's past with Jagger except for meeting Snow, Rowe, and Lucas. Ian was more than happy to get this meeting over with and get out of the bar.

Ian jumped in and gave Ernie a quick recap of everything that had happened at the restaurant as well as the attack on Ian at home.

Ernie's expression clouded and he sat up straight, glaring at Hollis and then Ian. "And you thought it was me?"

Ian chewed on his bottom lip for a second. He couldn't believe he actually felt a little guilty for accusing Ernie when he obviously didn't harbor any grudge against him. "Ernie, I know you made a very comfortable living from Jagger. And you were moving up while I was there. I know people have to blame me for taking down Jagger. We thought…maybe you wanted revenge for ruining your paycheck."

A slow sigh drifted from Ernie, and his shoulders slumped before he put both hands on the table. "I get ya. But you gotta know that I've been in this business since I was a kid. Sometimes the boss wins. And sometimes the cops win. If you don't get caught in the roundup, you count yourself lucky and go find a new boss."

Ian stared at Hollis across the table, and his husband shrugged at him.

"That's a really…down-to-earth view of things," Ian murmured.

"I ain't got no grudge against you, Ian. I know things was bad for you at Jagger's, and I had no interest in making things worse so long as you didn't cross the boss. I'm glad you got out, and I'm happy you've had all your success. I saw that magazine article about you. Very fancy."

"Thanks, Ernie." Ian could feel his cheeks heating with a blush.

"I really miss your cooking, too. You'd send all kinds of things down to the guardhouse, and I loved it all. I never ate so good. Some of the guys were sure you were gonna poison them, but I didn't care. It would have been a great way to go." Ernie shook his head, dropping his eyes to his hands folded in front of him. "I keep hoping that your restaurant will start using one of those delivery service apps. I'd love to try that food, but I don't want to make you uncomfortable."

And for that Ian was grateful. No one from Jagger's old crew had ever stopped into the restaurant as far as he knew. There had been several of Cincinnati's socialites who liked to attend Jagger's parties that would come into the restaurant, and Ian was always sure to make himself unavailable to the customers at that time. James had it down to an art if any of them was so bold as to ask for him. Ian refused to have his past shoved in his face while he was in Rialto.

"I'll look into it," Ian promised. He could at least do that if Ernie managed to give them some kind of viable lead.

"Well, if you're not pissed at Ian, do you know of anyone who might be? From Jagger's old crew?" Hollis pressed, putting them back on track.

"Nope."

"Have you been in contact with any of them?"

Ernie bobbed his head lightly. "Some. We mostly scattered after Jagger turned up dead. Seemed the smart thing to do. But I see them here or there."

"And none of them are pissed at Ian? Blame him for what happened to them or Jagger?"

Ernie made a face and spread his hands. "It's been three years now since Jagger was killed. The bastard deserved it and we all knew it. Sure, some mugs might have been pissed in the early months, but now? Pffft....No way. Who holds a grudge like that? We all got bigger problems to deal with."

And that was a good point. Who the hell would hold a grudge after so much time? And why go after Ian now? Three years had passed. There had been ample time to go after Ian then. Would have been easy too because Ian hadn't been watching his back after Jagger died. He'd been sure that he was completely safe.

Ian looked over at Hollis, who was staring at him with a deep frown. They were back at square one—without a single lead to go on.

"Thanks for your time, Ernie," Ian said, extending his hand. Ernie eagerly took it in both of his and pumped it a few times.

"Sorry about earlier," Hollis said, sticking out his hand as well.

"I get ya. You're just protecting your man," Ernie said easily, shaking Hollis's hand as well.

They stood, but before any of them could take a step toward the exit, Hollis stopped and held up a hand.

"Do you know what happened to any of the other kids that Jagger kept? Ones like Ian."

"You mean those in the house?"

Hollis nodded, and Ian didn't miss the uncomfortable way that Ernie looked over at him from the corner of his eye. It was an angle that none of them had considered. There were only a couple of others that usually stayed in Jagger's house besides Ian. Most of them didn't last long. Ian had been Jagger's favorite, but sometimes the bastard wanted a little variety. The only problem was that he got bored with them extremely fast, and they were usually passed around at the parties.

"It's okay," Ian reassured when Ernie seemed to hesitate.

"It ain't pretty. Most got hooked on drugs. They became dealers or mules for Jagger. Others left and just became rent boys on the streets. Both those lives…once you're in…"

"There's no real chance of getting out," Hollis softly finished.

"Ian is the only exception that I know of. He got out and did something better with his life," Ernie continued. "There's no real escape after meeting Jagger. He was like this sticky tar. That tar would get on you and just sort of drag you down."

Ernie's words made Ian feel sick, but he couldn't say that he was surprised by them. He'd already seen it firsthand with Kyle and Hanna Fogle. Kyle had fallen into Jagger's clutches when he was young. Jagger hadn't been interested in Kyle's sister, but he'd kept her to maintain a tight control on Kyle. The bastard had brainwashed both of them, got them working for him as arsonists. Ian was sure they wouldn't have ended up dead if it hadn't been for Jagger.

How many other Kyles and Hannas were there in the world? They'd blamed Ian for their falling out with Jagger. Were there other kids who blamed Ian for destroying their world because Ian killed Jagger?

Saying good-bye again, Hollis carefully ushered Ian out of the bar, but he was barely aware of it. Ian was running through all the faces of kids he encountered during his time at Jagger's. How many had there been with no escape? Had there been any that he could have helped to escape? Should he have been looking for them rather than worrying about starting his own restaurant? Or getting married?

The cold night air helped to pull Ian from his dark thoughts. Hollis kept his arm wrapped around his shoulder, guiding him to where he could see Rowe and Noah standing down the block. Ian's stomach churned and his heart hurt. He didn't want to admit it, but it was a damn good lead.

"What do we got?" Rowe asked the second they had joined them.

Hollis relayed the conversation they'd had with Ernie, both the parts about Jagger's old crew having no interest in him and the idea that the culprit might be one of the boys that Jagger tormented.

Ian didn't look up, but he could feel Rowe's and Noah's worried gazes on him. He wanted to be strong, pretend that it didn't affect him, but he continued to lean against Hollis, his arms wrapped tightly around his middle. Guilt had become a living thing in his chest. He'd been through this before, and his family had tried to convince him that there was nothing he could have done. That he needed to take care of himself in those early days.

But he should have done something.

When he escaped Jagger, he'd poured his entire existence into forgetting about those years. To living the best life he could as thanks for all that Lucas, Snow, and Rowe had done for him. He never wanted their sacrifice or the risks they took to feel like a waste. If he proved that he could pull himself up from the trash that Jagger had tried to make him into, then they would know that he'd been worth all the effort.

In all that struggle to be something more, he should have tried to save someone else too.

"Ian?" Rowe said cautiously.

"You need to tell Gidget that she should look through police records for someone between the ages of eighteen and thirty with an arrest record for drugs or prostitution. From there, we can see if any of them have links to Jagger," Ian said quickly. He wanted to distract Rowe from his silence.

"We're on it. I'm more concerned about you," Rowe continued.

"Don't be. I'm fine."

"You're not."

There was no point in denying it. He was so fucking far from fine. Fine was in another damn country for all that Ian was concerned.

"What if this is like Kyle and Hanna?" Ian whispered. "If this is another kid coming after me, we can't let anything happen to him. We have to save him."

"Ian, if he's trying to hurt you, even kill you—" Noah started, his voice soft and so sensible, but Ian didn't care.

"Doesn't matter," Ian snapped. "We have to at least try. Just talk to him. Try to help him." Ian had no plan in mind, but his resolve firmed. If this was a kid hurt by Jagger, then they would find a way to help him. Give him the same chance Ian had. Give him a second chance at life.

Hollis tightened his arm around Ian, squeezing him so he could soak in more of his husband's strength and warmth. "We'll try, baby. We need a solid lead first. I'll contact my friend at the CPD. The triplets will dig as well. Hopefully we find something useful soon."

Ian nodded, but he didn't have any doubts in his mind now that they'd finally kicked over this stone. Ian was sure that at the end of the trail to the person that was trying to ruin Ian's life, they were going to find someone who had their life ruined by Jagger.

## Chapter Fifteen

Ian pulled the lasagna from the oven and set it on the stove in Lucas's penthouse. He looked around the kitchen, and the nostalgia threatened to bring him down. His hand strayed over the counter's smooth surface in a gentle caress. So many new recipes had been tried in this kitchen. And so many had bombed, but Lucas had given a safe place to experiment. Countless breakfasts. Promising to come over for that first meal of the day twice a week had been the only way Lucas grudgingly accepted Ian moving out on his own. He hadn't even asked Ian to cook. Breakfast had been Lucas's guarantee that they'd see each other twice a week.

Those quiet meals together had been the starting point of too many arguments to count. Lucas didn't want Ian to move out. Lucas pushing Ian to open his own restaurant. Ian fighting Lucas over the amount of bacon he was allowed to eat. Lucas growling over Ian's dating attempts. Ian growling over Lucas's pathetic dating attempts.

The penthouse wasn't the first place he'd lived with the guys, but it was the last place he'd lived with any of them before moving out on his own. It was a refuge. A sanctuary.

It was home.

And tonight was their last night in the place. Most of Lucas's, Andrei's, and Daci's personal items had been moved into the new house Lucas had built in Indian Hill, a huge sprawling place with a big yard and more rooms than they could possibly need just for their family. There was even a cute little cottage being built for Andrei's parents at the edge of the property.

But before the doors could close on the penthouse, he, Lucas, Snow, and Rowe had decided on one last hurrah in their home before it went up for sale.

He gazed over the light honey wood and brushed nickel decor, then walked to the massive window that looked over Roebling Bridge and a wide swath of Cincinnati and the Ohio River. He'd miss this view and this gorgeous penthouse where they'd spent so much of their lives. They'd gathered on the balcony every year to watch the Labor Day weekend fireworks that were shot off from barges on the river. They'd watch snow falling in dancing swirls and bright flashes of lightning in brutal summer storms. Every holiday. Every major event. It all took place here.

And soon someone else would be living here where he had so many memories. It felt like *their* place. Made him sad to think it would be no longer.

Snow walked up to him and handed him a glass of wine. "Food smells good."

"I went with something easy, so we'd have more time together."

"Only you would think lasagna is easy, especially since I know you make that sauce early and let it simmer all day."

Ian shrugged and looked back outside. "I'm going to miss this."

Snow turned toward the window too. "So will I. I kind of hate that they're moving, but I certainly understand why."

Rowe and Lucas were in the living room, talking about some new toy Rowe picked up for Ward Security. Andrei had taken Daci out with his parents for the evening, so they had the place to themselves.

The little girl's presence was felt in the various pieces of baby furniture dotting the rooms. There was a high chair at the dining table and a playpen in the living room. Framed photographs had been taken down and packed already, but normally, the walls were covered with images of Daci, Andrei, and Lucas. The penthouse hadn't changed much when Andrei moved in. It continued to feel like the comfortable bachelor pad that it was. But that little girl had added a layer of warmth and love Ian hadn't thought possible.

He glanced at Snow to find the man frowning at the view as he brushed a hand down his gray sweater. Snow had gotten his nickname from his hair turning silver in his twenties, back when he was still in the Army. This penthouse had been a refuge for him as much as it had been for Ian, so he imagined the surgeon was feeling the same melancholy.

"Come on, let's join the others."

Carrying his wine into the living room, Ian settled on the black sofa, next to Rowe. Lucas, his hand idly holding a glass of some kind of amber-colored alcohol, sat in the chair closest to the fireplace. Snow took the other end of the couch. Ian looked around at his friends and had to smile. So many things had changed for them. It had started out as just the four of them, and now they all had husbands or boyfriends. Their lives were no longer solitary outside of their foursome.

"You remember that night Ian made the crab puffs and we got drunk here?" Rowe asked. "Let's do that again."

"I remember you face-planting behind the couch," Lucas murmured, a grin teasing the corner of his lips. His black hair was slicked back from his angular face, and he looked comfortably lazy in a pair of jeans and a blue sweater that made his eyes more gray than green.

Lucas sat sprawled in the chair, and Ian couldn't help but remember the night they were talking about—when Lucas had been so worried about Andrei, who'd gone undercover in an illegal cage-fighting ring. Lucas had been very different that night. Vulnerable. It was a word he'd never thought he'd use with Lucas. He was always an immovable wall of strength and determination, but when it came to the man who captured his heart, Lucas became vulnerable in all the best ways.

"Times sure have changed," Ian said softly. "We have a lot of memories of this penthouse."

Lucas's shoulders shook and he covered his mouth with one hand.

"What?" Ian demanded.

"I was thinking of the time Mel and Snow got so wasted they were singing 'Dancing Queen' at the top of their lungs while shaking their asses out on the balcony."

Rowe's loud bark of laughter filled the penthouse, and Ian's heart swelled to hear it. He knew Rowe missed his deceased wife, but he was glad he could now remember her with less pain and more joy. That woman was happiness personified, and it was all she would have wanted for her husband.

Snow leaned his head over, putting it against Ian's. "Half my good drunk memories are thanks to her."

"Only half?" Ian teased.

Snow lifted his head and grinned at Ian. "The other half I was too drunk to remember."

Everyone groaned and Snow snickered.

Rowe hummed. "Drunk Battleship."

"Fuck you!" Lucas shouted suddenly, and Rowe gave an evil cackle. "I was finding those damn red and white pegs all over the fucking house for months after that."

"Not my fault. Snow and Ian were cheating."

Lucas flipped Rowe off while Ian and Snow laughed. Ian couldn't argue with him. He and Snow had teamed up against Rowe in a random game of Battleship, and yes, they had cheated terribly.

"So many good memories," Rowe agreed.

"Bringing Daciana home from the hospital for the first time." Lucas looked down and patted the arm of the chair. "I fell asleep so many times in this chair while holding her after a late-night feeding."

"I wonder who will live here next. You're leaving it fully furnished, aren't you?"

Lucas nodded. "This furniture isn't all that old, so I might as well. Andrei and Ian have been shopping for the new house, so we'll be all set." He set down his drink and got up to walk to the bar. "I think this night calls for the Vintage Bourbon." He got the bottle down.

Snow groaned. "I can tell we're not getting out of here sober."

Rowe rubbed his hands together and got up to grab one of the drinks Lucas had poured.

Lucas handed Snow and Ian glasses and held his own up in a toast. "To new beginnings."

They clinked glasses and Ian took a sip of the expensive bourbon. It was definitely smooth, but he preferred the wine. He set his bourbon next to his Cabernet. "I've got two different glasses going on here, so yeah, I'd say we won't be leaving here sober. That lasagna should be ready in about fifteen minutes."

Lucas sat back in his seat and swirled the alcohol around in his glass. His gaze pierced Ian. "Enough time for you to fill us all in on what's going on since you were attacked."

Ian picked up his wine and took a sip. The red exploded on his tongue, and he sighed with pleasure. "I don't want to talk about that tonight."

"Too bad," Snow retorted. "I'd like to catch up as well."

Ian sighed. "Two of my employees were attacked."

"I know about that," Snow said. "Jude was on the scene. I want to know if you've gotten further in the investigation."

"As Rowe knows, we went out to confront one of Jagger's old enforcers and that was a dead end. Sort of. Hollis got a new idea as we were talking to Ernie. Maybe the person after me and my restaurant is actually one of Jagger's past kids."

"Why wait all this time if that's the case?" Lucas asked.

"Who knows?" Ian shrugged and cradled his wineglass between both hands. "Something must have set him off."

"You have been in the news recently with that magazine spread, and the restaurant is doing really well. All of Cincinnati knows you've got a new restaurant opening and is dying to get in." Rowe leaned forward, making the leather couch creak. "I can see jealousy being an instigator for all this. You have a lot going for you these days and as that brute said, a lot of those past kids ended up worse off."

Ian's heart clenched again at the thought of how much better he had it. "You guys are the reason my life is so good."

"You've made your own life good, Ian," Lucas said.

"But I wouldn't have gotten the start without you three. I like to hope I would have made something of myself once out of Jagger's clutches, but the truth is, I had help. The best kind of help. I love you all so much."

"Don't give him any more bourbon," Snow drawled even as he gave Ian a grin.

Rowe reached over and ruffled his hair. "Back at ya, kid."

"Not so much a kid anymore. I'm about to turn thirty."

"You're still a kid to us." Rowe got up to get another drink.

Lucas leaned forward to rest his elbows on his knees. "Do you remember any kids who seemed jealous of you back then?"

Ian shook his head. "It could have been any of them. But I've been making a list of those I remember. I wasn't around a lot of them—only during the parties." He frowned at those memories.

Snow curled his lip and Ian knew he was remembering one as well. Snow had gotten into several fights that night when he'd realized what was going on.

"Come on, let's take this to the dining room and eat. Andrei left us a big salad to go with it." Ian stood up.

Lucas chuckled. "The man's made it his mission to get me to eat salad every single day—even when he's not here."

"He loves you." Ian walked into the kitchen and got out a big knife. He cut into the lasagna, serving it onto plates he'd stacked earlier on the counter. Rowe got down bowls for the salad, and Snow gathered the different salad dressings from the refrigerator. By the time they all sat down, Ian hoped the mood had improved. Talking about Jagger's parties was enough to get them all down.

But Lucas wasn't done with the conversation. "We should be able to track some of them if you can remember any names."

"That's just it, I can't. I've been wracking my brain trying to remember, but a lot of that time brings up other memories. Ones I prefer not to revisit, you know?"

Snow scowled into his plate. "I hate thinking about that time, too."

"But if it helps with what's happening now…" Rowe pointed out as he forked a bite of food into his mouth. He chewed and swallowed, then followed it up with a gulp of bourbon. At the rate he was putting that away, he'd be face-planting again in no time.

Lucas must have been having similar thoughts, because he chuckled as he covered his salad with Italian dressing. He might complain about the salads, but he seemed to like them enough.

Ian tried his lasagna and smiled at the flavors. He'd changed up his sauce and he liked the improvement. He could taste the basil and garlic, and the pasta was perfectly cooked.

"Remember when you first moved into this place?" Snow asked. He picked up his drink and tilted it toward Lucas. "We thought you were crazy to buy it."

"All the freaking windows," Rowe muttered. "Still can't believe a sniper didn't take you out."

A slow smile spread across Lucas's lips. "Before Daci was born, Andrei spent a lot of time naked in front of those windows."

"Awww…and me without my binoculars," Snow mocked.

Rowe made a face at Lucas and Snow. "Seriously? He's my brother and COO now. I don't need that mental image."

Ian snorted. "Hollis is the love of my life, and I can still admit that Andrei is smoking hot."

"Mine," Lucas said with a low growl, but it was softened with a playful smile before Lucas took a bite of lasagna.

"Regardless, I hate that you're leaving it," Snow said.

"We'll still get together at the house, and you'll all have keys." Lucas paused and chuckled to himself. "Andrei said the man who made copies of the keys looked at him like he was insane when he said he needed eight copies."

"Big family," Ian murmured.

"Yeah, the last time I used my key, I got an eyeful of Andrei's ass." Snow smirked. "That wasn't a complaint."

Lucas laughed. "No, I can't imagine it was." He got up to snag the bourbon and bring it to the table. He refilled Rowe's glass and topped Snow's up before his own. He raised an eyebrow at Ian, but Ian shook his head. He thought the wine went better with their dinner. Lucas set the bottle down and went to get the Cabernet. He poured some into Ian's glass.

"I think he is trying to get us all drunk," Rowe said.

"Just wanting you all to enjoy this last night here." Lucas sat in his chair.

Again, that pang went through Ian's chest. "We have so many wonderful memories here."

"I know," Lucas agreed. "I was tempted to hang on to it, but it just didn't make sense."

"Your new home is gorgeous, so you probably won't even miss it." Ian forked another bite.

"Oh, I will. My family has gathered here for years. I fell in love with Andrei here. My daughter's first night home from the hospital was here. This place will always be a part of me."

"Oh brother, I need another drink." Snow reached for the bourbon.

"Hush, I know this is hitting you just as hard as it is us." Ian pointed his fork at Snow. "Even you and Jude have stayed here. Hell, you lived here at one time, same as me."

Snow grinned. "Yeah, okay, I am sorry to see it go. But we also have so much more to look forward to. And Lucas's new place has an indoor pool."

"Skinny dipping!" Rowe chimed in.

Lucas rolled his eyes, and Snow chuckled as he nodded. "Yeah, I wouldn't mind having one of those for me and Jude."

They ate in silence for a few moments, and Ian was glad to see them putting away the food in addition to the alcohol. He poured himself another glass. Hell, he'd have Lucas's driver take him home if he overindulged. He could crash here, but he didn't want to be away from Hollis all night—not after they'd had that fight.

By the time they were cleaning up the kitchen, both Rowe and Snow were weaving a bit. There was a lot of laughter and once again, Ian felt that swell of love he had for these men. They were saying good-bye to a part of their lives, but they would stick together for life. Of that, he had no doubt. They were his family.

Lucas wrapped an arm around Ian and hugged him close. "You have nostalgia all over your face."

"Ew, you should wipe that off," Snow said with a swagger into the living room. He snagged the bottle of bourbon as he went, with Rowe following close behind.

"I can't help it," Ian said with a smile. "So many good memories. I can't help but be sad that we won't ever be coming back here."

"We'll turn the new house into the penthouse," Lucas murmured, kissing his temple. "And we'll all have families to bring even more joy."

"And you guys say I'm the soft one."

"Shh. I'll never hear the end of it from Snow."

"He's been awfully quiet about his wedding tonight. I don't know if that's good or bad."

"Probably bad, but don't remind him."

Ian hugged Lucas, then went to grab his wine and join his friends on the couch. Snow was half-sprawled, and Rowe had his head on Snow's shoulder. They were looking at something on Snow's phone. Ian leaned over the back of the couch to see that Snow was flipping through images of the four of them over the years.

"We need to get some of these printed." Ian pointed to one of Lucas and Snow smiling. "Especially this one."

"That's a good idea," Snow agreed as he swiped to the next image. It was of Andrei and Daci, and the sigh over Ian's shoulder let him know Lucas had joined them.

"You have a beautiful family, Lucas." Ian patted his chest. "Absolutely beautiful."

"I'm a lucky man." Lucas leaned over the couch. "Send that one to me."

Rowe suddenly laughed. "Here we are, gathered for one last hurrah at the place we all considered part ours and we're oohing and aahing over pictures. We've turned into a bunch of saps." He paused as an image of Noah and his sweet smile came up. "Okay, okay, send me that one."

Ian cracked up and walked around to sit next to Rowe. He sipped his wine and leaned back into the couch, putting his feet up on the glass coffee table. He wiggled his socked toes and watched as Lucas went to his original seat. It felt so good to be here with them.

"Let's make a pact." Ian held up his glass. "No matter how busy we get with our new families, we'll always take at least one night every couple of months for just us four."

Rowe lifted his glass. "Agreed!" He took a huge gulp of his drink and hiccupped. "You know our significant others still have their nights out once in a while."

Snow snorted. "You mean the 'No Boyfriends Allowed' club? I can't believe they did that."

"What? Can't believe that Jude might need one night off from your grumpy ass?" Rowe teased.

"What the hell do you think they talk about?"

"Probably about the fact that my forever boyfriend hasn't met my parents yet," Rowe muttered under his breath.

"Or that I'm afraid to commit to a wedding date because I'm sure I'm going to fuck this all up," Snow admitted.

"Or that I'm fighting Andrei over being the sperm donor for our next child because my own family is so fucked up," Lucas added.

"Or that Hollis and I both need to go into therapy," Ian murmured. He looked up to find three sets of worried, questioning eyes. Ian smiled and shrugged. "The recent troubles have stirred up a lot of old Jagger baggage. Made us realize that we have stuff that we haven't worked through."

"Fuck," Rowe said with a heavy sigh and then threw back the rest of his drink. "I seriously hope their meetings aren't this big of a downer."

Lucas chuckled. "I doubt it."

"And ours won't be either," Ian added, keeping his tone upbeat.

"We can do our get-togethers on the nights they meet. When those of you with kids have babysitters."

Rowe looked down into his empty glass, eyes wide. "Wow, that sounds so weird. Babysitter. Kids."

"Still don't want any?" Snow asked.

"I'm surprised you do." Rowe poked Snow in the chest. "Mr. I'm Never Having Kids."

"Things change. I want it now. Jude will make a great father."

"So will you," Lucas added confidently. "And an interesting one."

"I haven't quite figured out how it will work with our schedules. Half the time, we're on together, so that's a lot of time to be away from a child." Snow sipped his bourbon.

"I'm sure Anna will step in for babysitting," Ian chimed in.

"Oh, there's no doubt about that. She's already screening surrogates."

Rowe snorted and spilled a bit of alcohol on his black Ward Security polo. He brushed it off absentmindedly. "Is that the way you're going to go?"

"We haven't decided, but more than likely we're going to adopt. If I left it up to Jude, we already would have. He's ready."

"Are you?" Ian asked because Snow looked a little green around the gills.

"Almost. I'm not quite there yet. I'm just really enjoying it being us still." He grinned. "I like the freedom to fuck him anywhere I like."

"Sex doesn't stop with a kid," Lucas said. "It gets interrupted sometimes, but there's still plenty of time to be together. I think you're going to love being a father, Snow."

"Well, I can't wait to be a foster parent. We're getting so close." Ian sipped his wine, feeling a pleasant buzz despite all the food he'd eaten. "But I won't even think of bringing a child into my life the way it is now. Not until we figure out who's messing with me."

"We'll figure it out, Ian. Don't give up on your dreams." Lucas gave him a smile.

"To dreams!" Rowe said, holding up his glass. "And to new beginnings!"

They all lifted their glasses. Ian settled back onto the couch and basked in the pleasure of being with these men as they said goodbye to the penthouse. He looked around and realized that the place really didn't matter. *They* were what mattered, and they'd always be together.

## Chapter Sixteen

Ian stood to the side of the entrance to Rialto's kitchen, watching as Isabella directed the controlled chaos with the expertise of a conductor overseeing the London Symphony orchestra. He'd just escaped his office and the pile of applications he'd been digging through in the hopes of lending a hand in the kitchen since both Sean and Wade were out for another day, but it was clear that Isabella had everything under control. He was almost afraid of being underfoot in his own kitchen.

He bit back a sigh and shook his head. He and Sean needed to have a meeting with that woman to discover if she wanted to remain at Rialto or take over as the *sous chef* for In Good Time. They'd put it off because of the recent chaos with the inspections, raid, bad reviews, and now the attacks on Sean and Wade. But it needed to get done.

Ian hated to admit that he loved having her at Rialto because he knew that his beloved restaurant was in good hands if Sean wasn't around, but she deserved her own kitchen, her own place to be queen.

And at the new place, she'd have a chance at trying some of her own recipes. He was curious to see what she'd do.

Moving her up also meant giving someone else in the kitchen a chance to move into her coveted spot and shine.

Feeling better about the decision, he made a mental note to chat with Sean when he returned and to schedule a meeting with Isabella. That just left him with the heavy task of filling out the rest of the kitchen staff for In Good Time and the holes that would be left in the Rialto kitchen should some of the staff choose to move over. James would handle the hiring of the hosts, servers, and bussers.

Being back at Rialto, Ian felt like he could breathe again. He was a step away from the chaos that seemed to be consuming his life. Rialto was a safe haven, a cozy slice of normalcy that gave him a sense of control and purpose when everything was trying to careen into insanity.

He started toward the main dining area when his phone vibrated in his pocket. Pulling it out, he glanced at the screen and frowned. Gidget. She had news. A knot suddenly tightened in his stomach. He should be excited that she had information that would help him stop this person who was trying to destroy his life and hurt the people he cared about. But there was a part of him that wanted to push it all to the back of his mind for a little while, to enjoy normal life again for just one day.

It was better to face this now. He knew that. The sooner it was taken care of, the sooner he could get all of his life on track. He returned to his office to get away from the noise of the busy kitchen.

"Ian here," he said as he shut the door.

"It's Gidget. How are you? Anything new happen?"

A smile tugged at his lips at her sweet concern. He'd always found it somewhat amazing that she was so at ease around all the rough and rowdy Ward Security bodyguards. Hell, it was amazing she managed to work with Rowe for so long, but he'd seen it with his own eyes—she was a perfect fit. "No, it's been quiet for the past few days."

"I heard through the grapevine that Wade is enjoying Jackson playing nursemaid," she said with a little giggle. "Is Sean okay?"

"Yes. He was in the hospital only the one night. He's still a little

# Rialto

grumpy about being forced to recuperate at home and has been sending me recipe ideas every day. He'll be back at Rialto on Monday."

"That's good. I cross-referenced the few names you gave me with police records on drug and prostitution arrests and I think I have a name for you. Max Hodgkins."

Ian flinched to hear that name cross Gidget's lips. Yes, he'd given it to her along with others, but to hear his suspicions confirmed still hurt. There had been a secret part of him hoping that Max had escaped this life, that he and Hollis had been wrong and they all escaped, but it was unrealistic.

"I remember him well," Ian whispered thickly.

"Looks like he was picked up once in the West End, and the second time was downtown, just east of OTR."

"If it's him, I wonder why he's taken so long to come after me."

"I don't know. I'm waiting on records from two others right now, but it's a start."

"Thanks, Gidget, I don't know what we'd do without you."

"You're welcome. I'm emailing you his police records now. They have the exact locations of where he was arrested. It'll give you and Hollis a starting point at least. I'm sorry it's not more definitive."

"No, it's a solid start."

He hung up and stood in his quiet office; the sounds from the kitchen were muffled but he barely noticed. His mind had slipped back to a lavish mansion more than ten years in his past. It had been a place of nightmares. The opulence was over the top and had felt so damn phony, but it was made all the worse by the guys walking around the place with their rough hands, crude manners, and guns. So many fucking guns. For so long, Ian had been afraid to move, to speak, confident that someone was going to shoot him at the first squeak out of him.

Max had already been there when he arrived. Had been trapped in that hell for a couple of years. He had looked a lot like Ian—Jagger'd had a type—but he'd been smaller and younger. He'd also been Jagger's favorite. At the top of his list as it were. That position came with certain "benefits" and freedoms that the other prisoners didn't enjoy. No one ever touched Jagger's favorite but Jagger. Ian hadn't understood that when he first arrived. Everything had been so new and scary. He'd just wanted to go home. It didn't matter if his parents hated him and had coldly ripped him away from everything he'd known. Hatred at home had to be better than being trapped at Jagger's.

But in a short time, better took on a new meaning. There was no going home. There was no escape. Better was about being Jagger's favorite rather than a party favor for Jagger's rich friends and associates. Better was having a room to himself rather than sharing a small, crowded one with ten other boys.

Life had been "better" for Max before Ian came along. Max lost his private room and little benefits to become just another party favor to be passed around night after night. The few times Ian had seen him at parties, Max had been outright hostile to him.

Ian's stomach churned and he put a hand on it. Even if it wasn't directly his fault, Max had a very good reason for hating Ian.

The phone still tightly gripped in his hand vibrated and he looked down to see an email from Gidget had just come through. He dropped down in the chair behind his desk and woke up his laptop so he could open the email and attachment. His heart skipped when he was faced with Max's mug shot. He looked nothing like the boy Ian remembered. This man was haggard and worn, years of pain, fear, and anger stamped onto his face like a grotesque mask. He stared at the camera, looking as if the weight of the world sat on his shoulders.

Ian's own shoulders slumped as if he took on some of that weight. It felt like he'd never be free of his past. He thought of his and Hollis's plans to foster children and wondered if this was where his focus should be. Wouldn't it be better if they tried to track down the kids that had suffered under Jagger's thumb? It was clear from Max's mug shot that not enough had been done to help these poor souls. No one had tried to find them, counsel them, give them a fresh start outside this depraved and damaged world.

But how would he find them all? He remembered less than half a dozen names now, and there had been so many that came and went. Even more after he escaped Jagger's clutches.

He stared at Max's broken image as he called Hollis, who was also working that night.

"Hey," he said softly when Hollis answered.

"Hey GQ, how's it going tonight? Restaurant good?"

Ian closed his eyes and let Hollis's wonderful voice wash over him like a soothing balm. Hearing that familiar murmur in his ear loosened the tension tightening his chest, making it a little easier to draw a deep breath. "It's quieter than usual, but nothing too alarming. We did have four cancelations for reservations. A little higher than normal and that worries me, but what can I do?"

"Nothing but your job. Just keep churning out amazing food, and people will keep coming to eat it."

The ghost of a smile tugged at his mouth. God, where would he be without Hollis? The man knew what to say to keep him moving when all he wanted to do was curl up in bed and pull the covers over his head.

"How's your night?"

"Oh, you know, the usual," Hollis drawled. "A little dumpster diving for incriminating evidence. A little sneaky surveillance of cheating spouses."

"Gidget called."

Hollis went silent for a moment. "She get a hit?"

"Found us a possible culprit. Max Hodgkins."

"Shit," Hollis swore softly. "I'm sorry, GQ. So sorry."

Ian nodded, swallowing past the lump in his throat. "Thanks." He'd mentioned to Hollis when they made the list together that Max was his main concern. The one person he could remember who seemed to dislike Ian the most. The other boys seemed relatively indifferent about his existence, too wrapped up in their own fears and worries.

When he could speak clearly, he continued, "She also found where he's been arrested in the past. Downtown and West End. I was thinking it might be a good idea to go down and see if I can find him."

"Not alone, you're not."

Ian smiled at Hollis's hostile tone. His need to protect Ian didn't rankle his nerves like it usually did, because Hollis was correct. He needed backup on this one both for his own physical protection as well as his emotional stability. Even if Max wasn't the perpetrator, Ian knew this wasn't going to be an easy meeting if they did manage to find the young man. "Of course not. When do you get off work?"

"I can take off now if you need me. We were just finishing up for the night." In the background, he heard the telltale squeak of Hollis's office chair and the shuffling of papers. Apparently, he'd managed to catch his husband in the office, maybe finishing up some paperwork for a client.

"Want to meet me here and we'll go?"

"Be there soon." Silence filled the air for a moment. He'd thought that Hollis had been about to say "I love you" or at least "good-bye," but there was nothing for a few long seconds like a thought had occurred to him. Ian had been about to ask him if everything was okay when he finally spoke again, his voice hesitant. "It might be a good idea to take one of the bodyguards. Or we can see if Rowe or Noah are up to their usual reindeer games? Those two are always game for a romp through the bad part of town."

Ian shook his head, though Hollis couldn't see him. "No, they would get too much attention. Can you imagine getting people to talk to us with Sven in tow? Or the Masters of Mayhem?"

"Don't you tell him I said this, but I have seen Rowe be sneaky before."

Ian snorted. "Sneaky is nice, but I was thinking more along the lines of subtle. Those two are about as subtle as a stick of dynamite."

"True. Very, very true." Hollis chuckled. "Okay, I'll have my gun."

Ian wanted to roll his eyes, but it was a good idea. If this Max was the one out to hurt him, it wouldn't be smart to approach him unarmed. Still, Ian wanted to help him more than he wanted to hurt him. Mostly he just wanted to know why the man had come after him. "I'll see you in a few."

## Chapter Seventeen

When Ian and Hollis climbed out of the car, Ian was rethinking his decision not to bring a bodyguard. Cincinnati had started to seriously cool off in the evenings as they closed in on the end of September. The trees were still green, and there were few signs that fall had reached the city besides a handful of stores displaying Halloween decorations.

But then, fall in Cincinnati tended to be an incredibly fleeting thing. Citizens were usually graced with one or two good weekends of colored leaves and moderate temperatures for corn mazes, pumpkin farms, apple picking, and haunted houses before the cold temperatures and gray skies whooshed in to claim the city for the next five months.

Pulling his leather jacket tighter around him, Ian stepped away from the car and took a quick look around him. Simply because it was the closest, he and Hollis had elected to check out the northeast side of downtown. They were outside the trendy reach of OTR and the sophisticated business end of downtown. No, here the streets were a little darker, and there were fewer cars rushing past them. The buildings looked largely empty, as if the business had moved to other parts of the city.

Little clusters of people lurked in shadowy doorways and the entrances to alleys. There were more than a few people stretched out on the sidewalk, wrapped in ragged blankets and sleeping bags, their faces turned away from what was happening around them.

Ian took in his surroundings and couldn't help but wonder if this was where he would have ended up if Snow, Lucas, and Rowe hadn't intervened. Would he even still be alive now? He couldn't imagine surviving on the street. No money. No home. No safe place. Would he have been forced to sell his body just to get by when Jagger was finally done with him? It wasn't like he'd had a high school diploma, an ID, anything.

No. Ian shook his head as a darker thought occurred to him. He wouldn't have ended up like this because Dwight Gratton would have killed him before he could have made it to the streets. Gratton had been obsessed with him. When Jagger was done with him, Ian was sure he would have been handed off directly to Gratton. And lost to his obsession, Gratton would have killed Ian.

"GQ?"

Blinking away those depressing thoughts, Ian looked over at Hollis, taking in his worried expression, and forced a smile. "I'm okay. Lost in thought."

"Do you want to wait a night? You've already put in a long day."

Ian shook his head before he stepped forward and gripped Hollis's forearm in reassurance. He was sure the contact helped to ground them both. "No, I'm fine. I promise. We can't put this off."

Squaring his shoulders, Ian walked to the first group of people he saw loitering on the street. There were three women talking in low murmurs. One was gesturing with a cigarette pinched between two fingers, while her two companions let out rough laughs at whatever she'd been telling them. The temperature might have been in the low fifties, but there wasn't enough clothing between the three of them to keep a single person warm. And their shoes…all of them wore these monster heels and platform shoes so that they teetered precariously on the fractured sidewalk.

Since talking to Hollis, Ian had mentally rehearsed what he would say, and nothing good was coming to mind. If anything, he

## Rialto

just needed to make sure he didn't appear to be interested in their... wares. Knowing his luck, one would be an undercover cop.

He'd briefly considered printing out Max's picture, but the only one included in the file that Gidget sent over was his mug shot. Not the kind of thing to convince people to open up to him. So, he had no images to share, and he hoped Max didn't have a different street name.

"Hi," he said to one of the women leaning against the brick wall of a building. The heavy layers of makeup did nothing to hide the wear and tear life had taken on her face. Somehow she didn't shiver in her short skirt and skintight white halter top with the red lace bra peeking through. But Ian wondered if life or drugs had numbed her to the cold. "Would you know if there's a Max Hodgkins around here?"

She looked him up and down before her gaze flitted to Hollis, who stood silently behind Ian like an avenging angel. He looked exactly like what he used to be. A cop. Her lips tightened and she shook her head.

Ian turned to the other woman standing beside her, but she did the same thing.

The one with the cigarette turned to him and gave him an ugly smirk. "Oh, honey, what do you want with a Max? It looks like you've already got all the cock you can handle. How bout I give you a taste of something sweeter?" She reached out with her long, curved fingernails toward his hair like she meant to run her fingers through it, but Ian jerked backward out of her reach, his shoulders slamming into Hollis's broad chest.

The cigarette woman cackled loudly, and her companions joined in, sending them rocking awkwardly in their heels in their amusement. Ian could feel heat filling his cheeks, but he didn't care what they thought of him. Not when Hollis's strong hand was gripping his shoulder, squeezing and reassuring him without saying a word.

"Nobody here knows a Max," a man said as he came out of the shadows. "You might as well move along."

Ian's heart sped up as he got a good look at him, taking in the large build and the shock of bright blond hair. He wondered if this guy worked security for the women. Then he realized it was probably their pimp. He nodded at him and pulled Hollis along down the street. The trio of women continued to shout catcalls and taunting comments after them as they walked away. They only grew quiet when a car slowed down and pulled over to the curb near them. A potential customer. He and Hollis were forgotten.

With Hollis at his side, Ian braved several more blocks and more alleys than he'd ever thought he'd venture down. They approached three more groups of people, a mix of both men and women, but there was no one willing to talk about Max. This wasn't going to be as easy as he'd hoped. Nobody admitted to knowing a Max. Either they were lying or he did, in fact, go by something else here. And they all clammed up as soon as they got a good look at Hollis.

"Shit," Ian said as they stood on yet another corner, looking up and down the street as he tried to decide which direction they were going to turn down next. They were getting too close to residential areas, and for better or worse, there were fewer people out. "Looks like this is another dead end."

Hollis squeezed his arm. "Give it time, we've only been at this an hour or so. Finding someone is never easy and especially when we're doing it like this. We need a photograph of the guy."

"All I have is the mug shot."

Hollis winced. "Yeah, flashing that around will get us nowhere."

Ian turned toward Hollis and folded his arms over his chest. "They can all tell you're a cop. Can you…I don't know…hunch or something? Look less imposing and official?"

Hollis laughed. "Hunching isn't going to change my carriage. They don't know I used to be a cop."

"Rowe and Snow both say you still stand and walk like you're a cop."

"That's 'cause Rowe and Snow are fucking deviants who spent too much time looking over their shoulders for cops when they were up to trouble."

"Yeah, but you've done undercover work. And now you're a PI. Don't you have to like…pretend to be unassuming and normal?"

Hollis made a face like he was fighting very hard not to laugh right in Ian's face, which he appreciated. Ian really couldn't blame him, because he wasn't sure there was much Hollis could do to look less intimidating than he did. And Ian had to admit that he loved how his man looked striding down the street as if he owned it. It was a fucking turn-on, not that they needed that right then.

"People just aren't going to trust you enough to talk. You're a stranger here." Hollis jerked his head down to the left. "There are a few more people gathered down there. We can try this block, and then we'll head to the car. Shoot over to the West End and cover that area for a couple of hours before calling it a night." He smirked. "I'll try to hunch."

Ian nodded and shoved his hands into the pockets of his jacket. Hollis was right, but he didn't want to head home until they found Max. He was afraid that these people would talk. If Max got word that someone matching Ian's description was looking for him, he might disappear completely. They didn't have a backup plan if this fell through, and Ian didn't want to wait around for this guy to strike again, hurting someone else he cared about, so they'd have a new lead to follow.

Their shoes clicked and scraped on the pavement as they headed to the next group. It was four men standing together. They were all short and slight in frame, giving Ian a glimmer of hope, but also a sick twisting of his stomach. Even if none of them were Max, were any of them former Jagger victims? Would he even recognize them if they were?

One of them turned so that light from a nearby streetlamp splashed across his face. His blond hair hung over one eye and he wore a threadbare T-shirt and was shivering in the cold. But Ian knew without a doubt that it was Max.

Ian hurried forward before the guy could take off, walking right up to him and getting in his personal space. "Max?"

Something flashed in his bloodshot brown eyes—surprise, recognition, and even rage—but it was all gone as quickly as it appeared. "You got the wrong guy, buddy," he muttered.

Up close, he looked worse than he had in the photographs. Dark circles rimmed his eyes, and his lips were pinched into a tight line.

Cheap cologne wafted up from him, but it wasn't strong enough to mask the stomach-churning body odor and hints of sex. Fuck, he'd been so pretty, so sweet a dozen years ago. Was this the effect of life on the streets or Jagger or both?

Hollis gripped the sleeve of Ian's jacket and tried to pull him back a couple of steps, but Ian shrugged out of his grasp. He didn't want to back off. They'd found Max. They could help him. "I don't think so. You're Max Hodgkins. I've been trying to find you."

"Don't know no Max."

Ian clenched his teeth for a second, hating the words that were about to tumble from his lips. "I know you remember me. I remember you. Jagger's Max." His voice softened on those last two words as he struggled to get them up his throat and past his teeth. They were too big and too ugly, but he had to get through to Max.

The guy's lip curled and the rage returned to his eyes. "So what? Yeah, I know who you are. Jagger's treasured little prince. What the hell do you want?"

"So you do remember me."

"Jagger's favorite. The Untouchable One. Hard to forget something like that."

Ian swallowed his own swell of rage at Max's words. He was trying to get under Ian's skin, make him angry, hurt him with his words. Max knew Ian had suffered while trapped in Jagger's compound. He'd taken his turn with Jagger's men when he'd fallen from favor. He'd suffered at the hands of Dwight Gratton. He had nothing to prove to Max.

"Looks like you got all fancy now," Max continued in Ian's silence. "Wanna experience things from the other side now? Want me to suck your dick? Twenty bucks." He managed to both sneer and wink at Ian at the same time. "Sorry. No freebies for old times' sake. Some of us gotta work for a living."

"That's not why I'm here," Ian snapped, barely pushing down his revulsion.

"Then get the fuck out of here. I'm working."

Ian grabbed Max's too-thin shoulder as he started to turn his back on Ian and forced him to remain facing toward Ian. "Are you the one who hit me? Who's trying to hurt my restaurant?"

Max's eyes narrowed, but something in the twist of his smirk made Ian's gut clench. He jerked his shoulder, pulling free of Ian's touch. "You're nothing to me. Why would I do that?"

Ian couldn't tell if he was telling the truth or not. The rage and hatred pouring off him was suffocating, but that didn't necessarily mean that he'd done anything to attack Ian in the past. It could just be an old hatred bubbling to the surface.

Hollis gently laid his hand on Ian's shoulder and pulled him back a couple of steps. This time, Ian let him as he became more aware of his surroundings. Waited quietly, watching. So were a few of the people around Max. One guy in red skinny jeans popped his gum, gaze locked on them. Another of the guys pulled out a pocketknife and started rubbing it with the edge of his T-shirt. Hollis's hand tightened on Ian's shoulder as if he were preparing to pull Ian behind his larger bulk to protect him.

True alarm crept through Ian, and he realized just how dangerous this whole situation was. He turned his attention to Max, his heart ramping up at the hostility blazing in Max's eyes. "I know you hate me—"

"I don't think nothing of you, you arrogant shit! You haven't changed at all. Still think you're the most important person around."

"I don't." Ian reached into his pocket and the guy flinched. "It's okay, I'm just getting my card." He pulled it out and held it up to Max as a car slowed down, then took off behind him. "Take it."

"I don't want it. You need to leave because you're scaring away business."

"I want to help you," Ian pressed, refusing to cave to the anger directed at him. He knew if he could just reach Max, get him to listen to him, he could fix this.

"Help me do what?" Max sneered, shoving his hands into his jeans pockets.

"Get out of here. Off the street. I can help you find a better job."

"I like my job just fine."

"Look, I had help to get out and I've managed to make a better life—"

The guy snarled, breaking him off. "You have no right to stand here and judge me or my life. Get the hell away from me."

Ian nodded and stepped back. He bumped into the warm wall that was Hollis, soaking in the reassurance and safety of his presence.

Max snickered at Hollis. "I see you got a man taking care of you. Still can't make it without a sugar daddy?"

"This is my husband. I told you I've made a better life. Jagger—"

"I don't want to hear anything about that pig. Glad he's dead. Killing him was the only good thing you ever did, but it still ain't enough." He took a step closer to Ian, and Hollis's hand tightened. "Just leave."

"Okay, I will. But take my card and call me. I can help you. Just think about it at least."

Max snatched the card from Ian's fingers and made a production of tearing it into pieces and dropping them. His track marks were highlighted in the streetlamp as he lifted his arms.

Hollis tugged Ian away, and they quietly walked to their car. Nobody bothered them. Max didn't follow them. Ian had no idea if he was the one terrorizing him, but his heart ached for the angry man. He'd been so hostile, so full of hate, that Ian still thought they were on the right track. Maybe confronting him had only made things worse.

They got into the car, Hollis sliding behind the wheel despite the fact that it was Ian's car. Ian didn't argue. Didn't even think about it. He was just grateful that he didn't have to navigate the downtown streets back to their house.

The locks thunked loudly in the silence and the lights flared to life with a little purr of the electric engine. As they drove home, Ian couldn't help but feel sad. That could have been him. Living on the streets and selling his body for drug money. He'd been truly lucky.

He reached across and put his hand on Hollis's thigh. "That wasn't fun."

"I got a bad feeling about that guy, Ian. He could be the one. A good liar. But he loathes you, and there was resentment there. Jealousy."

"Yeah, he was Jagger's favorite until I came along, so I kind of displaced him. He ended up being one of the boys passed around at the parties. He was hostile to me back then, too, but there was nothing he could do with so many eyes watching us at all times. He couldn't risk it."

"My gut is telling me we're on the right track."

"Yeah," Ian said quietly. "Mine is telling me that, too."

He stared out the window at the city lights as they blurred past his window and felt true exhaustion in his muscles. A loud voice in his head was telling him that Hollis was right; Max was the one targeting him and Rialto, but Ian didn't know what to do about it. He could only offer to help. He couldn't even go to the police. Not only did he not have enough evidence, but it would only make things worse for Max, and Ian didn't want that.

A fresh wave of guilt threatened to swamp him. Why had he gotten out and benefited from the protection of three powerful men? Why not Max? Or so many of the others trapped in that hellhole?

He felt guilty that he now had this fabulous life and a loving husband, while Max was standing on a street corner with track marks on his arms and not even a jacket to keep him warm.

Hollis put his hand over Ian's. "You know it's not your fault that he's living like he is, right?"

Ian forced a harsh, bitter laugh. "How'd you know what I was thinking?"

"I know you, baby, and your heart is big. Big enough to take in the entire world. He had a rough time, yeah, but he could do something to change his life now. He's an adult."

"One who went through hell as a teenager."

"So did you."

Ian nodded and bit his lip. He looked back outside, feeling the warmth of Hollis's hand and remembering the night before at Lucas's penthouse. He had so very much in his life. He was truly blessed.

And he had to find a way to extend a little of that blessing in Max's direction. He just had to figure out the best way to reach him.

## Chapter Eighteen

Ian relaxed in the passenger seat of Snow's Mercedes as they cut through downtown Cincinnati on the way back to Rialto. It was one of Snow's rare days off from the hospital, and he'd talked Ian into joining him for a meeting with an actual wedding planner.

Snow was finally willing to admit that he couldn't plan this wedding on his own, which only made sense. He and Jude worked some long and crazy hours. Neither of them had time to track down and try out various vendors for all the things they needed to make a wedding happen. And it was perfectly clear that Ian didn't have the time to deal with organizing everything for him.

Just the memory of sitting down with that poor woman as she tried to get Snow to answer her very reasonable questions was enough to make him squirm uncomfortably in his seat. The grumpy doctor had been unwilling to answer even the simplest of questions. Season of the planned wedding? Estimated number of attendants? Formal or informal?

Nope. Snow gave her nothing to work with. She'd been stuck showing him endless photos of other weddings she'd helped to pull together, both big and lavish and small and adorable. If Ian hadn't loved planning his own wedding so much, he would have happily handed it over to Kate. She freaking knew her stuff.

But Snow gave her some noncommittal responses and shuffled out, claiming to want to discuss it with his fiancé.

"Can I ask you a question and have you give me a seriously honest answer?" Ian said, breaking the silence as they sat at a red light.

"Of course. I'd never lie to you," Snow immediately replied. He even sounded hurt by the implication that Ian thought he'd lie to him.

But Ian was more concerned with Snow lying to himself.

"Do you want to get married?"

Snow jerked in his seat, twisting a little to look over at Ian before looking back out the windshield. His hands tightened reflexively on the steering wheel. "What? Of course I want to get married. I love Jude. I want to spend the rest of my life with him."

"I'm not doubting that you love and want to be with him forever. I'm asking if you want to actually do the marriage thing."

Snow opened his mouth, but nothing came out. He closed it again and expelled a long breath before shoving one hand through his hair and slumping in his chair. "I have never had trouble making decisions until this wedding thing. I love Jude. I want to be with him forever. And I want to make it legal and binding. I want to be his husband."

"Then what's getting you hung up?"

"The actual wedding part." He glanced over at Ian, his smile more than a little self-deprecating. "When have you ever known me to plan anything?"

Ian smirked back and gave a shake of his head while Snow pressed on the gas after the light turned green. "Okay, you've got a point there, but that's why there are wedding planners. To help narrow things down and handle all the different vendors you need."

"But they still need me to make decisions and…I can't. I think of Lucas's wedding—"

"You can't compare any wedding to Lucas's wedding."

"I know. It was amazing."

A ball of pride burned brightly in Ian's chest at Snow's words. He'd worked hard to pull Lucas and Andrei's wedding together. And yeah, it had been a stunning event.

"But that's Lucas," Snow continued. "It was more than a wedding for him. He was making a statement to the world. Did you know that one of those celebrity gossip TV shows carried photos from that wedding? A *gay* wedding was making headline news because that's what Lucas wanted."

Ian had heard about it. Even picked up a few of the magazines that carried pictures of the wedding just to read what they'd said about it. The praise had been so high that for just a moment, he'd considered opening his own wedding planning business, but he knew a large part of what made the organization of Lucas and Andrei's so successful was that he loved both men so much. He also chucked the idea because it would take him away from his Rialto too often.

"Even your wedding was a statement."

Snow's words shocked him, and he blinked at his friend. "You think?"

A smile lifted Snow's lips and he continued. "Oh, yeah. There was an understated grace and elegance, which is so you, but also strength. Two of the appetizers that were served were the same things you made that first night we met you at Jagger's."

Ian's hand tightened on the door armrest. It took him a moment to ask, "You noticed?" around the lump in his throat.

"Yes. And so did Rowe and Lucas."

"Why didn't you say anything?"

"Because we didn't need to. You were taking them back, reclaiming the last things that Jagger stole from you. We were so damn proud of you."

"Thank you," Ian whispered in a rough voice. "I hadn't expected anyone to notice."

"But what's my statement when it comes to Jude? What's the grand thing I'm supposed to be saying when I meet Jude in front of the Justice of the Peace? Every time I try to figure it out for the wedding, I lock up. I'm afraid that whatever I decide, it's not enough. He saved me, Ian. Gave me a life I didn't even think was possible. How am I supposed to show the world that in a wedding?"

Ian reached across the console and placed his hand on Snow's arm, his thumb rubbing across his wrist. "You don't. Jude knows all of that, and he's the only person who needs to know. The wedding is just a party to let everyone important to you celebrate your love for each other. It doesn't need to be more than that."

"So…if I wanted to throw a hillbilly barn dance in the middle of nowhere Kentucky…"

"Rowe would love you forever if you did," Ian said with a laugh. "And we'd all have a great time because we're together."

"Thanks, Ian," Snow murmured. He took his hand off the steering wheel and turned it to give Ian's fingers a quick squeeze before returning it to the wheel.

"What does Jude think about the wedding and your decision-making problem?"

Snow sighed. "He's worried. He wants us to make all decisions together, but I can't make any. I think he's starting to feel like he's guilted me into this marriage thing. I've told him he hasn't, but I know he's not going to feel better until we start figuring some things out."

"You'll get there," Ian said, feeling a little lighter about his morning out with Snow than he had. He glanced out the passenger window as they passed by shops while people hurried on their errands. They were still several blocks away from the restaurant, in a part of town that Ian wasn't overly familiar with. The sun was peeking out between the clouds, but there was a feeling of rain in the air.

As they stopped for another red light, Ian's eyes alighted on an increasingly familiar blond head of hair and thin frame. Max.

"Pull over! Pull over there!" Ian suddenly shouted. He lurched upright, shifting to the edge of his seat as much as his seat belt would allow so that he could get a clear view of Max.

"What?" Snow demanded. He was looking back and forth over his shoulder, trying to quickly change lanes through traffic so that he could reach to the curb where Ian was frantically pointing.

"It's Max!"

It had been two days since he and Hollis had found Max on the street. He'd told Snow about the meeting, and his friend had been less than pleased to hear about it and more angry that they weren't reporting him to the cops.

"What are you planning—"

"I just want to talk to him. And if you can't keep it civil, then you can stay in the car. Or better yet, just drop me here. I can walk to Rialto."

"Absolutely not! I'm not leaving you alone with him."

"And I'm not leaving him alone, period. He needs help."

Snow grumbled something under his breath, but Ian didn't catch it. He didn't care what Snow thought. Max needed his help. He needed someone to help him, and Ian was the only one likely to understand even a fraction of what he'd been through already.

The second Snow managed to pull into an open spot, Ian had his seat belt off and was jumping out of the car, ignoring Snow's warning shouts behind him. He briskly walked along the sidewalk, hurrying to catch up with Max as he shuffled along. His hands were shoved into the pockets of a ragged jacket and his head was down, as if he were trying to block out the world around him.

"Max! Max!" Ian shouted as he got closer.

Max jerked suddenly, spinning around. His entire body tensed as if he were preparing to bolt, but then he seemed to relax again when he caught sight of Ian rushing toward him. His face twisted into an ugly sneer and he stopped.

"What the hell do you want?" Max demanded when Ian was only a few feet away.

"To talk. Just to talk."

"I got nothing to say to you."

"Please. Just a few minutes." Ian frantically looked around the area where they were standing. His eyes lit on the one place he'd always sworn he would never go back to. The first time, he'd been out drinking heavily with a bunch of friends. Now he was going to propose stepping inside while stone-cold sober. The Awful Waffle.

He pointed down the block at the Waffle House with its classic yellow-and-black sign. "We can just go inside for some coffee. Maybe something to eat." He nearly said that it would be his treat, but he didn't think those words would go over well with Max. The guy had his pride, and Ian's existence seemed to stomp all over it.

Max's eyes followed where he pointed, and then he looked at Ian in surprise. Ian must not have been able to hide his revulsion as he'd hoped because Max let out an ugly laugh. "Sure. I could use a free breakfast." His gaze narrowed behind Ian's shoulder and he took a tentative step backward. "Who's that?"

Ian looked over to find Snow standing behind him, a hostile look cutting deep lines in his handsome face. Everything about his posture screamed threat, and that was the last thing he wanted. Ian surreptitiously jabbed an elbow in Snow's stomach as he returned his attention to Max. "This is my old friend, Snow. Snow, this is Max Hodgkins."

They seemed to grunt at each other, though Max still looked like he was preparing to bolt.

"We were just heading into…there," Ian said. He glanced at Snow to see the surgeon looking at him as if he'd lost his mind. Yeah, maybe the good doctor didn't care too much about what he put into his body, but he knew that Ian did. Didn't matter. Ian could do this for Max.

They walked awkwardly toward the little restaurant. Max made sure that he remained out of arm's reach over the short distance and led the way to the rear of the restaurant where he selected a small booth that put his back to the wall. Ian slid into the booth opposite of him and briefly glanced out the window to his left at the people walking down the street, oblivious to the tense meeting that was happening inside.

The place smelled of old grease, burnt coffee, and syrup. Everything looked clean, but there was still a dingy quality to it. He was pretty sure the Waffle House on this street had been there for decades, serving thousands upon thousands of tired customers through all hours of the day. An exhausted server wandered over with a nearly full carafe of coffee in her hand. She didn't even ask if they wanted coffee. Just started filling their white mugs.

"Want anything else?" she asked.

"I'll take a pecan waffle, two eggs scrambled, bacon, and large hash browns scattered, smothered, and covered. Also, keep the coffee coming," Max ordered without missing a beat.

Ian blinked at him and then at the server, who didn't look a bit surprised by the order. He was thrown for another loop when Snow spoke up next.

"I'll have a fiesta omelet and large hash browns—scattered, covered, chunked, and diced."

"Seriously?" Ian asked before he could stop himself.

Snow blinked at him, looking completely innocent. "What? I had a light breakfast."

Ian shook his head, stunned at how quickly Snow had pulled his order together. This was not the type of place he'd expect to see the grumpy surgeon, but then The Awful Waffle could have been part of Snow's more reckless partying days. Shoving the thought aside for later, he quickly looked down at the two-sided laminated menu, searching for something…lighter. He tried to ignore the something sticky his thumb landed on. Probably syrup. Maybe jelly.

"I'll have…the grilled chicken biscuit and grits."

The server gave the barest of nods before she returned to the cook to relay their order.

They were finally alone. Ian looked at Max. The other man took a drink of his coffee and lounged in his seat, his eyes watching the passersby out the window. He didn't look any better in the harsh light of day. His skin was too pale, and the circles under his eyes were darker. His cheeks were sunken in as if he'd not had a good meal in a very long time. If they accomplished nothing else today, Ian would feel good if he simply fed Max. His arms were covered, hiding away old scars that he'd gotten a glimpse of that night with Hollis.

He wracked his brain, trying to think of some way to get Max talking that wouldn't instantly upset him. Right now, Ian knew Max was using him for food. If Ian didn't speak, Max wouldn't either. He'd just woof down the meal that was served and then bolt.

"How long have you been free?" Ian softly inquired.

Max's ugly laugh rose above the low murmur of conversation filling the restaurant. There were only about a half dozen other people in the place, but Ian could feel them all stop and look toward their table for a second before returning to their meals and coffee.

"Free? You're going to have to be more specific than that," Max mocked. "You talking about when I got out of the compound? That'd be two years, four months, and seventeen days *after* you disappeared."

A shaft of pain sliced through Ian's heart at Max's bitter words. Ian had done nothing to get Max out. He'd been stuck there so much longer than Ian, left to continue suffering. Ian's only thought was to get away. He just wanted to be away from Jagger and Gratton and all those horrible memories.

"Or maybe you're talking about when I got free of muling smack and meth for Jagger? You know, in between my night job of taking cock in alleys. That was three years ago. Thanks."

The sarcasm in that bit of gratitude was so sharp, Ian could feel it slicing through flesh. Yeah, Max had benefited from Jagger's death in a way, but everyone at the table knew that Ian hadn't done it for Max. He'd killed Jagger to save his own skin. And Hollis's.

If he was honest with himself, there was some need for revenge mixed in as well.

"You being trapped at Jagger's is not Ian's fault," Snow said in a hard, low voice. Ian grabbed his arm, stopping him from saying anything else.

"Oh, I know. I just wasn't as cute as Ian. Not as sweet as Ian. Not as...well, just not the perfect damsel in distress. Not like Ian was," Max snapped. His cold eyes swept up Snow and down again. "Were you one of them? Heard he had these mysterious benefactors who jumped in and saved him from Jagger. Are you one of them?"

Ian squeezed Snow's arm again and started talking before Snow could admit that he was. Normally Ian would be proud to hear that Snow was one of the men who saved his life, but he was afraid Max would turn his venom on Snow next, making his life hell. No, he wanted Max to stay focused on him.

"Snow is a friend. That's all," Ian quickly said. "Look, I know that you've been dealt a raw deal in life, and it fucking sucks. I got lucky. I don't know why. I'm not saying that I deserved it. It's just how things worked out. I want to help you. Try to give you the same break I had."

Max curled his lip at Ian in disgust. "Not everyone needs to be saved like you. Some of us learn how to take care of ourselves all on our own just fine."

Their conversation was put on hold by the server arriving with a huge tray stacked with plates. She wordlessly set their plates down in front of them and then returned a minute later to refresh their coffees. Max dug in like a ravenous wolf who'd just stumbled out of an incredibly lean winter. Ian glanced over to find Snow digging into his omelet.

Ian picked at his. His stomach was churning and queasy from the conversation with Max. The soupy grits and biscuit that somehow managed to look greasy wasn't going to improve how he felt. Though he couldn't help but notice how Snow was devouring his hash browns like they were a gift from the heavens, his pale blues rolling back into his head with joy. Ian hadn't experimented much with the food, and he was wondering if he needed to make a special brunch for his friends that included them.

They didn't speak while Max ate. Ian was partially afraid he would upset him so much that he'd storm off before he finished. The guy needed food in his belly desperately. If anything, Ian prayed that maybe a full stomach would get Max to slow down and listen to his overtures of assistance. Not that Ian was putting too much stock in that insane thought.

Max had nearly cleared his plates when he looked up, but his eyes weren't on Ian and Snow. They widened as they latched on to something—or someone—just past Ian's shoulder. He paled, if that was at all possible, and pushed back into his booth, eyes frantically darting around the restaurant as if he were searching for some escape. But there was no escape. They were at the very rear of the building and the only customer exit was at the other end.

"What's wrong?" Ian demanded. He twisted in his seat, trying to see what had spooked Max so badly.

"It's nothing. None of your business," Max snapped, but it didn't have the same venom he'd used to hurl all his other comments at Ian. No, there was no fear lacing his tone.

Ian started to look again, but there was no need. A tall man with lean muscles stopped at the head of their table. His dark eyes moved quickly over Ian and Snow before they settled heavily on Max.

"Hey Maxine," he drawled in a somewhat high-pitched voice. "What are you doing here?"

"Nothing...I..."

"Can you imagine my surprise since you just told me that you didn't have the money you owed me, but somehow you've got money for a big ol' breakfast like this?"

"No—"

"I invited Max to breakfast. My treat," Ian interrupted.

"Well, ain't that nice of you," the stranger said. There was a grin on his face showing yellowed teeth and that a couple were missing from his smile. But there was zero warmth in his eyes. No, they were clearly making calculations. Probably wondering what kind of cash Ian had in his wallet. For a moment, Ian stopped feeling like a living, breathing human being and simply became a bank account. "I had no idea that our sweet Maxine had such caring friends."

"We've just recently become reacquainted," Ian replied smoothly. "I'm Ian and this is my friend Snow. Who are you?"

"Oh, I'm just your friendly neighborhood bill collector." In the blink of an eye, the smile disappeared from his face and his hand flashed out toward Max, grabbing a fistful of hair. He jerked Max's head so hard that it slammed against the edge of the booth. "And this little whore owes me money. A lot of it. He's been dodging me for a week now, and I ain't havin' it anymore."

"No, please, Carter! I'll get your money. I swear. Just another day!"

"I'll pay it," Ian practically shouted. Max instantly shut up and this Carter looked over at Ian, his eyes narrowing. "Whatever he owes, I'll pay it."

"No!" Max shouted back.

"He owes five grand," Carter said slowly, still not taking his eyes off Ian as if he didn't trust him.

Under the table, he could feel Snow squeezing his knee, trying to get him to stop talking. Ian knew he was putting himself in danger with this guy—probably Max's drug dealer—but Ian didn't care. If he didn't do something, this asshole was going to hurt Max. Good chance he was going to kill him. Ian couldn't let that happen.

"Fine. I'll pay it. Just let him go."

Before Carter could react, Max jerked his hair free with a little cry of pain and shoved Carter backward into the main counter that stretched the length of the restaurant. "I don't need your help! I don't need anyone. You're not paying for shit!"

Max launched to his feet and ran out of the restaurant, disappearing onto the street and out of view.

Ian turned his attention to Carter, who had picked himself up and was straightening his own shirt and jacket. He looked down at Ian with a sneer and clicked his tongue once.

"Looks like your old friend don't want your help. Wants to be on his own." He snorted. "You run into him before I do, you work harder to convince him to take your money. If he don't and I find him, it ain't gonna end pretty."

It was on the tip of Ian's tongue to offer to pay him right now on the spot, whether Max wanted him to or not, but he swallowed the words. He had a feeling this bastard would take Ian's money and then still harass Max into paying him another five thousand. The only way to save Max's life was to get him away from Carter completely, but there was nothing he could do if Max wasn't going to let him help.

Carter sauntered out of the restaurant and Ian sunk down in the booth, shoving his untouched food back. Snow's arm draped over his shoulders and pulled him in closer.

"What am I supposed to do? He won't let me help."

"Ian...he wants you dead," Snow said. He sounded like he thought Ian had lost his mind. And maybe he had, but he didn't care if Max hated him. Max needed help.

"I don't believe that," Ian said stubbornly.

"He attacked you in your home."

"He knocked me out," Ian corrected. "We both know it would have taken him only another few seconds to kill me if he really wanted me dead."

Snow sighed. "Ian…"

"I don't care. He's fought too long and hard to survive. He can't die like this. Not when I've just found him. He deserves a shot at something better."

Snow placed a kiss to the top of his head. "I know. I don't disagree with you. How about we swing by Ward's and talk to Rowe? Pick his brain a little."

"What little there is to pick," Ian muttered, but he couldn't deny he was at least starting to feel a glimmer of hope, thanks to Snow.

"His brain might be little, but it's packed with decades of devious knowledge."

"Thank God he's on our side."

And with a bit of work and convincing, Ian was going to get that devious brain on Max's side. He was going to save him. It wasn't too late.

## Chapter Nineteen

Ian sat behind his desk, pretending to look over some notes and contracts James had left him about the new restaurant, but his mind wasn't on it. He and Snow had met with Rowe, Noah, and Gidget for a couple of hours, brainstorming how they could possibly locate Max as well as try to uncover more information about this Carter guy. When Ian left with Snow to return to Rialto, there hadn't been a lot of good progress or answers. Gidget was going to get Cole digging around on Carter while she tried to find more information on Max. It wasn't much, but it was the best they could manage on the limited information they had.

Just as the restaurant was closing for the night, Max called, asking to meet at midnight after everyone had gone home. Hope had blossomed in Ian's chest, and he eagerly agreed to the meeting. It was probably too much to believe that one okay meal had changed Max's mind about letting Ian help, but Ian thought it was likely that Max was more scared of being killed by Carter. Didn't matter. Ian would take what he could get.

After getting off the phone with Max, he'd called Hollis.

Ian wasn't stupid. While Ian might be happy to assist Max, the young man might not be as eager to let Ian into his life. Hollis would protect Ian as well as offer another voice of reason.

Even if Max had nothing to do with what had been happening at the restaurant, Ian wanted to help him. He only vaguely remembered him from his time at Jagger's. He'd been quiet and so damn pretty with big eyes. Ian knew he was younger than himself by at least a few years and had spent too much time getting passed around at the parties. Ian had no idea how Max had found himself trapped in Jagger's clutches. Maybe he'd been sold by his parents as well. Or just kidnapped like so many others had been.

That wasn't important. Ian could help him start over. Find a better, safer, happier life.

The sound of movement in the restaurant had Ian's head popping up. He glanced quickly at his phone to check the time and found that it was way too early for Max to be there. As he was getting to his feet and starting to move around his desk, Hollis appeared in the doorway.

"You okay?" Hollis immediately asked.

"I'm fine. Everything is fine," Ian said. He continued around the desk and wrapped his arms about Hollis's waist. He tipped his head up, offering his lips for a kiss. Hollis relaxed against him and tenderly brushed his mouth over Ian's, warming his chilled lips.

"Has it gotten that cold outside?" Ian asked when they separated.

Hollis nodded. "We're definitely getting those first real tastes of fall. We might actually get our first frost soon."

"Mmmm," Ian hummed. "I guess I'll have to make sure I do a good job of warming you up when we get home tonight."

A wicked grin spread across Hollis's face as he backed Ian up while still keeping his arms wrapped around Ian's waist. "Really, now?" he drawled. Bending his knees, Hollis grabbed Ian by the thighs and lifted him, earning a surprised yelp from Ian, and sat him down on the edge of the desk. "Exactly what were you thinking of doing to warm me up?"

Spreading his legs, Ian pulled Hollis closer. The tantalizing scent of leather and the spicy hint of cologne teased Ian's nose. He closed his eyes and rubbed his face against Hollis's hard chest, trying to wrap his smell around him. This man meant everything to him. More than the restaurant. More than all his dreams for becoming a great chef. Hollis was home and happiness.

Hollis leaned down and captured Ian's lips in another drugging kiss that had Ian lifting his arms and wrapping them about Hollis's neck before hooking his heels behind his lover's calves. He loved their height difference. He wanted to fucking climb this man every chance he got. Hollis started to pull away and Ian bit down on his lower lip, holding him in place for a second before releasing him with a final lick.

"We probably shouldn't be starting this now," Hollis said with a low chuckle.

Ian sighed, hating to agree with him. The timing wasn't great. "Later. Tonight I'm going to crawl all over you and make you beg me."

"You know you own me."

Ian grinned up at Hollis. He did know it. But then, Hollis owned him heart and soul.

"I really don't want to ruin your mood, but I need to know. What is your goal for tonight's meeting with Max?" Hollis asked. Ian had told him about his surprise breakfast with Max that morning, and he had a feeling the only thing keeping Hollis from losing his temper was the fact that Snow had been there as well.

Ian leaned back a little and his hands slid down to rest on Hollis's chest. "What are you talking about? Our goal is to help Max."

Hollis pressed his lips together and stared silently at Ian like he was trying very hard not to frown while figuring out exactly what he could say without upsetting his husband. Yeah, that wasn't going to fly.

"Just say it," Ian snapped.

"Our focus should be on keeping you safe. You've been attacked in our damn home once already. We aren't completely sure that Max is the one behind the attacks yet. And now there's some other guy who's probably eyeballing you as well. Either Max's dealer or his pimp. Maybe both. I want to help him too, but not if it means that you're going to come in a distant second."

"We can do both. We can help Max and protect me," Ian said confidently.

Hollis didn't look so convinced, but he kept his comment to himself and instead asked, "What time was he supposed to be here again?"

"Quarter to midnight. What time is it now?" Ian twisted around and scooped up his cell phone, checking both the time and that he didn't miss any phone calls or messages while he was snuggling with Hollis. There was nothing new that had come in, and it was just now twenty until twelve. Five more minutes.

Hollis drew in a deep breath, his nose wrinkling while he turned toward the main restaurant area. "You don't have anything cooking in the kitchen, right?"

"No, not right now. Everything is cleaned up, and they all left nearly an hour ago. Why?"

Hollis released him and turned toward the door. He'd closed it when he entered the office, and Ian was sure he'd done it out of habit since the man had to sneak kisses every time he got Ian alone. Not that his entire staff couldn't guess exactly what was happening when it was closed.

"I smell smoke."

"That can't be right," Ian said, but he was also jumping to his feet and following Hollis toward the door. But now that he'd mentioned it, Ian could swear that he was catching little hints of smoke as well.

Hollis grabbed the doorknob but instantly released it, jerking his hand away like he'd been burned. "Fucking hot!" he snarled. Looking around, he grabbed a thick linen napkin that was resting on a shelf and used it to wrap the knob so he could quickly open the door.

Waist-high flames met them, lighting up the dark restaurant. They both leaped back in shock and horror. Ian's heart skipped a beat in his chest and then started zooming ahead in panic. His restaurant, his precious Rialto, was on fire!

Before either of them could move, smoke alarms started going off around the restaurant and the overhead sprinklers kicked on, dousing them in cold water. Ian turned to his desk and jammed his phone into his pocket before grabbing his laptop and shoving it inside the fireproof safe that was next to his desk. Everything was backed up on the cloud, but protecting the laptop would save them time.

From the corner of his eye, he saw Hollis leap across the room and snatch up the small fire extinguisher that had been hanging on the wall behind the door. There were two more larger ones in the kitchen, but they had to be able to reach them first.

"You need to get out of here! I can get us a path out of the office!" Hollis shouted.

Ian wasn't fucking going anywhere yet. But if he could get to the kitchen, he could help Hollis battle the flames. The smoke alarm and sprinklers were attached to the Ward Security system. The fire department would have already been notified of the fire and should be racing to their location.

"It's clear! Get out!" Hollis shouted. His voice was growing hoarse and raw from the smoke.

Ian grabbed another spare napkin and covered his mouth as he rushed into the main restaurant. There he could see little mounds of his magazine had been spread about the room and were lit on fire. By the intensity of the flames, he was pretty sure that whoever had started the fire had doused them with something like gasoline first.

But he didn't need to wonder who the culprit was for long. Max was standing in the open doorway leading to the kitchen. The light had been turned on, casting him in a strange mix of light and dancing shadows, but there was no missing the slightly maniacal grin stretching across his thin features.

"You deserve to fucking burn, Ian!" Max shouted at him. "This was supposed to be my life. You stole everything from me!"

"I didn't steal anything from you, Max," Ian called back. They couldn't have this argument here. They'd all die of smoke inhalation. Hollis was making progress with the damn flaming piles of magazines, but his little extinguisher was going to run out of juice soon.

"You stole Jagger from me the day you arrived! And then that millionaire and his friends noticed you. It should have been me!"

"I can still help you."

Max didn't say anything. He just turned toward the kitchen and ran. He was escaping. Ian twisted around to find Hollis tossing his spent extinguisher. Soot and sweat were pouring down his face. His clothes were sticking to him in the increasing heat of the restaurant. He didn't want to leave his husband to battle the flames, didn't want to leave his restaurant, but he had to go after Max. Couldn't let him disappear. There would only be more attacks.

Or worse, Max would die in the horrible life that he was trapped in.

"Go!" Hollis shouted, pointing toward the kitchen and the rear door. "I've got this!"

Ian was already confident that he couldn't possibly love Hollis more, but the man continued to surprise him at every turn. With a quick nod, Ian darted after Max. He shot through the kitchen and out into the relative darkness of the night.

The cool air was a brutal slap to the face. He sucked in a deep breath and immediately started coughing as his lungs fought to expel the smoke. In the shadows, he saw a flash of movement as someone about Max's size darted down an alley. Ian followed without hesitation, the hard soles of his shoes pounding on the uneven pavement.

The figure cut through the thin light thrown down by a street-lamp, and Ian could clearly see Max's blond hair and slender frame as he ran. Ian was slowly closing the distance on him. So long as he didn't jump into a car, Ian had a chance of catching him. Not that he was even sure what he was going to do once he got his hands on the asshole. He fucking set fire to Rialto! And to add insult to injury, he'd tried to fry both him and Hollis while they were inside. No one hurt his Hollis. There was a part of him that was dying to shake some fucking sense into Max. It was getting damn hard to be compassionate and understanding.

As they reached Vine Street, Max stopped in the empty street and turned to look at Ian, an evil grin on his lips.

"You think you can hurt me?" Max mocked.

Ian slowed his steps as he neared the sidewalk, trying to figure out what he could say that would reach Max. It was clear that Max was the one who'd been threatening his restaurant and staff. He had a sneaking suspicion that the magazine spread had been the final straw for an old hatred that had simmered just under the surface for years.

But there had to be a way to get through all that irrational hatred. A way to talk some reason and sense into him so that no one else got hurt.

Ian lifted both of his empty hands toward Max and took a deep breath. But before he could even say a word, a large black van screeched to a violent halt just a few feet away from Max. Neither of them had seen it approach; their attention had been locked on each other.

The side door slid open with a loud metallic clang, and two men dressed all in black wearing ski masks jumped out. They ran straight for Max. The young man was frozen for a second and then attempted to run, but it was already too late. He screamed and kicked, fighting against the men who quite easily picked him up and hauled him toward the van. Ian lurched forward a moment later after recovering from his shock. Max…was being kidnapped. Just a second ago the bastard had set his restaurant on fire and blamed him for everything going wrong in his life. Now he was being grabbed by strange men in black. It was as if Ian were stuck in some crazy dream.

Before he could even get to the street, the van was roaring up Vine Street. Max's desperate screams could be heard over the squealing tires before the sliding door slammed shut again. Standing in the middle of the road, Ian locked his gaze on the license plate and repeated it over and over again while he pulled out his cell phone.

It was just his luck that someone from Ward Security was calling at exactly that moment.

"Ian!" Gidget's panicked voice came through when he thumbed on the call.

"H-Q-Q four-thirty-two!" Ian shouted back.

"What?"

"H-Q-Q four-three-two! Black van. I think maybe a Ford. Looks like it could be something used for deliveries, but there are no markings. Just black. It's headed north on Vine Street. I think it might have turned east on West Seventh."

"Got it," Gidget immediately said. "Who—"

"Someone dressed all in black grabbed Max after he set Rialto on fire and threw him in the van. I can't follow. I have to get to Hollis." Ian had already turned toward the alley he'd just exited and was jogging down the narrow path back to his husband with the phone pressed to his ear.

"He's outside. I can see him on the camera in front of the restaurant. The fire department is there."

Gidget's reassurance sent a wave of relief through Ian, nearly knocking his knees out. He wobbled and slowed, pressing his free hand against the wall to steady himself. He'd hated leaving Hollis alone to battle the flames, but he'd also known that they could lose their one and only lead. Well, lead no more. Max was definitely the one who wanted to hurt Ian.

But Max had more problems than just Ian.

"Is Max with a gang? Did he have help?"

"No, he was taken against his will. Kidnapped."

"What?" Gidget gasped and Ian fought the urge to growl. He didn't have time to explain everything right now. Especially since he wasn't entirely sure what the hell was happening.

"Just try to track down the van. Find out where they're taking him. We need to rescue him."

"Okay…"

Yeah, he got it. He sounded insane. He wanted to rescue the guy who just tried to kill him and his husband. Ian wasn't thrilled about his restaurant going up in flames or the risk to their lives, but Max could be saved. He was hurting and he was lashing out the only way he knew how. That was a gift from Jagger. The only things they learned with him were pain, suffering, and violence. Max was in pain and he thought it was Ian's fault, so he wanted to make Ian suffer. But there was another way.

Unfortunately, Ian couldn't show him that until they got him out of the clutches of whoever had him now.

"Call Rowe and Noah. Get them and whoever else you can get ahold of to Ward Security tonight. Once I get things under control with the fire department, Hollis and I will be coming there. We are getting Max free tonight."

They just had to figure out who had him and where he was being stashed. He prayed that they didn't immediately kill him and dump the body.

## Chapter Twenty

Ward Security was a buzz of activity and chaos. A mix of emotions filled Ian that he had no hope of untangling until they found Max. It was a combination of the adrenaline from the fire, worry over what the *damn fire* had done to his restaurant, and flat-out panic over what could be happening to Max. He felt like he could crawl out of his own skin.

When he walked into the IT room, Ian was surprised to see Lucas and Snow since it was close to two o'clock in the morning. In addition to them were Rowe, Noah, Dom, Garrett, Gidget, and Quinn. They had a roomful, and once again, Ian was struck by just how much support he had in his life. Support that Max had never had. He nodded his thanks to Dom and Garrett, two of Rowe's security agents.

"Rowe called us to come here instead of Rialto." Lucas grabbed him and hugged him. "You smell like smoke."

"That happens when someone sets your restaurant on fire." He hadn't even had time to dwell on the fact that his restaurant was so damaged, but it would hit him later. Hard.

"Is it destroyed?"

Ian shook his head. "No, but we'll be shut down for a time.

Luckily, the sprinkler systems and Hollis got a lot of the fire out fast." His husband had probably saved Rialto. He looked at Hollis, who was still covered in soot. They hadn't even taken the time to change clothes before rushing to Ward Security after they finished with the firemen and police.

Rowe clapped Hollis on the shoulder. "You can shower here and borrow some clothes from Noah. He has extras in the office."

Hollis gave him a tired smile. "I will after this is all over."

Ian looked at Gidget, who was fully dressed as if she'd never left work and looked more bright and chipper than the rest of them. "I'm sorry to have you here so late. Your little boy okay?"

"I have a neighbor who is there for emergencies, so we're all good." She tucked a strand of blonde hair behind her ear.

"Any luck tracking that van?" Ian asked.

She turned, caught her skirt in the rollers of her chair, and yanked it out. Once she was finally situated, she pointed at her screen. "I have the location where they stopped. It's an old warehouse in the West End, known for being a drug den. Nasty place."

"Maybe it was people Max owed money to. This Carter guy," Ian mused as he stared at the building on Gidget's computer screen. It looked like any abandoned warehouse he'd ever imagined, only this one had lights shining in the windows. *They were still there.* "We have to help him."

"Do we know anything about this Carter Snow and Ian met?" Hollis asked.

Gidget winced and looked over at Rowe, who was scrubbing a hand through his hair.

"Gotta say, Ian, when you fucking pick them…" Rowe muttered under his breath.

"What the hell is that supposed to mean?" Ian snapped.

But Rowe didn't look at Ian. He kept his eyes on Hollis, who was standing next to Ian with his hand on his shoulder. "CJ Thorpe mean anything to you, former cop?"

"Son of a bitch. Are you kidding me?"

Ian twisted around to see Hollis pace away a couple of steps and then turn back. He'd shoved both hands through his hair, leaving it standing up in all directions thanks to the sweat and dirt that still covered him. His eyes were wide with what looked to be shock, and his mouth just sort of hung open.

"What? What's going on? Who's CJ Thorpe?" Ian demanded.

Hollis stared at him wordlessly, the emotions flitting across his face moving from shock to worry to sadness, creating a sinking feeling in Ian's stomach.

"Thorpe is Cincinnati's major drug mover," Noah said into the silence that had lengthened in the room.

"He was nothing more than a brainless goon when Jagger was around, because Jagger was the major mover and shaker in the city. He took care of all his competition," Hollis continued.

"But when Jagger was killed…" Rowe said, his voice trailing off.

"This CJ guy filled in his place," Ian finished, his heart clenching.

"I'd heard as much from some old friends on the force," Hollis confirmed. "And he took a page out of Jagger's book when it came to being the city's drug powerhouse."

"What do you mean?"

Hollis looked down at his husband, his frown deepening. "It means that he's violent. Brutal. He has no qualms about killing or torturing people. The fact that he's allowed Max to run up a debt of five g's makes me think that Max is usually good for the money or that Max is doing more than just solicitation. He's probably selling or muling for CJ as well."

"Do you think he plans to kill Max?"

"Eventually. The fact that he hasn't already means that he either thinks he can get his money out of Max or Max has something he wants…maybe product. Once he gets what he wants, Max is dead."

"But we're still going to save him, right?" Ian turned to look at the other men watching him around the room.

Lucas cleared his throat. Dressed in jeans and a black sweater, he had his hands in his pockets. His handsome features were pulled tight in a fierce frown. "This Max is the one who hurt you? The one who's been systematically trying to destroy Rialto?"

Ian nodded, knowing he'd need to explain his feelings. "He was one of Jagger's boys. I kicked him out of his spot as the favorite, and he feels that it should have been him you guys met and saved at that party."

"And you want us to save him?" Snow asked. He looked tired as he leaned against a table, as if he'd just gotten off a shift at the hospital. Like Lucas, he was in jeans and a sweater, his silver hair disheveled.

"He's a victim, too," Ian insisted. "He didn't get the chance to get out like I did. Didn't have a millionaire backing his first restaurant or protective friends to help him get back on his feet. I've been so damn lucky, and I just want to pass some of my good luck on. So, we'll go get him and break him out of that place."

"It wasn't luck, Ian," Lucas said. "We love you."

"Oh, it damn sure was luck that you two happened to go to that party when I was there. That you loved something I'd cooked and sought me out in the kitchen. You may love me now, but all that was pure luck."

Rowe scrubbed a hand over his face. "You want us to infiltrate a known drug den. Tonight. Take down Cincinnati's main drug dealer with little to no reconnaissance?"

"It has to be tonight." Ian threw his hands into the air. "Who knows what they're doing to him!"

"He's probably already dead, Ian." Rowe shook his head. "These kinds of guys don't play around."

"We don't know that. And I won't be able to live with myself if I don't try to help him." Ian knew he sounded belligerent, but he could also tell they weren't all totally with him on this. Not that he could blame him. He was demanding they risk their lives for a guy who had been trying to destroy Ian. "You've got some new toys you want to try out, right?"

Rowe perked up a little, but it was Dom who spoke first. "Ooooh...the new doorbuster and the lighter night-vision goggles. They need a field test." Ian saw Dom and Garrett grin at each other like a pair of kids at Christmas.

"Maybe I'll let you pick the code names," Ian pressed when Rowe didn't look totally sold. Dom and Garrett were a good start, but he knew he needed Rowe and Noah in on this mission. He'd be happy if Lucas and Snow returned home to their respective spouses.

Rowe twisted a little to look over at Noah. "You wanna go take down a drug lord?"

Noah shrugged nonchalantly, but Ian could see that he was barely holding back his grin. "It has been months since we blew up that building. Could be interesting. Also…code names."

"I want a good one," Ian interjected.

"You're not going!" Rowe and Lucas said at the same time.

Ian narrowed his eyes and got ready to argue as fury erupted in his chest, but Hollis surprised him by speaking up.

"This is Ian's mission. Hell yes, he'll be there. And he should get to pick the code names."

Dom spoke up. "He should get to come. You can put him in body armor." The redhead was sitting in one of the chairs next to the conference table.

Garrett snorted and ran his hand over his short black hair. "We're all gonna be in body armor if we're going into a place like that. Those dudes will be armed to the teeth."

"Then let's do this." Rowe rubbed his hands together. "I've got all kinds of goodies we can break out. Body armor, sniper rifles, and some new tranq guns."

The others burst into questions.

The talk over just what would be needed nearly frightened Ian out of going, but he didn't let it. He'd been left out of a lot of these missions over the years and this one was his, dammit. His restaurant had been set on fire, and he felt responsible for the situation Max was in, even though logically he understood he wasn't. Not entirely.

Max had made his choices in life after getting free of Jagger, but Ian had been honest when he'd said he was the one lucky enough to meet Lucas, Snow, and Rowe. And while he'd never wish that were different, he could understand where Max was coming from.

"I managed to find some floor plans for the place," Quinn announced into the noise of the room.

All the guys and Gidget quieted and gathered around his computer to study them. Hollis rubbed his hand up and down Ian's back, and Ian leaned into him. This was taking too long, and all he could think about was Max and what he was going through right then.

*Were they beating him?*
*Was Rowe right and had they killed him already?*

All the shit Max had done to him paled when compared to that. He leaned harder into Hollis, who wrapped an arm around him. He was thankful his husband had spoken up in his defense. Lucas, Snow, and Rowe would always try to protect him. Not that Hollis didn't feel the same way—they were just on equal footing, and Hollis never let him forget that.

"We need to hurry," Ian said, feeling antsy and worried.

Rowe nodded and led everyone down to his toy room to get them outfitted. Ian held back, his hand on Hollis's arm to stop him from following.

"You okay with all this?"

Hollis smiled down at him and cupped his face. He kissed him briefly. "Yes. You have a big, big heart, and it's one of the reasons I love you so much."

"But I'm putting everyone in danger over this, and a part of me is feeling pretty damn bad about that."

"These guys wouldn't do this if they didn't feel it's right on some level. Even I feel bad for the kid."

"He's not a kid—he's probably around twenty-seven years old. Remember, I was a little older than Jagger liked them when he got me."

Hollis grimaced. "Yeah, but Max never got to be a kid. Like you." Hollis kissed him again. "This is someone who had all his rights taken away, and then he was thrown out onto the streets after living a nightmare. I can understand why you want to help him."

"It could have been me, Hollis."

Hollis pulled him in for a hug. "But it's not you, and I for one am glad. I never would have met you if you hadn't taken the life path you did. I'm the luckiest husband on Earth."

Ian smiled into his sooty jacket. He hugged him back and pulled him toward the door. "Come on, let's go look at what Rowe's showing everyone."

All the guys picked out their "toys." Gidget and Quinn were going to work remotely with them and watch for cops. Gidget was also going to work her magic and take the power down at the site.

Ian was given two guns, one a tranq and one real. They felt weird in his hands, but he didn't share that feeling, not wanting everyone to be more nervous than they already were about arming him. Years ago, Ian had gotten some shooting lessons from Lucas and Rowe as a "just in case." Ian had been sure he'd never hold a gun again after those lessons, but life takes strange turns. Lucas and Noah took him into the firing range for a quick refresher course, but Ian knew he'd need a lot more than one lesson to be comfortable shooting a gun.

It wasn't long before they were piling into SUVs and driving through the dark, quiet streets of Cincinnati. There was a strange hush to the city this early in the morning, but Ian knew a lot of that strangeness was linked to what he was about to do. Raid a known drug den.

He looked over at Hollis to find his husband watching him closely. His man was worried about taking him on this mission despite his earlier words. Not that he blamed him. Ian was a freaking chef, after all, not an ex-cop.

As they drew closer to the warehouse, Ian's nerves threatened to eat him alive. He ran his sweaty palms down his slacks.

A memory of flames licking their way through Rialto flashed through his mind, and his heart threatened to break. Ian violently shoved that worry to the side. He needed to keep his head in this. Not only was his life on the line, but the lives of his family and friends. He wanted all of them returning home safe and sound at the end of this.

They parked several blocks away and one by one, the men drifted into the night carrying their weapons. Ian, gripping his gun with sweaty hands, followed on Hollis's heels.

## Chapter Twenty-One

Hollis crouched down behind a car, a gun clenched tightly in his right fist as he tried to ignore the cold. It had rained earlier in the evening, leaving the pavement damp and peppered with puddles. His shoes were already soaked. But the physical discomfort was nothing compared to the fear and panic battling it out in his chest. Ian was squatting behind the car with a gun.

*Ian was holding a gun.*

His sweet, loving, soft-hearted husband had a gun.

It was something he never thought he'd see or even have to contemplate. There was no one kinder or more loving than Ian. Hollis couldn't fathom Ian ever shooting someone.

But there had been no way any of them was going to allow Ian into this drug warehouse without a weapon to protect himself. As it was, they'd already cleaned Rowe out of body armor. Noah and Lucas had pulled Ian aside and given him some tips on using the weapon along with a few minutes in the firing range. Hollis knew they were all praying that Ian never had to squeeze the trigger. That the gun was a last resort in case the entire operation went pear-shaped fast.

There had been no point in calling the cops. Trying to explain everything and then convincing them to lead a raid on the place for one poor guy with a history of drugs and prostitution was a waste of time Max didn't have. There was a small part of Hollis that wanted to just leave Max to the drug dealers holding him. The guy had hurt Ian, Sean, and Wade. He'd made his choices in life, and he had to suffer the consequences. Particularly if they put Ian in danger.

But Hollis could too easily see Ian's point of view.

Were it not for a small whim of fate or luck, that could have so easily been Ian. If Jagger had chosen Max over Ian. If Lucas, Snow, and Rowe had met Max instead of Ian, would they have helped him, saved him? Would Ian have been left behind to be tortured for several more years before being tossed to the streets without a penny to his name?

Hollis knew in the end, it had been Ian's drive and determination that got the man to not depend on Lucas and the others. He worked hard to become a great chef and open an amazing restaurant. He worked hard to have the incredible life he had.

But it also didn't hurt that Ian had a great base from which to rise. Lucas, Snow, and Rowe gave him a loving, stable environment from which to recover and find himself.

Max never had that.

He could now, though, if he'd just listen to Ian and let him help.

Of course, that was assuming they all got out of this insane plan alive so they could even offer to help Max.

A hand gripped Hollis's shoulder and squeezed. He twisted around and saw Ian's worried eyes watching him while a weak smile lifted the corners of his mouth. Hollis wished he could reassure Ian that he had no regrets. That he was there because he'd do anything to make Ian happy, that he was there because it was the right thing to do.

But there was no denying he'd prefer that his heart was far from this place, maybe even back at Ward Security with Quinn and Gidget.

But Ian had a right to be there. As much as any of them did.

Max didn't deserve to be left behind a second time.

## Rialto

"All right, kids," Rowe drawled in their ears through the coms they were all wearing.

Hollis smirked and looked over his shoulder at Ian, who rolled his eyes. Hollis had heard so many tales about the infamous Rowe and Noah assaults with the crazy weapons and code names, but he'd been involved in only the small one with Rowe, Noah, and Ian down in Kentucky and then the crazy operation at Union Terminal against Jagger.

Good to know that if the police got wind of this, they were all going to jail together.

"Is everyone in position? Check in," Rowe continued.

Ian winked at him, some of the worry and fear finally leaving his eyes. "Dorothy and Toto are in position outside the western entrance. No guards."

There was a low snicker, but it was too soft for Hollis to identify. Yeah, he was Toto to Ian's Dorothy, but he didn't care. As soon as the plan was being sketched out, Ian quickly announced that he had the theme for code names decided. No one grumbled. Apparently, it was becoming understood that the family member behind the mission got to pick the code names.

It didn't hurt to hear the enthusiasm in Ian's voice. He was finally being included in a mission, in the secret plans of Rowe, Snow, and Lucas. Hollis just could have done without risking Ian's life in the process.

"Wicked Witch and Flying Monkey outside the front door," Noah said, referring to him and Dominic. "Two visible guards."

"Glenda on the roof," Garrett announced. "No guards, but the door is sealed shut. I'm going down through the skylight."

"Shit. I knew I should have picked the roof," Dom muttered. "Did you bring the flamethrower?"

"No, Wicked Witch confiscated it," Garret grumbled.

"Damn straight I confiscated that. It's not a toy!" Noah snapped. "Plus, I didn't get to play with it before it ran out of fuel."

"Focus, gang," Rowe interrupted, putting them on track again.

"Scarecrow is in the crow's nest," Lucas said darkly.

Hollis had been initially surprised to hear that Lucas was taking up the sniper position, when it was supposed to be one of Noah's specialties, but apparently Lucas was damn good with a gun, particularly at a distance. He also suspected that it was Rowe's attempt to keep the daddy out of the line of fire as much as possible.

"Confirming two guards out front. I can see at least two more people walking around in a room on the second floor. I'm blind to the rest of the warehouse. No one approaching," Lucas continued.

"Wizard in position and sees all," Gidget chimed in from her remote position at the office. "They've got a security system. Fancy one. Lots of cameras. Everything is quiet in our part of town on the police bands. Standing by."

"Lion and Tin Man at the south entrance. We've got one guard," Rowe finished the roll call.

"I don't understand why I had to be the Tin Man," Snow mumbled.

"It's a perfect fit for you." It sounded like Ian was just barely holding back his laughter.

"Should have made him a member of the Lollipop Guild," Lucas added.

"Shut up, *Scarecrow*."

"Shut up, everyone," Rowe snarled. "Wizard? You ready?"

"Yep!"

"Work your magic."

Hollis held his breath as he waited. A couple of seconds ticked by with nothing, and then it was like watching a wave of darkness sweep over the city as one block after another went down. There were no lights for as far as they could see. An eerie hush fell over everything, suffocating and thick. The sounds of cars was softer and farther away than they had been. Crickets and other night creatures stopped stirring and seemed to hold their breaths. They knew something was about to happen and they wanted to watch.

"Oops…" Gidget whispered. "That was a little bigger than I was expecting."

Someone chuckled and Hollis swore that it was Garrett or Dom. It confirmed that Gidget managed to take down more of the electrical grid than she'd been initially aiming for.

# Rialto

"Don't worry about it, Wizard. How much time do we have?"

"At least five minutes, but I'll try to stretch it longer."

"Go!" Rowe ordered.

Hollis rocked on the balls of his feet and launched himself forward, moving directly toward the door he'd been watching. He heard only the tiniest scrape of rubber sole across the pavement as Ian followed. His heart pounded in his chest, and his fingers tightened around the gun in his hand. This one was loaded with tranquilizer darts, but they each had a second gun and two magazines loaded with real bullets.

For now, they were going in quietly and taking down their drug dealers with tranq darts. As Noah had said, they were starting off civilized since they weren't cops, but they were willing to fuck shit up if things went south.

Hollis had a feeling that it wasn't going to take much for the whole mission to go to hell fast, but he was hoping it wouldn't.

"Two guards down. Flying Monkey and Wicked Witch heading inside," Dom said. His voice was deadly serious and cold. Something Hollis was sure he'd never hear from the man.

"Glenda is holding position," Garrett said with no small amount of frustration. Hollis couldn't blame him. A large man crashing through the skylight would throw the entire mission out of the covert category fast. He was one of their last lines of defense if things went to shit.

"Tin Man and Lion inside. One down," Rowe whispered.

Hollis reached the side, the metal handle cool even through the leather gloves he was wearing. Very carefully he turned the handle and winced to hear the loud whine as the door opened. While it wasn't locked, the door apparently wasn't used often or maintained. He was pretty sure he'd announced to everyone in the warehouse that someone was coming through the side-fucking-door. *Wonderful.*

"Down!" Ian barked and Hollis immediately dropped to his knees, his head tucked down to his shoulders. In the darkness, he could see Ian lift his gun in both hands and squeeze off a round. The guy who had been standing in the now open doorway grunted. He was a monster of a man, standing close to seven feet and as wide as a refrigerator. He looked down at the dart that was sticking out of his chest.

Ian gave a little shrug and fired a second dart into his chest. With all his bulk, the fucker probably needed it.

The man swayed and fell forward. With one hand, Hollis grabbed the guy's bicep and made sure he fell as quietly as possible.

"Nice job, Dorothy," Lucas said from his perch. "Pay attention, Toto."

Hollis looked over at Ian to see him give a little shake of his head in the darkness, but Hollis couldn't argue with Lucas. He needed to pay better attention if he was going to keep Ian safe.

"One guard down. Dorothy and Toto inside," Ian relayed to the rest of the team.

By his count, six of them were inside the warehouse while Garrett was standing by on the roof and Lucas was positioned on a nearby rooftop with a sniper rifle and a high-power scope. Rowe really did have the best toys—not that he'd ever tell the man that to his face.

The interior of the warehouse was pitch black. Hollis pulled on a pair of incredibly heavy night-vision goggles, since all the lighter ones had been grabbed, and tried to tamp down the same giddy thrill he'd felt when Dom had handed him a pair at Ward Security. *Really...the best toys.*

The entire world was bathed in a strange green light, but he could now see the towers of boxes and crates. The open area in the middle of the room was filled with long tables and what looked to be a very organized drug packaging and processing outfit.

It was fucking gutsy to have all this shit out in the open. Hollis's old cop senses were tingling. Either CJ was a complete moron, or the bastard was confident because he had a cop or two in his pocket.

People ran around, knocking into shit and tripping over metal folding chairs in their haste. A few were smart enough to pull out their cell phones and turn on the little flashlight app so that slender shafts of bright light swept over small swaths of the warehouse. They were the first targets. The lights needed to stay out.

As one guy ran close to their position, Hollis took aim and

## Rialto

squeezed off his first round. The man stumbled as he passed, twisting around to touch the meaty part of his shoulder where the dart hit. They were lucky most of these guys appeared to be wearing T-shirts despite the cold air of the warehouse. Less padding the darts had to sink through to get to flesh. He was pulling the dart out of his arm when he went down in an unconscious heap.

Ian and Hollis moved through the warehouse, sweeping along the west side, while Snow and Rowe moved from the south and Noah and Dom moved in from the north.

"Someone is here!" The angry voice echoed from the second floor. Hollis looked up to see a figure standing against the railing of a catwalk that spanned the main floor of the warehouse. Gunfire opened up and Hollis ducked down, barely holding in check his need to pull Ian to him to cover him with his larger frame.

"Fuck!" Rowe snarled. "Change guns!"

"Target is on the second floor," Lucas called out. "They're moving him. Southwest corner."

"There's a staircase near me. I'll go!" Ian shouted. "I need Tin Man with me."

"Coming," Snow instantly said.

"They could use a distraction," Hollis snapped as a bullet thudded loudly into the wood crate he was hiding behind.

"Glenda!"

"Here comes Glenda, bitches!" Garrett roared a second before the sound of breaking glass filled the warehouse. That insane bastard had jumped through the skylight and was plummeting through the air with two machine guns belching out bullets as fast as they could be fired.

Ian grabbed Hollis's arm and squeezed for a second. Hollis's heart skipped a beat, and he swallowed hard against the lump in his throat.

"Be safe," Hollis said hoarsely.

"Always," Ian murmured, and then he darted away into the darkness and thunder of gunfire.

Hollis had to pull his eyes away and force his attention to providing ample cover for Ian and Snow. All the drug dealers had turned their attack to the lunatic falling through the air on a nylon rope to the ground, missing the two men who were closing in on the staircase leading to the second-floor offices. Ian would be safe. Ian would come back to him in one piece.

∼

Sliding around a large tower of crates, Ian ran as fast as he could while wearing the damn goggles. It wasn't an easy thing. They were so heavy that they bounced on his head as he ran, forcing him to steady them with his free hand while gripping a gun in his other. None of this felt natural or normal, and for that he was grateful. He belonged in his freaking kitchen. Not in some drug den trying to rescue a guy who was trying to destroy his life.

Of course, Ian could argue that Snow had no business being there. He should be at the hospital, prepping for his next surgery. But that didn't explain the big grin on his face as he reached Ian at the staircase. This was an adventure. And Ian was a part of it.

"You're freaking insane," Ian whispered with a laugh as Snow reached him at the bottom of the stairs.

"I think we're all a little insane for doing this, but here we are," Snow said as he passed by Ian and charged up the stairs ahead of him.

Ian's step was lighter on the metal, making only a murmur of sound behind Snow's pounding tread. They rose above the firefight on the ground floor, and Ian forced his thoughts away from Hollis and the rest of his family. He was only half listening to the chatter back and forth as his companions counted off the men they took down, whether by bullet or tranq dart. They were keeping a count, but the problem was that they had no idea how many people had been in the warehouse before they entered.

As they reached the second floor, Ian smiled at Snow, who looked over his shoulder to check on him. Before Snow could turn back, a man ran out of an open doorway and lifted his gun, pointing it directly at Snow. Ian didn't think or speak. He launched himself into Snow's stomach, slamming him against the wall, while

Ian covered him with as much of his body as he could. He tensed, waiting to feel the bullet tear through his flesh, but it never came.

Behind him, a window broke and Ian opened his eyes to see the man who'd been aiming at them spin around as something unseen hit him in the chest and shoulder. He stumbled backward and went tumbling over the waist-high metal railing before plunging to the concrete floor below.

"You're welcome," Lucas said in a low drawl.

Snow groaned. "Never gonna let me live that down, right?"

"Nope."

"Thank you," Ian whispered, not caring that his voice was shaking. It had been too damn close. Snow's arms briefly closed around him, hugging him. Snow's voice might be calm and even bored, but Ian could feel his heart pounding like mad under his ear.

"Be careful," Lucas admonished. "I think the target is in the room that fuck just came from. I've got no visual."

"Got it," Snow said evenly, releasing Ian.

The instructions were clear. The moment they stepped into that room, they were on their own. No more backup.

Ian followed Snow to the doorway the man had stepped out of to find two men in jeans and T-shirts shoving piles of money into what looked like two large overnight bags while holding their phone flashlights on their work. The lighting was horrible, but Ian could make out the angry and frantic expression twisting Carter's...or rather, CJ Thorpe's face.

From the doorway, Snow fired several rounds into the room. Ian was stunned to see that he was still using the tranq gun, but maybe he shouldn't have been. Any bullets Snow put in, there was a good chance he'd have to take out later if they survived.

Both men shouted and grabbed their guns. But while one dove behind the desk for cover, Carter lunged for Max. He wrapped an arm around the smaller man's neck and pulled his limp body up so that he was little more than a human shield. Ian's heart skipped a beat to see Max's seemingly lifeless body dangling in front of Carter. Max didn't even flinch or cry out at the rough handling.

"I don't know who the fuck you are, but you ain't getting out of here alive!" Carter shouted. He extended his gun past Max's beaten and bruised face and fired into the open doorway. Ian and Snow pulled away. Ian prayed the walls were thicker than they appeared.

"We just want Max," Ian called out when the bullets ceased for a moment.

"The whore?" There was no missing the surprise in Carter's voice.

Ian clenched his teeth to hold in the torrent of angry words he longed to unleash. Max was more than what he'd been forced to do in order to survive. When he could speak evenly, he replied, "Give us Max and we'll leave. No more trouble."

"Who are you?"

Ian glanced at Snow and his friend was shaking his head fiercely, glaring at him in warning, but Ian ignored it. "Take the opening," Ian whispered, and then he was moving around Snow's larger body. He inched slowly into the doorway so that Carter would be able to at least make out the shape of him in the darkness that was only thinly cut by the bright moon. "You remember me, right? From Waffle House," Ian said to Carter.

Carter lowered his gun a little and his mouth fell open in surprise. "Pretty boy? What was your name again?"

"Ian."

"That's right. Ian. What the fuck—"

"I came to pay you that five grand Max owes you."

"Are you fucking shitting me? All this…you attack my house? My people? For this little whore?" Carter barked out an ugly laugh. "And you think five grand is gonna cover it. Oh, fuck no!"

"Ten grand," Ian snapped. His damn palms were sweating so much, fingertips trembling in fear.

"Try again."

"Fifty."

"I had no idea he was such a great fuck," Carter cackled and then suddenly stopped. "But try again."

No matter what he offered, it wasn't going to be enough. He knew that. He could only hope that Snow was ready. "No. Enough. We're taking him."

## Rialto

"Move now," Snow whispered.

Ian dove for the opposite side of the open doorway at the same time as Carter jerked his gun upward. From the corner of his eye, Ian saw Snow slip from the other side of the doorway and fire two darts at Carter. The man shouted and managed to squeeze off. Ian rolled out of the way, but his eyes immediately came back to Snow. His friend gave him a quick thumbs up to prove that he was unharmed.

The firing suddenly stopped, and they both peeked into the room to find Carter and Max collapsed on the floor, unconscious. They both charged into the room. Snow kicked the gun away from Carter's limp fingers before they kneeled down next to a bloody Max sprawled across the floor. Were they too late? Had Ian just endangered the lives of his family and friends for nothing?

Max flinched and tried to curl up in a ball when Snow pressed his fingers to his throat to check for a pulse. Ian breathed a heavy sigh of relief. Even through the night-vision goggles, Ian could clearly see that Max's face was horribly cut and swollen from the beating he'd suffered. Blood was splashed across his ragged clothes, and there was an ugly rattle in his breathing as he gasped for air against the pain.

"We've got the target. He's alive," Ian announced.

"But he's in bad shape," Snow added. "Watch the door while I check him over. I need to be sure that it's safe to move him."

"*Not* moving him isn't exactly an option, Tin Man," Rowe said over the earpiece, his sneer very evident in his words. "We need to hurry!"

Ian took up position in front of Max and Snow, making sure they were blocked by his body should anyone come through the open doorway.

"I'm not making him worse by moving him," Snow snapped.

"Do you want me to call an ambulance?" Gidget offered.

"Not yet—"

"Oh, darn it!" Gidget cried. "Lights in five seconds!"

Ian grabbed his goggles and ripped them off before he could be blinded. He could hear the others cursing the electric company for having their shit pulled together so fast.

Light suddenly glowed behind his eyelids and Ian blinked several times, trying to get his eyes to quickly adjust to the dim, dirty light of the room. The warehouse behind the doorway looked brighter, and he hoped his friends were adapting.

"Ian?"

Ian whipped around at the sound of Max's surprised voice. The beaten man was staring at him through the one eye that wasn't swollen shut.

With more speed than he thought possible, Max grabbed the gun Snow had set down while he examined Max and pointed it at Ian's chest. Snow straightened, pulling away from Max, while Ian took a step backward, holding both of his hands up. His damn back was to the doorway, making everyone in the room vulnerable to an intruder.

"What? Why are you here?" Max demanded. The nose of the gun trembled, but his finger was resting on the trigger, making it too damn dangerous for Snow to jerk the gun away. Ian wasn't sure if it was Snow's tranq gun or a real gun, but he really didn't want to find out the hard way.

"We came to rescue you," Ian said as gently as possible.

"Bullshit—"

"We don't have time for this! My friends and I are risking our lives to save your ass. I'll not have them die because you're too busy being an idiot."

Max's busted lips parted in surprise, and Ian had to admit that it probably wasn't the best approach when someone was holding a gun on him.

"But…why? I attacked you…burned your restaurant…"

"I know. You're angry. You have a right to be angry. You shouldn't have suffered alone for so long. I was lucky. I have people who helped me. Loved me." Ian slowly lowered his empty hand and stretched it out to Max. "Let us help you now."

"But…"

"No buts. Let me help."

Ian held his breath as he waited for Max to decide whether his hatred of Ian outweighed his need for help. The seconds stretched, feeling like an eternity, before Max gave a jerky nod. He removed his finger from the trigger. Snow instantly jerked the gun away and seriously looked as if he were contemplating turning it on Max.

"Dorothy? Tin Man? What's going on?" Rowe demanded.

"We're good. Clear us an exit. We're coming down," Snow replied.

"Get moving, gang," Gidget announced with new urgency. "A call just went in about gunshots."

Ian listened with only half his attention as the men he'd invaded the warehouse with pulled back to the exit and prepared to cover his and Snow's escape with Max. Lucas was already moving to pull the van around. The gunfire on the main floor of the warehouse had slowed and was now only the occasional pop.

Snow tucked his gun away and carefully pulled Max up to his feet before placing him across his shoulders in a fireman's carry. Max moaned softly as Snow settled him. It was a good thing Max was roughly the same size as Ian. Snow made it look like he was hefting a rag doll. But he had to keep both hands on Max and the railing. He was completely dependent on Ian to keep them covered and safe as they descended to the first floor.

With a nod from Snow, Ian led the way out of the room, sweeping his gun from side to side as he watched for anyone who might be waiting to attack. The second floor was clear. Ian briskly led the way down the stairs to find Hollis already waiting for him with Rowe leaning against him, blood soaking Rowe's left arm.

"You've been shot!" Ian cried as he reached the ground floor.

"Shhhh!" Rowe hushed, but it was already too late.

"Who? Who's been shot?" Noah demanded.

"It's just a little graze," Rowe replied. "I'm fine."

"It's not a graze," Snow growled. "I'll take a look at it in the car."

"I knew it! I fucking knew it!" Noah ranted. Rowe was going to be lucky if Noah didn't shoot his other arm, he sounded so pissed.

They quickly made their way out of the warehouse with the rest of the team flanking them every step of the way. When they reached the main doors, they exploded outside to find Lucas waiting in the black SUV. Doors were pulled open and about half of them piled in while others started running toward where the rest of the vehicles had been stashed a few blocks away. Noah paused at the SUV for only a moment to glare at Rowe. With a shaky smile, Rowe placed his hand against Noah's cheek.

"I'm fine, babe. I promise."

And then Noah was gone without a word.

"Cops are en route. About two minutes away," Gidget chimed in.

Ian climbed into the back seat next to Max while Snow and Rowe jumped into the middle row. Hollis was in the front seat next to Lucas, but he was keeping his eye on Max. Lucas sped away, and Ian started to breathe a sigh of relief.

They were less than a block away when there were a series of loud booms that sounded like they were coming from the warehouse. Ian twisted around to stare out the back window to see flames and smoke billowing from the large building.

"Rowan!" Lucas growled.

"What?" Rowe said and then hissed in pain as Snow worked on Rowe's gunshot wound. "Quinn and Cole cooked up these new transmitters they wanted me to test out."

"What was that? Dynamite?" Hollis asked.

Rowe snorted. "Dynamite. Really? No, that was C4."

"Are you fucking kidding me? You were running around the warehouse with fucking C4?" Lucas continued. "You could have blown us all up."

"It was just a little C4," Rowe mumbled softly, sounding so much like a scolded child. "It was just enough to distract the cops. No one in the building got hurt."

"I can't believe you took the flamethrower away from me, and he's allowed to play with C4," Garrett added, reminding them all that they were still wearing microphones and earpieces.

A hand landed on Ian's arm, drawing his gaze back to Max who was staring at him with what kind of looked like confusion, but it was hard to tell with his face so battered and swollen.

"Why?"

It was the same question he'd asked in the warehouse. Ian got it. Max had threatened Ian's life. Threatened his restaurant and employees. Anyone else would have left Max to be brutalized and killed by those men.

But Ian also knew the kind of life Max had suffered already at the hands of Jagger. He knew he was there partially out of guilt. He felt guilty for not saving Max so many years ago, for not looking for him sooner.

That wasn't the only reason, though. He believed in paying it forward. More than a decade ago, three amazing men saved his life when they didn't have to. They gave him a shot at happiness, love, and his dreams. He wanted to give Max that shot now.

"Because you're more than the life you've been living," Ian said softly. "You're more than what Jagger forced you to be and do. I want to help you get a second chance. But you have to want that second chance too."

Max nodded gingerly, tears starting to fill his eyes. "I do. I don't want this. I've…I've been so lost. I don't know what to do…"

Ian carefully wrapped his arm around Max's shoulders and pulled him in close. "I know. You're not alone anymore. I've got you."

"We've got you," Hollis added from the front seat, bringing a teary smile to Ian's lips.

Snow's head turned and he stared at Max for a moment before giving a little nod. "Yes. We've got you."

## Chapter Twenty-Two

Less than forty-eight hours later, Ian glanced into the back seat to find Max staring out the window, his narrow features pensive as he tapped out some kind of rhythm on his thigh with his fingers. He was in for a bad time with withdrawals, but he seemed more than willing to go through it. He would just need a helping hand. He'd already started showing symptoms with nausea, tremors, runny nose, and more. Ian had sat up with him the night before, and it had been awful. The violent mood swings were threatening to get worse, and Max needed more help than Ian and Hollis could provide alone.

Light-brown eyes met his, and Ian was struck again by how much they resembled each other, though Max was thinner and had lighter hair. Ian's heart broke to think about how small and helpless he'd been with Jagger. How fucking young.

"Thank you again for doing this," Max said softly. "Especially after everything I did to you."

"I had help myself. People sometimes need help to get past the really rough stuff." He glanced at Hollis, who was busy navigating the intense traffic. Ian had all the support he could ever need. He smiled at his husband, who threw him a smile back.

It took them over an hour to get Max situated at the rehabilitation facility. They had spoken with nurses, doctors, counselors, nutritionists, and more. But those weren't the only members of Max's support team. That morning, Ian had gotten him a new phone and programmed the numbers for himself, Hollis, Rowe, Noah, Lucas, and Snow. They were all there to help him fight. By the time Ian and Hollis climbed into their car to leave, Max looked a little frightened but also determined to see this thing through.

Ian expected there'd be bumps in his road, but at least Max seemed willing to try. If he pulled through this and got clean, Ian planned to offer him a job. He'd talked with the man a lot the last couple of days and Max had been angry, jealous, and so hyped up on drugs, he could barely function. Ian got the feeling he wasn't that bad of a guy. He certainly seemed thankful for all they were doing.

As Hollis drove them home, Ian reached out and took his hand. He threaded their fingers together. "Have I told you lately how lucky I feel to have you?"

"I'm the lucky one," Hollis replied, tightening his fingers.

They drove in silence for a while until he noticed that Hollis kept glancing at him. "What?"

"How are you feeling about the foster thing now?"

"I still want to do it at some point, but the last few weeks have shown me I was taking on too much, and I still have some baggage I need to work through."

"We both do."

"I think we need to go ahead and finish the classes but hold off on the rest until we work through some of it. I need to get In Good Time off the ground and turn more of the work at Rialto over to my manager. If we're going to have children, I want to be around more."

"I've already talked to Shane about fewer night jobs, and he's on board with me. But as for working through the baggage, are we talking therapy?"

Ian nodded. "I still plan to go back. I hadn't realized we were pushing so many emotions down when it came to my time with

Jagger. I thought I'd really gotten past all that. But I still carry a lot of guilt."

"What happened to you wasn't your fault."

"No, but I feel like I should have done more for the people who'd still been trapped there. Max is a perfect example of that."

"What happened to Max isn't your responsibility either. And what you're doing for him now is wonderful."

"All I'm doing is paying for his rehab."

"And planning to visit him. And offering to be a support during the process."

Ian shrugged. "I can make time for him."

"And planning to offer him a job. That could easily backfire."

Ian sighed and ran his free hand through his hair. "I know. But I have to try."

Hollis lifted their joined hands and kissed the back of Ian's. "I love you."

"Love you, too."

He shivered when Hollis kissed his hand again. The butterflies going crazy in his belly were so welcome. He hoped he'd always feel them when Hollis loved on him.

And speaking of loving, Ian wanted to go home for some of that. They'd had Max in their place and hadn't really had the time to connect following all the chaos with Rialto and then the rescue.

Of course, when Ian hadn't been hovering over Max in his recovering, he'd been hovering at Rialto. The destruction hadn't been horrible, but it still made his heart clench. A company had been called in to deal with the smoke and water damage. James was in the middle of hiring a contractor to make the necessary repairs. The earliest estimates coming in were that it would be two weeks before Rialto could reopen. As part owner, Lucas was already butting in, trying to squeeze out an earlier timeline.

For now, Ian was leaving James and Lucas to hash it out. There wasn't much he could do until the repairs were done. This forced mini-vacation could be a good thing. He could turn his attention to his new restaurant and his sexy husband.

"How about you take me home for some makeup sex?"

"Nothing to make up."

"Then just the sex."

Hollis grinned. "I'm up for that."

They didn't let go of each other all the way home and once they got inside the condo, Hollis pressed Ian up against the closed door. He cupped his neck and stared down at him. The love shining in his eyes sent Ian's butterflies winging through his stomach again. He loved this big, protective man more than anything on Earth.

Hollis kissed his forehead, then his eyes and nose, before pressing their mouths together. Ian opened for him and Hollis's tongue slid into his mouth. The kiss was slow and sensual, making Ian's toes curl in his shoes. He slid his hands up Hollis's back, tugging him closer. Hollis kept kissing him over and over. It didn't take long for Ian's cock to harden.

When Hollis reached for the buttons of Ian's shirt, Ian was already breathing heavy. His husband unfastened them slowly, bending down to press kisses to each batch of skin he revealed. He latched on to a nipple and swirled his tongue around it before moving to the other.

Ian gasped and held the back of his head.

Hollis dropped to his knees and opened the fly of Ian's jeans. He tugged them down to his thighs, then ran his hands over Ian's hips. "Such sexy hips." He ran his finger over the muscle there before cupping Ian's testicles. He caressed them as he ran his tongue around the head of Ian's cock.

It felt so good. Ian's head hit the door, but not for long because he wanted to watch. There was nothing sexier than Hollis going down on him. Blue eyes locked on his as Hollis took more of him into his mouth.

Ian moaned, still cupping Hollis's head. He added his other hand and directed Hollis's movements. The soft groan from Hollis vibrated around him as his tip hit the back of Hollis's throat. Ian pulled almost all the way out and pushed back in. Hollis hollowed his cheeks, the suction feeling so fantastic, Ian shuddered. His mouth was warm and wet and tight, enticing Ian to pump his hips more.

Hollis reached around to grasp his ass, one finger brushing over his hole. Ian held his breath as Hollis lifted his hand to Ian's mouth. Ian sucked on his fingers, getting them nice and slick. Hollis took those damp fingers back to his ass and slid one finger inside him even as he sucked harder on Ian's cock. He hit Ian's prostate, and Ian couldn't stop the long moan that escaped his throat.

"Fuck," Hollis bit out when he pulled off. He stared up at Ian. "Love this."

"I do, too," Ian panted. "Don't stop."

"Never." Hollis took him deep again as he pushed his finger in and out of Ian. He lifted his head, ran his tongue around the head of Ian's cock, then sucked him down. His slow movements were going to drive Ian crazy, and he started pumping his hips even as he clenched on the finger inside him.

Hollis picked up the tempo and Ian gasped again and kept thrusting into that wet heat. He went faster and faster as Hollis added a second finger and pressed onto his prostate. When his orgasm barreled through him, Ian yelled and hunched over Hollis. Pleasure exploded and he scrunched his eyes tight as wave after wave of it overtook him. Hollis swallowed him, taking everything he gave, then licked him clean. He slowly pulled out his fingers and Ian clutched at them, not ready to have them gone.

Hollis chuckled and the sound was broken with lust.

Ian took a moment to get his vision back, to get his breath back. He stared at his husband and saw that he'd opened his pants and was stroking himself off. "Mine," he whispered, pushing Hollis to his back on the floor. He tugged Hollis's jeans down and nuzzled his balls, kissing around them before pulling one into his mouth. He sucked it, getting it nice and wet before he kissed up to Hollis's hip.

"You're killing me, baby," Hollis said, his voice raspy. "Suck me."

"You know I like to savor my treats."

"Savor faster. Watching you lose it has me on the edge."

Ian could tell. Hollis was breathing hard, his hips writhing on the floor. Ian grasped the base of his dick and licked the pre-cum at his tip. "Mmm," he said as he slowly took Hollis deeper into his

# Rialto

mouth. He ran his tongue over the silky, soft skin and Hollis jerked against it. He hollowed out his cheeks and kept going until the spongy tip met the back of his throat. He swallowed around it and Hollis cried out.

Fuck, he loved doing this. Loved the noises he could pull from his husband. Hollis gave himself over to sex in a way that awed Ian.

Hands landed in his hair as Hollis clasped his head. He thrust up into Ian's throat and Ian choked. Hollis groaned and pulled away, then did it again. Ian let himself gag, knowing how hot that sound was when on the other end. Then he went to town on Hollis. He sucked and licked and let him slide into his throat, moving fast, the way Hollis liked it.

"Fuck, baby!" Hollis thrust his hips up over and over, his panting loud in the silence of the condo. A long, rumbling groan sounded just before Hollis's back bowed off the floor. Hot semen hit Ian's throat and he swallowed. And kept swallowing as his husband unloaded into him. When he was done, Hollis collapsed onto the floor, gasping air into his lungs. He sprawled there a moment before he tugged Ian onto him. He wrapped his arms tight around Ian and kissed him, no doubt tasting himself on Ian's tongue.

They kissed for a long time before Ian slumped against him and buried his face in Hollis's neck. He smiled because they hadn't even made it to the bedroom. God, just knowing how much his husband wanted him made him so damn happy. He let the joy swamp him, and he lifted up to look into Hollis's dazed blue eyes. He smiled. "Love you with everything in me."

"Hell, Ian...I didn't even know what love was until you. You're my everything."

"You're my everything, too. Promise me we'll be like this forever."

"Oh, it's for forever." Hollis grinned. "We're going to be eighty and still all over each other because I'll never get enough of you."

"Promise me."

"I solemnly swear that I will ravish you in the doorway even when we're old."

Chuckling, Ian got to his knees and looked at Hollis, who still wore his clothes, with his jeans pulled around his thighs. His dick, soft now, lay against his thigh. It was still shiny and wet-looking. Ian ran a finger over it, then sent both hands up under Hollis's shirt. He put one over his beating heart, loving the bump against his palm. "We're going to have a good life together. I have a feeling we've seen the last of my past interfering. A good feeling."

"So do I." Hollis laid his hand over Ian's, and he could feel the warmth of his skin through the shirt. "So, after a little time, we'll resume all the steps to becoming foster parents and we'll do this thing we both want."

"I can't wait to have a family with you."

"We already are a family, GQ. You and me? We're family."

They were. And they had a big extended family with all their friends. Ones who dropped everything to help each other, support each other.

All the tension Ian had been carrying through this experience with Max drained out of him and he leaned down to press his lips to Hollis's, pulling back just enough to see him. Their breaths mingled between them as he stared into the prettiest blue eyes that looked at him with so much affection. He still had Rialto to get straight, still had the new restaurant to open, and yes, he still planned to finish the steps needed to get foster kids in his home, but right then, he wanted to wallow in Hollis's affection. He stood and held out his hand to help Hollis up.

"Come on, husband, let's take this to the bedroom."

## Epilogue

*Thanksgiving, 2020*
*(One year later)*

Ian gripped the steering wheel of his new SUV as he carefully maneuvered the vehicle around a particularly tight turn into Lucas's neighborhood. He loved his new car, but the thing was just so much bigger than his old Volt that its size took some getting used to. His eyes might tell him he was safely in his lane, but his body was screaming that they were taking up the entire road.

"Should I have driven?" Hollis asked from the passenger seat. There was no missing the laughter in his tone.

"No, I'm fine. I'm only going to get used to it by driving it," Ian said primly.

A giggle from the back seat drew Ian's eyes to the rearview mirror and the twins that were still safely secured in their car seats. Ian's heart swelled every time he saw their smiling faces, and he was pretty sure that was never going to change.

Tyler and Thomas were three-year-old foster kids who had been placed in their home just a month ago, and Ian was already in love with them both. Honestly, it hadn't taken him long at all to adore the kids. And he was thrilled to see Hollis fall for them just as hard.

That wasn't to say that there hadn't been plenty of rough moments and stumbles along the way. There had been nightmares, coloring on the walls, food disagreements, and even a few fights between the twins.

But there had also been snuggles, cartoons, bedtime stories, toys, splashing in the bath, and so much laughter. Ian was sure he'd already laughed more in the first month of the twins being in their house than he had in the last six months.

Ian turned his attention to the road and smiled as the large mansions flashed past their windows with their perfect lawns even at the start of winter. They deserved the laughter. The past year had been filled with chaos, but also fun. In Good Time had launched without a hitch to lots of enthusiasm on the part of Cincinnatians. He didn't think it was going to be as popular as Rialto, but Ian didn't mind. It meant that fewer people were being turned away each night because there wasn't room for them.

Ian cut down on his hours at both restaurants so he could help Max as he worked his way through drug rehab. That had been ugly as he battled both withdrawal and old demons in therapy that was long overdue. It had been enough to send Ian back to therapy for once-a-month sessions. Max had stirred up old memories, old nightmares, and old doubts. Talking it out with a therapist helped him get a handle on those traumas again.

Max was starting to get on his feet. He'd moved in with Rowe and Noah. The Masters of Mayhem had been there to help through rehab and offered him a safe place to simply be himself, while providing some quiet oversight to make sure he didn't backslide into bad habits when he struggled. He was also working as a server at Ian's new restaurant. If everything continued to progress, Max announced that he was going to start some online classes in the summer for a business degree.

At the end of the street, Ian directed the SUV down the long, winding driveway to the sprawling red-brick mansion with the black shutters and elegant double doors. Lucas never did anything small.

But then, he had a sneaking suspicion that there was a very deliberate reason in Lucas's mind for the giant house. He wanted to fill it with family—both with his made family as well as any children that he and Andrei had.

Ian parked the SUV behind Snow's Mercedes and sighed. "We're the last ones to arrive."

Hollis unbuckled his seat belt. "Andrei did warn us that it takes longer to get out of the house with a kid."

"Yeah, but thirty minutes to get ready? That's insane."

Hollis snorted. "Only because they decided to make a game of taking off their shoes and hiding them from you."

Ian sighed, but he was still smiling. This was the first time the twins were meeting the entire family, and Ian wanted to be prepared for anything. He'd made a few dishes for Thanksgiving dinner while agreeing to hand the turkey and some of the sides over to Andrei's mother, Sonja. He'd also spent time prepacking bags for the twins such as clothes, toys, and other random things. Everything had been ready…except for the boys.

That had been a thirty-minute production getting them dressed, into coats, and into their car seats. He'd been exhausted before they even left the driveway.

Ian popped the trunk and got out of the car. They'd get the kids inside first and then send someone out to fetch the food he'd brought. His main focus was making sure the boys were comfortable. The holidays were turning into big gatherings each year, and he was worried about Thomas and Tyler being overwhelmed.

He held Tyler's hand while Hollis had Thomas as they walked up to the massive house. Climbing the stairs, Ian laughed to see Daciana's tiny face pressed to the window beside the door. Her dark eyes were wide as she took in the little boys. She was only weeks away from her second birthday, and she was a lively little one that kept her fathers on their toes. She disappeared when they were only a few steps away, but Ian could hear her high-pitched voice calling for someone. From their distance, Ian wasn't sure if it was English or Romanian she was speaking. Probably a mix.

Ian opened the door and they were immediately hit with a wall of joyous voices and laughter. Tyler's hand tightened in Ian's and he scooted closer, clinging to Ian's pant leg with his other hand. Ian looked over at Hollis to find that he was now carrying Thomas. Yeah, the family could be a bit overwhelming, but Ian was hopeful that the boys would feel at home within a short period of time.

The soft patter of small feet could be heard approaching them. Daciana appeared around the corner, wearing an oversized pink T-shirt that read Kung-Fu Princess, and sparkly purple leggings. Her dark hair hung down her back and was wild. Lucas had gotten quite good at braiding his daughter's hair, but it never seemed to stay that way for long. She looked torn between rushing toward Ian for a hug and hesitating because of the unknown little boy.

The whole matter was settled a second later when Andrei walked around the corner holding a three-month-old boy with a head full of dark hair.

Stefan had been born at the end of summer after yet another lengthy search for a new surrogate. Lucas and Andrei admitted that they wanted a second child right away, so the siblings would be close in age as they grew up.

Tucked against his father's chest, Stefan was comfortably sleeping through all the noise. Everyone had teased Lucas that his son didn't resemble him besides the dark hair, but it looked as if the little guy was already developing his biological father's stern frowns.

"Welcome to the chaos," Andrei greeted in a low voice so as not to disturb Stefan.

Before Ian could reply, Daciana was whispering something loudly to her father, but Ian didn't catch a word of it. Definitely not English. Andrei smiled and replied in Romanian.

"No one warned me that we were going to need subtitles," Hollis teased.

"Sorry about that," Andrei murmured. "We encourage her to speak Romanian at home, but we're still working on not speaking it around people who can't understand her." He then turned his attention to the boys and smiled. "And who did you bring to join our special day?"

"This is Tyler," Ian said, placing his hand on the head of the little one clinging to him. "And Hollis is holding his brother, Thomas."

"It's very nice to meet you, Tyler and Thomas. We've set up a playroom off the kitchen and built a huge blanket fort. Would you like to go see it?"

Tyler and Thomas looked at each other and gave small nods but didn't yet release either Hollis or Ian.

"We'll help get them settled," Ian said as he worked to take off Tyler's coat and then his own.

"I'll take them to the playroom if you want to get situated in the kitchen," Hollis offered, holding out his and Thomas's coats.

Ian smirked and accepted the garments. "I promised that I wasn't going to spend all my time cooking this year."

"Uh-huh…keep tellin' yourself that, baby," Hollis teased as he took Tyler by the hand and started to walk toward the area Andrei had indicated while Daciana ran ahead of them.

"Where are Rowe and Noah? I was going to send them out to fetch the food I brought."

"In the pool. Last we heard was something about skinny dipping. Snow went down to get them." Ian groaned and shook his head. "But I think Max and Jude are handy."

"Good. That will give me a chance to hold this one," Ian said, extending his hands toward Stefan.

Andrei chuckled and carefully shifted the sleeping baby so that he was now snuggled against Ian's chest. The warm and delicate weight had Ian's heart melting. They were already talking about adopting Tyler and Thomas, but Ian could understand the allure of surrogacy. Holding a tiny one like this, knowing that it was your own flesh and blood.

Ian laughed when he caught sight of Andrei's shirt and then winced, afraid he'd woken Stefan.

"Don't worry about waking him. He's due for a feeding."

"Nice shirt."

Andrei snorted and looked down at where it said, "Call Me Big Poppa."

"Rowe brought them for us. He got Stefan one that said, 'Future

Ward Security Bodyguard' but Stefan already spit up on it. Wait until you see Lucas's."

They walked to the great room, where several people were relaxing. From there, he could see Sonja and Lucas's sister, Nicole, working on the food in the kitchen. Hugs were given out and Andrei quickly directed Jude and Max to Ian's car for the rest of the food. The air was thick with the scent of turkey, yeasty rolls, and other wonderful spices.

There was a part of Ian that ached to head straight into the kitchen and take over. Thanksgiving was his jam. He loved making all the food for the holiday and then listening to everyone exclaim how wonderful it was. But he held back. It was clear that Sonja and Nicole had everything under control, and there was a bigger part of him that wanted to hang out with family for a while before wandering over to the playroom to spend time with Thomas and Tyler.

Lucas appeared from an adjoining room and Ian took a step back as he laughed. The always perfectly dressed Lucas was wearing a pair of comfortable jeans and a black T-shirt with white writing. It said, "Call Me Big Daddy."

"Rowe strikes again," Lucas muttered, but he was smiling as he pulled Ian into a careful hug. As he stepped away, he brushed a loving finger across Stefan's cheek.

"It's a good look for you."

"I'd say fatherhood looks good on both of us," Lucas replied. He nodded toward the room he'd just come from. "I just saw Hollis with the twins. They're adorable."

"You met them?"

Lucas made a face. "From a distance. They didn't want to stop playing with Daciana in the fort."

Stefan shifted against Ian's chest and gave a big yawn before letting out a soft cry.

"Mine!" Milos, Lucas's father-in-law, shouted as he jumped to his feet. The older man hurried across the room and carefully lifted Stefan from Ian's chest. "I was promised this feeding."

"His bottle is prepared—" Andrei started, but Milos was already waving his free hand at his son as he walked toward the kitchen.

"I know what I'm doing. I fed you plenty of times. And our little Daci. Go away."

Lucas chuckled and Andrei rolled his eyes.

"There's no shortage of help during the day," Lucas said.

"Yeah, just try finding some help when it's three a.m.," Andrei grumbled.

"Does this mean you're going to slow down now?"

Andrei and Lucas looked at each other, slow guilty smiles spreading across their faces.

Ian gasped. "You're not pregnant again, are you?"

Andrei placed both hands on his flat stomach and looked down. "I don't look pregnant, do I?"

"Be serious!"

"No, we're not pregnant," Lucas said evenly.

"Do you have a surrogate?"

"Not officially, though we have someone we're considering."

"Word has gotten out regarding how well Lucas pays," Andrei mumbled.

"But we are also looking into adoption," Lucas added.

"That's wonderful." Ian threw his arms around Lucas, hugging him tightly.

"It's still a ways off. We want to wait until Stefan is at least two before we add another child to our family."

The volume of noise in the great room jumped as Snow, Rowe, and Noah entered. All three had wet hair. Rowe and Noah looked to be in their usual street clothes, but Snow was wearing a pair of sweat pants and a soft, gray sweater that Ian knew belonged to Lucas. Apparently getting a naked Rowe and Noah out of the pool had meant that Snow went into the pool. Probably fully dressed.

Ian walked over to the newcomers and gave out hugs, complimenting Rowe and Noah on their gifts to the Vallois family. Snow grumbled at Rowe and Noah, promising to get them back for the dunking, which they just laughed off.

Snow dropped onto the couch and Ian joined him.

"Not running to the kitchen?" Snow asked in surprise.

"Nope. Relaxing this year."

Snow wrapped an arm around Ian's shoulders and pulled him in closer. "It's about time."

Ian had to agree. This was nice. In all the years since he'd come into this family, he'd never had this on Thanksgiving. He was always in the kitchen, worrying about the food being prepared just right or worrying about the place settings, or a hundred other little things. There had never been time to sit and talk with his family. That always came after dinner when they were stuffed and in danger of falling into a food coma.

Looking over at his friend, Ian caught sight of the gold band on Snow's left hand. Something he'd been sure he'd never see in his lifetime, but Jude changed a lot of things for the grumpy surgeon. "Anna forgiven you yet?"

After nearly a year of indecision, they'd each gotten a call late one night from Snow and Jude, informing the family that they'd hopped on a plane for Hawaii and were now married. *They'd freaking eloped.* Ian had been a little sad that he'd not been there for Snow's big moment, but if he was honest with himself, he wasn't really surprised. Snow and Jude weren't into big, flashy events or being the center of attention. They'd wanted something just for them.

There were only a few pictures, but they were gorgeous. Just the two of them with an official saying their vows on the beach with a beautiful backdrop of blue skies and gentle waves. A perfect peaceful moment.

Snow groaned and dropped his head against the sofa. "Yes and no. She says that she has, but she wants to throw a big party this spring for the entire family."

Ian giggled at the idea of Snow surrounded by all of Jude's family. But after the life that Snow had before Jude, Ian was sure that Snow could use all the love he could get from those loud and boisterous people.

And Anna was the mother he needed whether Snow was willing to admit it or not. That woman adored him and babied him as much as she did her own sons.

"What about your house? Adjusted to the little ones yet?" Snow asked.

Ian shrugged. "We're getting there. Every time I think we've got it all covered, they cook up something new to surprise us. I love it!"

"I'm assuming those were the voices I heard in the fort with Daci…"

Ian nodded.

Jude laughed as he approached them. "I have a feeling that they're going to be eating dinner in that monstrous thing." He then looked over at Ian. "All your food has been handed over to Sonja and Nicole. They said to tell you that they've got it under control." Jude dropped down on the sofa next to Snow and threaded his fingers through Snow's. Both of them looked tired after spending the afternoon with Jude's family.

A few minutes later, Sonja and Nicole announced that dinner was ready. Ian jumped up and helped Hollis prepare plates for Thomas and Tyler. They managed to get them to the table, but seating had to be rearranged so that Daciana was next to the twins. Stefan was tucked in his nearby Pack 'n Play and asleep again with a full belly and clean diaper.

With his own plate piled full of food in front of him, Ian stopped and looked down the long table at the family spread around him. More than a decade ago, he'd had his first Thanksgiving with this family. Then it had just been him, Snow, Lucas, and Rowe around a small table loaded with food he'd cooked.

Now there were so many of them smiling and laughing. His family had grown so much over the years, and he'd never expected this. Hoped, maybe, but never really thought it was possible.

Across the table, he caught Hollis staring at him with a knowing smile. Ian lifted his glass and his smile grew to see the others do the same as if they'd expected it from him.

"To family."

Ever wonder how Lucas would react if Andrei cut his hair or what would happen if someone took Rowe's duct tape away?

Get the answers to these questions and much more straight from the characters! Download BETWEEN THE SHEETS: CHARACTERS SHARE WHAT HAPPENS BETWEEN THE BOOKS for free for a limited time.

Or start binging stories about Rowe's bodyguard team at Ward Security. Read *Psycho Romeo*, book 1 of Ward Security, now.

# About the Authors

## Jocelynn Drake

*New York Times* Bestselling author Jocelynn Drake loves a good story, whether she is reading it or writing one of her own.

Over the years, her stories have allowed her to explore space, talk to dragons, dodge bullets with assassins, hang with vampires, and fall in love again and again.

This former Kentucky girl has moved up, down, and across the U.S. with her husband. Recently, they've settled near the Rockies.

When she is not hammering away at her keyboard or curled up with a book, she can be found walking her dog Ace or playing video games. She loves Bruce Wayne, Ezio Auditore, travel, tattoos, explosions, and fast cars.

Check out all her books at JocelynnDrake.com or join her newsletter and get regular updates on all upcoming books.

## Rinda Elliott

Rinda Elliott is an author who loves unusual stories and credits growing up in a family of curious life-lovers who moved all over the country. Books and movies full of fantasy, science fiction, and romance kept them amused, especially in some of the stranger places.

For years, she tried to separate her darker side with her humorous and romantic one. She published short fiction, but things really started happening when she gave in and mixed it up. When not lost in fiction, she loves making wine, collecting music, gaming, and spending time with her husband and two children.

She is the author of the Beri O'Dell urban fantasy series, the YA Sister of Fate Trilogy, and the paranormal romance Brothers Bernaux Trilogy. She also writes erotic fiction as Dani Worth. She can be found at RindaElliott.com.

Jocelynn and Rinda can be found at: www.DrakeandElliott.com

Or you can sign up for their newsletter at DrakeandElliott.com/newsletter .

They are found on Facebook as Drake and Elliott and on Twitter as @drakeandelliott.

And don't miss out on all the sneak peeks and speculation at the Facebook Group, Unbreakable Readers.

# Also by Jocelynn Drake and Rinda Elliott

## The Unbreakable Bonds Series

*Shiver*

*Shatter*

*Torch*

*Devour*

*Blaze*

*Fracture*

*Ignite*

*Rialto*

## Unbreakable Bonds Short Story Collections

*Unbreakable Stories: Lucas*

*Unbreakable Stories: Snow*

*Unbreakable Stories: Rowe*

*Unbreakable Stories: Ian*

## Ward Security

*Psycho Romeo*

*Dantes Unglued*

*Deadly Dorian*

*Jackson*

*Sadistic Sherlock*

*King of Romance*

*Killer Bond*

*Seth*

*Wicked Outlaw*

## Pineapple Grove

*Something About Jace*

*Drew & Mr. Grumpy*

*All for Wesley*

## Weavers Circle

*Broken Warrior*

*Wild Warrior*

*Blind Warrior*

# Also by Jocelynn Drake

## Lords of Discord

*Claiming Marcus*

*Saving Rafe*

*Waking Bel*

*Embracing Winter*

*Healing Aiden*

## Exit Strategy

*Deadly Lover: Special Edition*

*Vengeful Lover*

*Final Lover*

*Forbidden Lover*

*Accidental Lover*

## Ice and Snow Christmas Series

*Walking on Thin Ice*

*Ice, Snow, & Mistletoe*

*Snowball's Chance*

*Defrosting Jack*

# Also by AJ Sherwood & Jocelynn Drake

### Scales 'N' Spells Series

Origin

Breath

Wish: A Novella

Blood

Made in the USA
Las Vegas, NV
12 July 2022